D1529016

PROPERTY OF

THAT, EXCEPTING IN RARE CASES, YOU MIGHT AS WELL SEND TO THE FOUNDLING HOSPITAL AND BORROW A BABY AS TO BORROW A BOOK WITH THE IDEA OF ITS BEING ANY GREAT SATISFACTION. WE LIKE A BABY IN OUR CRADLE, BUT PREFER THAT ONE WHICH BELONGS TO THE HOUSEHOLD. WE LIKE A BOOK, BUT WANT TO FEEL IT IS OURS. WE NEVER YET GOT ANY ADVANTAGE FROM A BORROWED BOOK. WE HOPE THOSE NEVER REAPED ANY PROFIT FROM THE BOOKS THEY BORROWED FROM US, BUT NEVER RETURNED.—

* * *

DON'T WORRY YOUR FRIENDS BY BORROWING THIS BOOK. BUY ONE.

* * *

FOR·SALE·BY·ALL·BOOK·DEALERS OR BY MAIL ON RECEIPT OF PRICE BY PUBLISHER.

PESCHEL PRESS ~ P.O. BOX 132 ~ HERSHEY, PA 17033 ~ EMAIL: BPESCHEL@GMAIL.COM ~ WWW.PESCHELPRESS.COM

The Casebook of
Twain & Holmes

ALSO FROM THE PESCHEL PRESS

THE 223B CASEBOOK SERIES
Sherlock Holmes Victorian Parodies & Pastiches: 1888-1899
Sherlock Holmes Edwardian Parodies & Pastiches I: 1900-1904
Sherlock Holmes Edwardian Parodies & Pastiches II: 1905-1909
Sherlock Holmes Great War Parodies & Pastiches I: 1910-1914
Sherlock Holmes Great War Parodies & Pastiches II: 1915-1919
Sherlock Holmes Jazz Age Parodies & Pastiches I: 1920-1924
Sherlock Holmes Jazz Age Parodies & Pastiches II: 1925-1930
The Early Punch Parodies of Sherlock Holmes
The Best Sherlock Holmes Parodies & Pastiches: 1888-1930

THE RUGELEY POISONER SERIES
The Illustrated Life and Career of William Palmer
The Times Report of the Trial of William Palmer
The Life and Career of Dr. William Palmer of Rugeley

ANNOTATED EDITIONS
The Complete, Annotated Secret Adversary
By Agatha Christie
The Complete, Annotated Mysterious Affair at Styles
By Agatha Christie
The Complete, Annotated Whose Body?
By Dorothy L. Sayers

OTHER BOOKS
The Dictionary of Flowers and Gems
Suburban Stockade

ALSO BY BILL PESCHEL
Hell's Casino
Writers Gone Wild (Penguin)

The Casebook of
Twain & Holmes

Seven Stories From The World Of Sherlock Holmes, As Dictated By Samuel Clemens

To Amanda, Dont let your hair get too grey over the idjits. Bill Peschel

Bill Peschel

PESCHEL PRESS ~ HERSHEY, PA.

THE CASEBOOK OF TWAIN AND HOLMES. Copyright 2018 Bill Peschel. All rights reserved. Printed in the United States of America. No part of the notes or essays may be used or reproduced in any manner without written permission except in cases of brief quotations embodied in critical articles or reviews. For information, email peschel@peschel press.com or write to Peschel Press, P.O. Box 132, Hershey, PA 17033.

Cover design by Bill Peschel. Colored by Lily Peschel

www.peschelpress.com

ISBN-13: 978-1719550918
ISBN-10: 1719550913

Library of Congress Control Number: 2018945754

First printing: July 2018, version 1.2

Table of Contents

Introduction i
Acknowledgments iii

The Stories

Our Man in Tangier (1867) 5
The Adventure of the Dancing Man (1868) 38
The Adventure of the Jersey Girl (1878) 59
The Adventure of the Stomach Club (1879) 93
The Adventure of the Missing Mortician (1882) 124
The Adventure of the Fight Club (1887) 164
The Adventure of the Whyos (1894) 199

Combined Bibliography 231
Copyright Acknowledgments 233
About the Author 234

Introduction

"A little before noon, he sent for Clara to find Paine, and when Paine arrived, Mark Twain indicated a pair of unfinished manuscripts and whispered, 'throw away,' and pressed Paine's hand, and that was the last moment Paine had with him."
— From Ron Powers, *Mark Twain* (2005)

In his remaining years, Mark Twain devoted his energies to dictating his memoirs, a monumental outpouring of stories and opinions that he told, not in chronological order, but as they came to him. Although he embargoed them for a century, excerpts were printed in his lifetime. The Mark Twain Project at the University of California, after years of careful, meticulous work, published the *Autobiography* in three volumes.

But not everything has been collected. Around 2000, I bought a box of old papers at a warehouse auction in Carlisle, Pa. There was nothing about the box that suggested there were treasures within. It contained a jumble of handwritten papers, receipts, advertising circulars, crumbling newsprint, and other ephemera. As an amateur historian, I'm fascinated by such mundane papers. It certainly held no value to its original owner, who had scrawled "BURN THIS" on the side.

An examination of the pages, however, revealed that they were nothing less than Mark Twain's tales of his adventures with Sherlock Holmes and his circle. Dictated to a secretary as part of his autobiography, he chose for some reason not to publish them. Apparently, the box was given to his longtime maid Katie O'Leary. Instead of following instructions, she took the box home. Perhaps she frugally intended to use the paper to light her household fires. Eventually, the box was sealed and stored and passed through the family over the years until it was disposed of in Carlisle.

At least, that's my story, and I'm sticking to it.

But if the process from the Twain home to Carlisle was long, what followed was just as arduous. The first story, "The

Adventure of the Whyos," was published as an ebook single in 2011. The rest of the stories appeared in the back of volumes in the 223B Casebook series that were published over the next eight years.

Will there be more stories? Like Dr. Watson, I, too, have a tin box, only it is made of electrons. It's filled with stories for which the world is not yet prepared. There's the excursion into the lair of the white worm under the streets of New York, the case of the Irish anarchists that crossed two continents and threatened the crowned heads of Europe, and the story of Twain and Sherlock's visit to Hannibal that was hinted at in "The Case of the Missing Mortician." The decision about publishing these stories will depend, as it always does, on you the reader.

Bill Peschel
May 2018

Acknowledgments

The task of recovering, transcribing, annotating, and publishing these curious stories fell to many hands, not all of whom wish to be identified in these pages. They know they have my thanks and gratitude for their help.

Posthumous thanks must be given to Katie O'Leary, the Clemens' longtime maid whose frugality led to the preservation of these papers. The auction house on Petersburg Road, across the road from the single-strip airport, is no longer in business, but my fond memories of attending the weekly auctions there made a once-young copy editor feel a little less lonely in an unfamiliar area.

George Macdonald Fraser's Flashman novels, which combined the fictional and the historical (with footnotes!) was a direct influence on this series. If you've never met Flashy, by all means remedy this by checking them out

Finally, thanks be to my wife of many years, Teresa, who patiently read and commented on each of my stories. She knows my heart belongs to her; so does my gratitude.

Get the newsletter: If you want to learn more about my books, my researches and the media I eat, sign up for the Peschel Press newsletter. You'll get an intermittent chatty letter about what we're publishing plus a glimpse behind the scenes at a growing publishing house. Visit www.planet-peschel.com or www.peschelpress.com and look for the sign-up box.

Got a review? If you like this book — or even if you don't — could you leave a word or two at the online book retailer of your choice? I would really appreciate it.

Our Man in Tangier

Our Man in Tangier (1867)

———◈———

Like many entries in his autobiography, Twain was inspired to tell this story after reading something — in this case a travel book about Morocco — that sparked his memory. He had visited the country early in his literary career. In 1867, he booked passage with a tour group to the Middle East aboard the steamship Quaker City. *He made a deal with a Sacramento newspaper to publish his letters about his experiences, and they were expanded into his first travel book* The Innocents Abroad *(1869).*

From July 4 to 17, the Quaker City *crossed the Atlantic and stopped at Gibraltar, the British possession on the Spanish side of the strait. Twain and five of his fellow passengers took the opportunity to cross the Mediterranean to Tangier. Although he described it as "a foreign land if ever there was one," he left only a sketchy account of his activities in* Innocents. *This story explains why.*

> "I started with no special object. Anyone with very little experience of travelling other than by railways could do the same. It would be desirable that they should first make themselves familiar with the general conditions of the country, and it is certainly an advantage to know something of the language."
> — From Frances Macnab, *A Ride In Morocco Among Believers and Traders* (1902)

THIS IS SOUND ADVICE. I wish I had heard it 40 years before, when I was carried ashore the Tangier beach on the shoulders of a Moor who reeked of sweat, salt, and spices. It would have meant a totally different story than the one I'll relate. If I had known more about the landscape and its people, and a few words of Arabic, I would have avoided the sad eyes in the *hareem*, the kidnappings, the serious end of guns and swords, and suffering the storyteller's worst curse: knowing a keen story and unable to tell a soul.

I blame Mycroft. That boy had more devilment in him than Huck, and he came by it naturally too, through his blood. If I had known what he was going to get me into, I'd have shoved that fresh-faced child into the Mediterranean halfway between Gibraltar and Tangier. I would have gotten away with it, too. I could have sworn my *Quaker City* companions to silence, and the Moors wouldn't care what one white man does to another, so long as they're not involved.

We boarded the small steamer in Cadiz, Spain.[1] The boat was not as spacious as the *Quaker City*. It was not spacious at all. There were too many bodies filling the deck. Most of the space was covered with an awning and every square inch of it was taken up with a body, sitting, laying, and standing. We covered the spectrum of skin tones, from pale white to printer's ink black and every shade in between. Of clothing, apart from the Western duds in our party, we saw sashes, skullcaps, turbans, trousers, pantaloons, slippers, boots, long robes and bare legs. Moorish merchants and Muhammadian vagabonds. A rag-shop of a congregation.

Our party stood at the bow soon after casting off, our cigars cheerfully contributing to the cloud that trailed the steamboat. Young Blucher, who was from the Far West and on his first voyage, joined us at the rail. Like a young boy out in nature, he came across an interesting creature and brought him home. This was a young man in a white linen suit and a straw Panama hat. He looked like a young bull, a head taller than Blucher, and his curling locks brushed his collar. He introduced himself as Michael Herndon, late of Oxford. He was off to see Europe, and he wanted to look into Morocco. I mentioned we were doing the same and that we originated with the *Quaker City*. His eyes lit up.

"Why, you're famous," he told me.

I told him I was pleased to hear that my Jumping Frog story was not only on everyone's lips in America, but it had

---

[1] A port city in Spain, about 77 miles northwest of Gibraltar.

caused a stir in his country as well.

He said nothing to that. I figured he was stunned by my presence. He had probably never met a famous writer before, Oxford not quite measuring up as a center for literature as New York.

By now, you've no doubt spotted Mycroft Holmes, traveling under an alias. The reason he did this I'll reserve for later. Rather than cause confusion, I'll set his alias aside and refer to him direct.

He pulled out of his coat a Spanish newspaper and pointed to an item on the front page. I was unable to read it, not knowing the lingo. I ciphered through it, though, but could not see my name. Presumably they translated it into Spanish, and I made a note to check a dictionary to see how "Mark Twain" would fare. But I did see "*Quaker City*," "Generalissimo Sherman" and "padre Beecher con Brooklyn Church of the Brethren" listed.

"We've heard of Sherman and Beecher's roles in the abolition of slavery," Mycroft said. "Are they here?"[1]

Blucher spoke up, "Certainly! You're talking with Sherman right now." He slapped my shoulder. "As for the good reverend, he's back on the boat, but you know, you could pass for his double."

Mycroft lit up with joy and thrust out his hand.

"General Sherman, it is an honor to meet you. You look not at all as you do in the papers!"

"It is the uniform, I suppose," I said. "There's nothing like a uniform to give a man weight and tone."

"They make you look handsomer, too." The boys exploded

---

[1] William Tecumseh Sherman (1820-1891) was one of the most notable Union generals during the Civil War. He led the march into the heart of the Confederacy that resulted in the capture of Atlanta, followed by Savannah, effectively cutting the South in two and contributing to the re-election of Abraham Lincoln. Henry Ward Beech (1813-1887) was a notable preacher who was one of the earliest advocates for the abolition of slavery. Among his activities, he raised money to send rifles to pro-abolition forces in the Kansas Territory, saying that would do more good than a hundred Bibles.

in laughter at that, and that made me hold my tongue. I could have told him that Sherman and Beecher were supposed to join the tour — I signed on in the expectation of reporting on them — but they made their excuses at the last minute. I could have made this clear to him, but he was so duped by my impersonation, and so full of good words about my general-ship during the war that it would spoil a good joke to have it end so soon, so I accepted the compliments on Sherman's be-half. And therein lay the seeds of my downfall, as you shall see.

All because that ass Blucher spoke up and invited him to join us while we toured the city, and he happily accepted.

"I'm sure that Gen. Sherman's will open doors that would remain barred to an Oxford student," Mycroft said in a way that made me pause. If you've read the stories, you'll wonder how he could be so easily taken in. To that I'll answer that he was older, wiser, and far more knowledgeable, that man capa-ble of running the British government (to borrow Doyle's phrase). When I met him, he was just beginning to bloom. The brains were there, alongside his skill at pulling strings. He just needed seasoning.

My suspicious thoughts were interrupted by my first meeting with our guide, Si el Aziz. He was a thin, small man who dressed himself in a Western-style suit that would have marked him for a swell in San Francisco. Blucher found him in the Cadiz shipping office when he bought our tickets to Tangier, and he came highly recommended as a guide, partic-ularly from himself. In addition to his services in arranging the tickets and acting as our go-between with customs offi-cials and other thieves, he also bought and sold trade goods between the two ports. In the hold he had three trunks stuffed with tobacco, liquor, and newspapers. The first two were for the locals and the last for the lonely Europeans who hungered for news of the outside world. Considering that we paid for his passage, he stood to reap quite a windfall.

He had just finished stowing his cargo, so he accepted a

cigar from me while Blucher and he talked about how we'll see Tangier. He had a particular habit of poking his finger into the air and saying, "Yes! Yes!" to most questions we asked him. Our every request would be granted ("Yes! Yes!") and the mysteries of the Orient would be revealed to us.

When the business was settled, Blucher made the introductions. I continued in my guise as Sherman, and the devil in him extended the joke to identify Mycroft as Rev. Beecher. Mycroft was clearly stunned at his promotion to the clergy, and tried to raise an objection, but the English tend to be docile in the face of the unexpected, and once Blucher explained to Si our international reputation, he grew even more eager to lead us. The only way to capture his excitement would be to violate the norms of English grammar and include exclamation points in the middle of his speech, like this:

"I shall make sure! you fine gentlemen! should see the treasures of Tangier!" he said. "Yes, yes, your famous names! [pounds the chests of Mycroft and myself, raising the dust of the desert] will open doors! in my country, I'm sure! In the meantime, would you like English and American newspapers?"

He pulled from his satchel his collection of folded papers and spread them like a giant fan. There were a couple London *Times*, some New York papers, even some *Harper's Weeklys* from the previous year. We declined the offer. We were bound for foreign lands and wanted no reminders of home.

"I believe I would like some papers," came a new voice from over my shoulder, speaking English with a German accent. He was older than Mycroft, tall and sallow-faced, but what really drew the eye was the dueling scar that neatly bisected his cheek.

"Yes! Yes! A man who must stay informed is an intelligent man," Si said with rapture and the deal was concluded.

The talk grew more general. Mycroft took Aziz aside to talk privately by the railing and the German caught my eye. He introduced himself as Dietrich, a Prussian from Konigsberg. He had studied at Heidelberg, where he picked up the dueling scar as a member of one of the student clubs renowned for their dedication to swordplay. He was traveling in the same way Englishmen acquired culture through the Grand Tour of Europe, after which he would become a soldier. Although stiff in manner, Dietrich exhibited a willingness to ingratiate himself and experiment with his English. It was rusty, but serviceable for his needs, and we amiably shared our plans for the day. I encouraged him to let us take him in tow, but he said he had tasks of his own to perform.

Soon we reached the shore of the city out of sight of the harbor, where the boat dropped anchor. We were somewhat taken aback by this, but we were reassured that this was how the thing was done here. A boat with three men pulled up for Si el Aziz. He had disappeared after talking to Mycroft. He reappeared in long robes with a red sash, Persian slippers, and a gold chain that he tucked under his clothes. His Western clothes were in a suitcase which he dropped into the longboat. He ordered the men to take his three chests and put them in his boat. Then he jumped in and was rowed away.

We called to him, and he shouted for us to await the Moors, who were approaching, and ride one of them to shore.

"Come! Come!" he called to us in English. "We are burning sunlight! There is much of Tangier to see! Yes, yes!"

That is how we set foot on our first truly alien shore, borne on the backs of Moors the short distance from the shallow-drafted steamboat. I reveled in the sensation of standing on *terra incognita*. I was eager for the adventure ahead. Dietrich was ahead of us. He had taken the first Moor available, and was already striding across the shingle and soon lost amid the natives.

[In the manuscript, Twain pasted a page from *The Innocents Abroad*.]

This is royal! Let those who went up through Spain make the best of it — these dominions of the Emperor of Morocco suit our little party well enough. We have had enough of Spain at Gibraltar for the present. Tangier is the spot we have been longing for all the time. Elsewhere we have found foreign-looking things and foreign-looking people, but always with things and people intermixed that we were familiar with before, and so the novelty of the situation lost a deal of its force. We wanted something thoroughly and uncompromisingly foreign — foreign from top to bottom — foreign from center to circumference--foreign inside and outside and all around — nothing anywhere about it to dilute its foreignness — nothing to remind us of any other people or any other land under the sun. And lo! In Tangier we have found it. Here is not the slightest thing that ever we have seen save in pictures--and we always mistrusted the pictures before. We cannot anymore. The pictures used to seem exaggerations — they seemed too weird and fanciful for reality. But behold, they were not wild enough — they were not fanciful enough — they have not told half the story. Tangier is a foreign land if ever there was one, and the true spirit of it can never be found in any book save *The Arabian Nights*. Here are no white men visible, yet swarms of humanity are all about us. Here is a packed and jammed city enclosed in a massive stone wall which is more than a thousand years old. All the houses nearly are one- and two-story, made of thick walls of stone, plastered outside, square as a dry-goods box, flat as a floor on top, no cornices, whitewashed all over — a crowded city of snowy tombs! And the doors are arched with the peculiar arch we see in Moorish pictures; the floors are laid in varicolored diamond flags; in tesselated, many-colored porcelain squares wrought in the furnaces of Fez; in red tiles and broad bricks that time cannot wear; there is no furniture in the rooms (of Jewish dwellings) save divans — what there is in Moorish ones no man may know; within their sacred walls no Christian dog can enter. And the streets are oriental — some of them three feet wide, some six, but only two that are over a dozen; a man can blockade the most of them by extending his body across them. Isn't it an oriental picture?

That's what I wrote, and if you read the rest of the chapter with care, you'll see there wasn't much detail. Of what I *read* there was plenty. Of what I *saw* I said little. There was the amusing description of one of our party attempting to enter a mosque on the back of an ass, and if it weren't for Si's intervention, he would have been chased through the town and stoned. Between that and the moment late in our visit when we met the American Consul and his family, I remained silent.

Here's what happened in between.

At the mosque, there was much muttering among the Moors and significant discussions with Si, and many dark looks directed at the heedless Blucher. Finally placated, they went into the mosque to take up their prayers and Si resumed leading us through the narrow and twisty lanes of the city.

He led us through the merchants quarters, where shopkeepers set out their wares on carpets laid on the ground and busied themselves with their work crafting more stock for their shelves. The streets were tight and we pushed our way through.

Then we found ourselves moving through narrower passages where the Moors had fled. Si had lost the thread of his chatter and his "Yes! Yes" was remote as a lighthouse on an off-shore island. We asked Si where we were going. He said, "To Paradise, Ifir, if Allah wills it."

I wasn't sure what he meant by that. His intention was clear soon enough when we stopped at the end of an alley.

"What do we do now, Si?"

"We wait, yes, yes, we wait," he said. "These two," he said, indicating Mycroft and myself. "The rest of you should run." He banged on one of the doors and shouted something in a burst of Arabic up at the second-floor windows.

"Whatever the devil for?"

"So you will not be killed." The doors opened all around us and the alley was filled with Bedouins. Hands were laid on us and we were invited with the aid of a few shoves to join them inside.

I expostulated. I pleaded. I roared. I was young and vigorous then, and let fly with a volley of abuse about anything of theirs at hand.

Mycroft batted my shoulder to get my attention. "Keep quiet! Your temper could get us killed."

This may be laying on more than half. I asked him what he meant.

"I believe they intend us no harm, but only if we cooperate."

I fell silent. Si had vanished, but Mycroft for all his youth seemed sure of his facts. This was my mistake. I should have followed my instinct and dashed his brains on the nearest doorframe and lit for daylight.

We were granted a tour of the home, but we did not greet the mistress of the house. We were not even permitted to leave our visiting cards. We were hustled out the back door and across the street into another building. As we passed from the darkened home and into the bright sunlight, I could see the backs of our companions racing up the road with men trotting after them, their bedsheets flapping and swords glinting in the sun.

We were hustled down another alleyway. I complained again about our handling. Mycroft not only said nothing, but he seemed to encourage them, moving easily to their rhythm and gazing at the sights around him, like a museum visitor who wanted to miss nothing.

We stopped at a low door. They pounded on the blue-painted wood and waited. There was an uncomfortable moment as our captors averted each other's eyes. What if no one was home? they were thinking. What should they do with us?

They started at the scraping of a heavy piece of wood being pulled back. The door opened a scant few inches and a woman's face revealed herself, briefly. She quickly veiled herself. Hasty, excited words were exchanged, and the door was pulled open and we were admitted.

They led us to a wide, shaded porch in a courtyard. At the center, a fountain sprayed water, providing a cooling contrast to the heat. We were led to low divans and ordered to sit.

"Now this is more accommodating. Tell the waiter to fetch us a couple of beers," I said. Mycroft shushed me.

We were joined by the owner of the establishment. We were considerably wider than he was tall. We could tell his status because his sheet was snowy white, his hands were unmarked by work, his face suffused with good food and unmarked by care. He was pleased to see us. He tried a few words of Arabic and French on us, then stopped when he saw that he wasn't striking home.

He clapped his hands and called out, and he was joined by a younger man. He was a slimmer edition of the host, but with a protruding nose that reminded one of Roman busts in Italy. He listened intently to the older fellow, then turned to us and said in English, "I am Abd Ghailan. You are welcome to the house of Hassan Herach. Peace be upon you." It was clear that he was familiar with the words, but not the music. His pronunciation was off-key, but he still made himself more understandable than some miners I knew back in Frisco.

"And peace be upon you, Hassan Herach," Mycroft said.

There was a long burst of Arabic between Hassan and Abd. "We hope your stay will be comfortable, but not long," Abd said. "You are honored guests until we can pass you along to the rebels, General Sherman."

That pulled me up short. I was expecting to hear my name, not that name.

"We are grateful that you have agreed to help lead the revolt—"

My mouth hung open like a trout angling for a worm.

"And that, *inshallah*, you will help us charge the palace and depose the sultan."

My mouth flapped a couple of times, and I was startled to hear words, only it wasn't me, it was Mycroft speaking for me.

"General Sherman is looking forward to the campaign, as much as he enjoyed capturing the port city of Savannah in America. It would please the general if he knew the disposition of your forces. He would like to begin planning the battle as soon as possible."

Abd delayed turning to his master to ask, "The general seems to have a question to ask?"

Mycroft said, "Let me inquire" and leaned into me. "Is there a problem?" he inquired mildly.

"I'm not Sherman," I hissed at him.

"Mmmm?" If there was any surprise in his response, he took great care to hide it. "Then this would not be a good time to mention it."

Before I could get steamed at his be-damned attitude, Mycroft said to Abd, "What the general means is that he is here under a *nom de guerre*. He looks like a shabby American tramp, but it is only a disguise for the brilliant soldier you need to overthrow the sultan."

That stopped me like a poleaxed bull. I burned a look at Mycroft that should have set his hair on fire. Abd turned and directed a blast of Arabic at Hassan, who beamed at us like a farmer appreciating his prized sows.

"He is pleased with your response," Abd said. "My master

would wish you to take food and rest until we hear from the rebels." He waved his arms and called to the servants. At Abd's orders, they led us down the hall into a comfortable room with divans and hangings and deposited us there.

I was puzzled and furious. I took refuge in a cigar and asked Mycroft for his opinion on the day's events. He kept himself busy pacing the chamber and carefully examining the walls.

"It appears your fame has spread, General Sherman, and you have been recruited into the army of the rebellion. Someone must have overheard you on the boat. We'll remain in Hassan's good graces so long as you keep up appearances. If he knows you're shamming," and he stopped his perambulations very close to me and said softly, "then I don't think we'll get out of here alive."

"He can't do that!"

"Why not?"

"We're guests here. I'm an American citizen."

"Who's just been told that Hassan Herach is plotting to overthrow the Emperor of Morocco. That's dangerous knowledge to have in your head. He may decide to keep it up there, and put it on a shelf for safekeeping."

This unsettled me considerably. There were a number of things I wanted to experience on this journey, and a beheading was not on the list. Meanwhile, Mycroft had spotted a barred window high up on the wall and a pile of baskets.

"If I can get up there, but I dare not pull them down on me. Here now, kneel and give us a leg up." I eyed him dubiously. I told him the view wasn't going to improve by getting closer to it.

"The view! I'm not — look, trust me and get down."

Having nothing better to do at the moment, I complied. He took a couple steps back. I could hear him shuffle his feet. I next felt the impact of a foot in the small of my back. He launched himself atop the baskets and my shoulders wrenched downward from the force. I must have ate a basket.

I'm sure I spit a straw at him.

I rolled over and sermonized some on the sin of stomping on a person's back without warning, but he was ignoring me. He was waving through the bars and chattering with someone in the street. I couldn't hear what he was saying. I took the trouble to roll myself up into a standing position and lit a cigar. I smoked and considered that not much had changed in the U.S.'s relations to the mother country.

He finished his chat and jumped lightly down. He was grinning as if he had been told the most marvelous joke, until he caught a whiff of my stogie. He blanched a little and waved at the smoke.

"What's got you amused?" I said.

"You'll see," was all he would admit, and he kicked at a bag of dates to test its freshness and settled himself on it. "Are you finding Tangier to your liking, Mr. Clemens?"

I blew out a cloud and considered. "Their attention to my comforts has been lacking, and I'm powerfully famished, but otherwise they are a hospitable people." Now that matters had quieted down, I got to thinking about what had happened and commenced worrying.

"The Arabs pride themselves on that point. I'm sure your friends are fine."

"That's comforting—," and I stopped at the new direction this conversation was taking. "What makes you think I care a tinker's dam for them?"

"You were thinking about them."

"I was not," I said, but with not much conviction.

"You had ceased roaring at me, which meant you were thinking," he said with more than a trace of smugness. "You were eying the barred window, but your face did not convey calculation, but concern. It wasn't about yourself that bothered you, but your friends."

"All right, since you put it that way. How do you know they're all right?"

"If our host's friends really meant to do them harm, they

wouldn't have let them reach the street. You'll recall as we were hustled out the back way that the gentlemen with the swords were within striking distance of them, yet did not attack."

"Is this how they commonly treat strangers?" I said.

He shrugged like a Frenchman. "This is not a Cook's tour you were on.["1]

"What happens to us next?"

But my question was not destined to be answered, at least by Mycroft. Out in the streets, a roaring could be heard, a ulululuation as if by a thousand voices. It was a mob, coming to call on the house.

I hopped up and down in my agitation. Mycroft stood up, shook out the wrinkles in his pants, and calmly turned to face the door.

"We, my dear sir, are about to be rescued," he said.

The door burst open. We were flooded with Tangierians. Unlike the first group we met, these seemed wilder. Their beards were longer and unkempt. Their robes were striped and foul. They appear to have bathed as often as Forty-Niners. They had clearly come for us, and they carried us off.

They placed us at the head of the parade. The men pressed around us, waving their swords and staffs in celebration. We were hustled down a narrow street in the merchants quarter. We had brief glimpses of street vendors with their stock on rugs before them, lit braziers the jewelmakers used to melt small pots of silver and bronze, alcoves and small carts bearing fruits and sweets. They scattered like flies at our flow of humanity until we left them behind to gape in wonder before they shrugged at the passing madness and returned

---

[1] Travelers participating in a tour organized by Thomas Cook & Son. The elder Cook (1808-1892) took advantage of the expanding British railway network to organize tours that included discounted train fares and food. The venture was so successful that "Cook's trippers" were looked down on as vulgar tourists being herded about to gawk at the natives and scribble graffiti on ancient sites.

their trade.

We stopped at another wide thick door. Dagger handles pounded on the panels. This was opened by a blackamoor slave, absurdly tall compared to the height of the door, and against the human wave he fell back impassively as if such events occurred daily.

This time, the majority of the party remained in the foyer while a half-dozen men escorted us through darker, smaller rooms. We were pushed up a set of stairs, and after the leader pounded on another door, were escorted through another set of quarters. Here for the first time, we saw women. Many of them. *Hareem,*[1] I thought, but this was no fantasy painted by English salon painters. These women were not clothed only in spangles or jewels, but from head to foot in heavy black hajibs. Some left their faces unclothed, and the younger women looked fresher, but all exhibited signs of carrying a heavy burden, like horses worked past their prime. That they barely noticed our passing, noisy and rough as a pirate crew, made me thoughtful when I recalled it later.

We were rushed through these rooms even faster — I suspect the men were singularly uncomfortable in these quarters, and we found ourselves in another storeroom, but with a ladder that gave access to a hole in the ceiling. Up that! We were on the roof. A flat roof at that, with a low wall around the edge. The hatch slammed behind us.

This time we were guarded by two men. They were seated against the wall, occupying what little shade the roof edge afforded us. They barely acknowledged our presence apart from a glance in our direction. They didn't seem to care that we would try to escape. I strode to the edge to test them. They did not move. I looked over the edge and saw why. It was a three-story drop to the street below, and their attitude was

---

[1] A Westernization of the Arabic *ḥarim,* meaning most popularly a sacred, inviolate place. Although popularly associated with Islam, the practice of secluding women existed for thousands of years in the Ottoman, Greek, and Persian empires.

clearly "go ahead and try. But watch that first step."

We could yell, but who would hear us? Who would come to our aid? We could leap for another building's roof, but that demanded more nerve than I could muster at the moment.

I looked around. Mycroft had settled himself next to the two men. He seemed to be trying to tell them a joke, because they were laughing. Mycroft wasn't, however. In fact, he didn't seem pleased at all.

I had lost my cigar in the parade, so I scratched a match on the wall and lighted another and observed, "This is a peculiar turn of events."

"It is?" Mycroft said. His hair was tousled and his face was shining with sweat.

"Yes. We have been rescued, it would appear, but we have been left imprisoned. Can you account for that?"

"There is something in what you say. Unfortunately, we won't get it from them."

We returned to quiet, leaving me to smoke in peace until the roof door opened with a crash. A head popped up, nodded to us. The swordsmen escorted us down and led us to the home's courtyard. There by a rectangular fountain with rows of single jets hissing water, was a large rectangular blanket laden with food in baskets and piled high on plates. Waiting for us at the head was a thin older man dressed in brilliantly colored robes. Next to him sat his assistant, a younger man who glared at us as if expecting any moment to have to strike us down. We sat on the carpet opposite them as if filling out a foursome for bridge.

The older man's head was covered with a cloth cap, and the hair that wasn't covered by it was grey and cropped short. He nodded to his assistant, who waved his hands at the spread.

There were fewer utensils on the board than I encountered my first time heading west by wagon. Mycroft spied my hesitation and said, "Follow my lead." Following the custom of these people, we ate with our right hands, carefully rolling balls of rice and popping them into our mouths like grapes. We drank cups of sweet tea and smiled to show there were no hard feelings; of stealing and imprisoning us on their part, and at being held captive and threatened with skinning on ours.

It was a jolly party, except during the first few courses Mycroft was clearly weighing a matter over in his head. He would eye me, eat a handful of rice, mumble a few words of gratitude to our host, and be received with the glare of a maiden aunt. Finally, with a huff of resignation, he spoke a few words of Arabic.

If I had a knife and fork, I would have dropped them. The effect on our host was electric as well. He spoke for himself, and Mycroft answered. Soon, they were holding a regular old confab, the burly assistant glaring at me and myself trying not to drop my food in my lap.

Mycroft broke his conversation to translate: "This is Ishmael Muhammad. He is a merchant. His aide de camp is Rais Uli, who promises to kill us if we offend his master. Ishmael commends us on our good fortune to be rescued from his rival, who is a dog who deserves beheading for his insults to us. He begs us to be patient. He has sent word to the sultan that we are his guests, and that for the proper payment we will be returned unharmed."

"How did he know we were on offer?"

"Ah," he adjusted himself into a more comfortable position. "It seems that word of our arrival had spread through the *souks* — their marketplaces.

"So why us?"

"Because Europeans in Tangier are protected by the consuls who have influence with the emperor. We, however, have no influence. We are valuable only as a source of currency."

I confessed that I was perplexed about Morocco's customs. Was kidnapping the common method of welcoming guests?

"Not for everyone," Mycroft said. "You've come here at an

interesting time. Morocco and Spain fought a war a few years back. It did not go well for Sultan Muhammad IV. The treaty called for an indemnity payment to Spain that was 20 times the government's annual budget. He's been squeezing the inland tribes who owe him fealty as well as everyone else, and they're resisting."

"But what does that have to do with us? We're not Spaniards."

"The chain of logic is simple, once you know enough facts to construct it. The tribes resist the sultan. To do that, they need weapons; good, sturdy, expensive, European guns. They need money. They can't rob much here. There's not enough gold to go around. So they kidnap foreigners."

"So does this mean I can stop claiming to be Sherman? Considering I'm not to be drafted after all."

"I'm afraid so."

We bantered about a number of subjects. Knowing I was an American, Ishmael wanted to know about the rivers of gold and silver discovered in California and Nevada. I sketched an outline of my adventures in that line, and he asked if it were possible to find similar veins in the mountains of Morocco. I averred that I wasn't a geologist and couldn't say. I suspected that if gold had been discovered, it had been long dug out and moved away. Morocco had been inhabited for thousands of years. Gold laying about in its streams like the one at Sutter's Mill would have been found and exploited long ago. He nodded and muttered, "Inshallah" — "If Allah wills it" — the standard phrase about luck good or bad, for maladies inflicted or received.

After we had eaten and drank our fill, we were invited to rest. We couldn't refuse such hospitality. Led by a slave with a lantern and rope, and followed by two guards, we were taken to a room with a couple of low divans and low tables nearby. Without bothering to shuck our clothes, we were flopped down on the larger of the two and our arms tied behind us at the wrists. The slave left the room and closed the door. The bolt slid into place, and we said nothing until the *shuush-shuush-shuush* of the slave's slippers faded to silence.

My eyes adjusted to the gloom, and I saw cracks of light peeping through the wooden panels barring the window. It was muggy. The air was saturated with moisture. I sneezed several times from the dust. The quiet stimulated my brain-pan[1] and I reflected on events during our journey that had been puzzling me. Next to me on the divan, Mycroft was squirming as if his clothes were infested with lice.

I told him, "I been cogitating about your stories, and I'm wondering if you know more than you've been willing to share. I didn't have it on my itinerary that I was to be shanghaied. It doesn't suit me.

"Yet here I am, snaffled not once but twice, along with a stranger who, after showing ignorance of the language and politics, seems at home in this country. You certainly didn't get all that gossip about Sultan Muhammad from afternoon tea in Oxford. Send up a flare if I'm sighting land, will you?"

He said nothing but emitted a sharp whistle that cracked my ears. He was paying more heed to the window than to me.

"Indications to the contrary, you're not a fresh-faced whelp looking for a spree. You got more under your hat than your hair. Now, if I knew more about what you're looking for, I might be amiable to help. You're looking for some thing. Someone who's been kidnapped? No. If they'd be wanting ransom, you'd know who did it and where to look. So it's the person behind the snatchings. You don't know who, because if you did, you'd go asking in every nook and cranny. But you don't, so you're blundering around like a schoolboy, which I'd say you are, because you haven't the foggiest notion of where to begin."

He stiffened at that. I had struck a blow, so I pressed my advantage. "I suppose when I get out of here, I'll have a chat with the American consul about you. Did you know I'm writ-

---

[1] A non-medical name for the cranial cavity. The word has been traced back to the 12th century, from the Old English *braegenpanne*.

ing letters to a Sacramento newspaper back home? This'll make a thrilling story, especially after I work my imagination on it. 'British spy drags American into Moroccan nightmare!' Yes sir," I sucked in a cloud to give that shaft time to settle in, "once that gets to the New York newspapers, it'll hit London like a comet. It'll make them sit up and take notice. And where will you be when it does? Back at Oxford?"

"All right, you've made your point, but what I tell you cannot be revealed to another soul."

I nodded. "I'm not who I say I am."

"Do tell."

"And I didn't give you quite accurate information."

"That's a given."

"There's been an increase in kidnappings for ransom here. We suspect someone's using it to buy weapons for the hill tribes, possibly for a revolt against the sultan."

"What for?"

"Could be anything," Mycroft said. "The sultan has given up reforming the country after the Spanish debacle. He's retreated to his harem, his poetry, his intellectual interests. A change of rulers could shift the balance to France, Russia, even the Ottomans. Piracy could return, focused on British shipping passing through the straits.

"I concluded it was the Prussians, with this new fellow called Bismarck directing foreign policy, but Whitehall says it's the French. They discount the Prussian threat entirely. I want to prove them wrong."

I let that sink in and concluded he had gone crack-headed from the heat. To explain why, I must adopt the manner of a pedagogue.[1] I don't know what the world will know a century from now. At the time, Germany didn't exist. There was the North German Confederation ruled by Prussia with the help of Bismarck. Bismarck was barely a year in power as chancellor under Willy the First. The struggle everyone was watching

---

[1] A teacher, particularly a strict or dogmatic one.

was between Britain and France, with Russia throwing their weight with whoever benefits them the most. So listening to Mycroft in the semi-darkness of our makeshift cell rattling on about the dangers of Prussia made as much sense as saying fairies are real.[1]

"So when you came along, Clemens, introducing yourself as Sherman, I saw a way of getting deep inside Tangier culture. Si el Aziz knows the city well and arranged for our capture. He was supposed to rescue us once I gave him the sign, but that did not happen like I planned."

"And is Aziz going to rescue us?"

"That I do not know. Which means we need to leave."

"The vote is unanimous. Shall we walk out like this?"

"Best to leave the ropes behind. Let me give a pull here—"

"It's sturdy rope—" and then his wrists separated and he held his hands before me.

"A knife blade concealed in my sleeve." Mycroft examined the hole at the arm end of his coat. "My tailor will be distraught. Can't be helped. If you will turn?" He held up the blade and grinned like a maniac.

When the feeling was restored to my arms, we examined the barred window. With the help of the blade, Mycroft picked the heavy lock, threw open the panels and we climbed into the alley. We reached the street and stood there a moment trying to decide which way to run when we heard the hiss of "My-kul! My-kul!" Si el Aziz was in the alley across the street, beckoning us to follow him.

We trotted to catch up with him. The sun scalded my head, and made the coolness of the narrow alley all the more welcoming.

"Hurry! We must hurry!" he said, his robes fluttering be-

---

[1] Twain's summary of the political situation at that time is accurate, although this is the earliest evidence of German interest in Morocco. In 1905 and 1911, German acts over Morocco raised European tensions and, if a few decisions had gone the wrong way, could have sparked World War I years earlier.

hind him. "Have you fulfilled your mission, yes, yes?"

"Enough," Mycroft said. "I must see the British consul. Hay will know what to do."

"That is good, very good," Si el Aziz was gasping as he led us through the twists and turns, deeper into the close-packed block.

"Is this the way back to the port?" I said.

"It is very important that we go this way, yes, yes," he said.

I chewed over that statement as we hurried. I was having my doubts about this affair, especially when it seemed like we were never going to get out of this congestion. We passed parties of veiled women, Moors bearing heavy bundles on their heads, gangs of raggedly dressed children slipping through the semi-dark like silverfish.

Then there was a turn down an alley lit by a blaze of light that assaulted our eyes. We stumbled toward the end like we were entering heaven. The noise of crying merchants mingled with the braying of donkeys and camels deafened me.

Then we reached the street and into the arms of several robed and masked men, who seized us. We were tossed like cordwood onto a wagon. Blankets were heaped on us, and a few backsides sat on us as a suggestion to stay in place. The teamster yelled at the donkeys, and we rolled to an unknown destination.

It was stuffy and smelly underneath the blankets. I spent my leisure trying to breathe as little of it in as possible. Si el Aziz had become too enthusiastic about his job. He was supposed to arrange one kidnapping and one rescue, and he threw in a second on his own hook. I began to suspect that he had not been playing fair with us, and I would certainly not tip him when we were finished with him.

Moreover, I was not pleased with Mycroft's role in this falderal. I had signed onto the *Quaker City* tour to visit foreign lands, but not while wearing bonds and gags. I most certainly did not asked to be kidnapped, held at sword-point, threatened with beheading, and held for ransom. I am certain I did not ask for that on the application form.

There were many questions buzzing around in my head, and I hoped for more time on this side of life to ask them. My ruminations were interrupted when the wagon turned sharply. We stopped feeling the blazing heat of the sun. The wagon stopped suddenly, we heard the clashing of wooden doors closing, and we were handled like packages out of the wagon and dropped to the ground, where we were allowed to stand and dust ourselves off.

We were in a large barn, surrounded by our captors, fingering their cutlery and regarding us as a butcher regards a sheep with a certain future. One of them nodded toward a door and we obeyed. We walked into a room, followed by three of the men. The door was slammed shut, and we turned to see the two assistants, Abd Ghailan and the evil-eyed Rais Uli, accompanied by another man whose facial features were obscured by a blood-red head scarf.

This was curious. They had been clearly working for their employers. Were they working for them still? Or was it someone else now? And what did they want with us?

They talked among themselves between shifting glares our way. Since my hands were free, I unholstered another cigar and set it alight.

Mycroft made a face like he had bit into a lemon. "Must you smoke so much?"

"I have never regarded myself as an excessive smoker," I said with the surety of a saved soul. "I never smoke when I am asleep, and I do not smoke more than one cigar at a time."

We were clearly in a stable of some kind, and the room was used to store tack and saddles. There was a small table and a couple of chairs against the far wall. The men were blocking our way to the only door out of this space. Being a seasoned kidnap victim by now, I elected to sit and rest.

The three men stopped their discussion at rising cries from within the barn. Even not knowing the lingo, I could conclude they were friendly greetings for a new arrival. Maybe there would be lunch.

"He is coming!" Abd Ghailan said. [Mycroft told me this later.]

"He is coming?" Rais Uli said. The third man said nothing but snorted and tucked his loosened scarf behind his neck.

"Who is coming?" I said.

"Their leader," Mycroft said. "Perhaps the mind behind this unrest." The blood drained from his face. I turned.

Dietrich walked in.

"I'm very pleased to meet you again." He dropped his newspapers on the table and sat down. After so many years, I could still see the *Harper's Weekly* on top, the only thing so recognizably American that seemed so out of place here.

Then he turned to me and said, "Gen. Sherman, it is a pleasure to see you again. But I do have one question I would like to ask."

His smile sent a chill through me. There was no mirth in it. There was no genuine pleasure in seeing me.

"If you are the general," and he reached over to the *Harper's Weekly* and flipped over a few pages, "then who is this Sherman?"

There he was, on the page, a woodcut of the man boarding a ship bound for Mexico aboard the *Susquehanna*. The issue was more than six months old, but that wouldn't excuse the fact that I resembled the man who gifted Savannah to Lincoln for Christmas like a strawberry resembles a pumpkin.[1]

"So! What should we do with my two spies," Dietrich said.

---

[1] Ironically, Twain would meet Sherman at a dinner in Chicago in November of 1879. The Army of Tennessee held a reunion to honor Grant. At 2 in the morning, Twain rose, the last speaker, to deliver a toast to "the babies." It was such a success that Sherman congratulated him afterwards, saying "I don't know how you do it!" It is probable that Twain prudently did not tell Sherman about his masquerade in Morocco.

DEPARTURE OF LIEUTENANT-GENERAL SHERMAN FOR MEXICO—HIS RECEPTION ON BOARD THE UNITED STATES FRIGATE "SUSQUEHANNA." Sketched by A.R.Ward [See Page 742.]

Outside, we could hear the call to prayer. "With our plan to cast Britain out of Morocco and then from Gibraltar nearly complete, I can't afford to keep you around." He was talking to himself as if he was thinking through the logic of his intentions. "I shall sell you to a slaver."

To our shocked faces he said, "Do not be too scared. European men bring a high price as house servants. If you resist, they'll put you to work in the fields. By the time you escape, there will be a new emperor on the throne." He called out a name, and through the door appeared Si el Aziz, our treacherous guide. "Tell Ayush Et-Lezra here to take them to the slave market. Find a slaver bound for Marrakesh. Take whatever price is offered."

"Yes, yes!" Si said. He translated the orders to the man in the red scarf, who nodded.

"Good day, general," Dietrich said, and this time he meant it, and they left the room.

But then a peculiar thing happened. Instead of leaping upon us like his fellow Moroccans had been doing all day,

Ayush stayed rooted in place. He looked down at his sword, deep in thought. Abd Ghailan and Rais Uli exchanged questioning glances. These desperados seemed reluctant to carry out their Dietrich's order.

It reminded me of Black Bart, who I knew in San Francisco. He was a desperate man. Nothing scared him. He showed fright over nothing, except nuns. Whenever the mothers of Mary appeared, Bart minded himself so carefully it would make a dog laugh. We would have, too, except he wasn't afraid of us, and we were definitely afeared of him.

Ayush sidled over to me. Turning his back on Mycroft, he snorted, then spoke softly, and to my shock in English.

"A question, may I ask? If you were free, out in the street, what would you do?"

"Do? I'd kick up so much dust racing for the ferry that you'd think a sandstorm was coming."

He could feel a sneeze coming on, but pressed to say, "You wouldn't, say, you understand, tell the consul?"

"Why you blithering wretch! Of course I—"

A hand clamped over my mouth.

"Of course we wouldn't!" Mycroft said. Ayush loose a sneeze that puffed his scarf out of place. Then he sneezed again.

Mycroft paused, his head tilted like a coon dog hearing something in the bushes. The ruffian's nasal music had stirred a chord of memory in Mycroft. He said, "Binky? Is that you? Of *course* it is!"

The beast slumped at being found out. He pulled his scarf back, revealing a deeply tanned face. "Fiddles! You always were hard to fool, Ego."

"Dust never suited your sinuses, and don't call me that."

"Only if you drop that Binky nonsense. It won't do in the field."

"Done. What are you doing in the back of beyond? Whitehall didn't—"

He made a shushing gesture. "Security, you know, one

hand can't be seen washing the other—"

"A bloody bollocks, if you asked me."

"Yes, well," Binky dropped the tip of his sword and rested on his pommel like a farmer hanging over the fencepost. "Have you seen Twiddles? You were so close. How's the pater—"

Their confab was interrupted. Dietrich came back in, trailed by Si el Aziz. "What is going on here? Why are you talking to them?" He drew his gun. "I give an order; it shall be carried out."

Binky turned back into Ayush Et-Lezra and said, "*Sidi*—" meaning "Master."

"Take them out of here! Perhaps they need encouragement even if this will lower his price," and he pointed his gun at Mycroft's feet.

He froze. Binky's sword pricked the center of Dietrich's throat. "I wouldn't do that old chap. Seems that Ego's a mate of mine."

Dietrich burst into a Teutonic curse that no one could understand, then told Si el Aziz, "Tell Abd and Rais to kill the heretics!"

Then Rais spoke —

"I'm sorry, Herr Dietrich," he said in heavily French-accented English. He sheathed his sword and bowed to us. "Jean Armand Joyeuse of the Ministry of War. If Been-key is playing it that way, I cannot do otherwise," he added with a smirk.

Binky groaned.

Dietrich looked mad enough to bite the barrel of his gun. With the sword still poised at his throat, he couldn't rant too hard, but instead eyed the third man.

He shrugged. "I am still Abd Ghailan," he said. "But Spanish military."

Mycroft said, "I could almost feel sorry for you, Dietrich. You went to great trouble to build a mine underneath the throne of Morocco. Wormed yourself in, secretly ran guns, flattered, bribed, and recruited your allies. Your dreams of a fine coup fizzled because you couldn't tell a native Moroccan from a European in cork and greasepaint."

Dietrich recovered himself well, though. He stood ramrod-straight and defied everyone. He glared at Binky with disdain. "Know that I go to my death a Prussian soldier."

"Oh, don't be like that, Herr Dietrich," he took the Prussian's gun and stuck it in his waistband. "This inning is over. You'll have your revenge on another field." His friends chimed in with their support as well. You'd think they were commiserating with a rival on the cricket field, which stirred Dietrich's hash. His face darkened like a thundercloud, and he shivered like a boiler nearing eruption.

Then he exploded. "You have won this time, but I assure you that we will learn from this! England will not dominate us forever! We will—"

His steam was up and he was building into a fine flow of invective, but he was drowned out by shouting from the street. A drumbeat of hooves rose in volume, accompanied by a chorus of cries in Arabic.

Binky said, "Monsieur Joyeuse, please to look out off the window and tell us what you see."

"There is much turmoil in the streets. A troop of the emperor's guards approach. It is time for us to fade into the crowds."

As if to confirm his statement, the door flew open. The rest of the crew, true Moroccans this time, stormed in to cry the news.

Binky sheathed his sword. "We must go," he told his fellow spies. He hastily shook Mycroft's hand. "I'm a member of White's.[1] Stop by for a drink? Come on, lads, time to evict, stage right, pursued by a bear."[2]

---

[1] A London club for upper-class gentlemen founded in 1693 as a place to dine, drink, gamble, gossip, and network. It is one the world's most exclusive clubs, not surprising considering one of its members is Prince Charles.
[2] One sign of an upper-class Oxbridge-educated gentleman is the ability to quote from the classics. In this case, it's a stage direction — correctly

Dietrich was gibbering by this time, stamping his feet and shouting, but he was drowned out by cries of the villains and the storming for the doors.

I patted his shoulder and said, "you'd best run. The Emperor of Morocco is not going to reward you for your work among the heathens."

He stiffened, and I thought for a moment that he would strike me. But the shots fired outside reminded him of the danger he was in.

"General Sherman, you and your friend must come to Germany, so you may receive the hospitality you deserve." He fled.

More gunshots could be heard outside, but it didn't sound like there was much anger behind it. The uproar quieted, replaced by the rapid-fire volley of marching feet coming down the hall. Into the room came a brash young man in a tan suit and white pith helmet. Pale sandy hair, sun-blistered nose, handsome face. I didn't need Mycroft to tell me he was an American. I didn't know at the time, but I was seeing the grown-up Tom Sawyer.

Behind him stomped two members of the Emperor's Guard, spears at the ready. Tom's eager blue eyes shifted among us and he piped out: "Are you the captives?"

I didn't speak to Mycroft again until we were on the boat back to Cadiz. There was no opportunity. We were taken to the American consul, while Tom and Mycroft went to John Drummond Hay,[1] the long-time British consul who had great

phrased "Exit, pursued by a bear" — from Shakespeare's *The Winter's Tale*. Binky's quote belies the fact that the bear's appearance interrupts Antigonus as he is abandoning the infant Princess Perdita. The baby is rescued by a shepherd, while Antigonus is killed by the bear.
[1] As Envoy Extraordinary to the Court of Morocco, Sir John Hay Drummond Hay (1816-1893) was one of the great diplomats of history, chiefly by keeping Her Majesty out of hot water there, giving the empire room to find trouble elsewhere. At 28, after spending four years in Constantinople,

influence with the emperor. Everything was smoothed over, but by the time the bloodhounds were sent after Dietrich, he had disappeared.

When all of that was done, we were aboard the small steamer, chugging across the Mediterranean. Tangier was fading away on our stern, the low buildings radiating a dull reddish-gold. To the west the sun was beginning to set beyond the Pillars of Hercules,[1] a brilliant yellow light fading to a corona of gold-brown before darkening to eternal night. Above the stars were gleaming like pinpricks of diamonds. I was using the last of the light to get a few more impressions into my notebook.

A hand reached around me and grabbed my notebook. Mycroft quickly paged through it, ripped out the relevant notes, and cast them to the wind. I expressed my opinion of his act in the most vigorous language. I tore my slouch hat off and stamped on it. Arabs within earshot kneeled to pray and beseech Allah to spare the vessel from God's wrath.

"You cannot tell anyone what happened," he handed back my notebook after I stopped ranting. "As a representative of Her Majesty's government, I should warn you that she will remember how she is treated in the press."

"Especially when they're the ones doing the fooling? Disguising themselves as natives? Plotting to bring down a king? Oh, that's a grand joke."

"It had its amusing aspects, but thanks to our intervention we prevented that happening. It won't help anyone to write about this, especially you."

Hay was sent to help the Consul-General in Morocco. He proved so useful that within a few months he was given the job that he would hold for the next four decades. In addition to overseeing British interests, he would help the sultan negotiate treaties with other countries as well. His affection for Morocco was made clear after he retired, when he continued to spend part of the year there.

[1] The ancient name given to the promontories that flank the Strait of Gibraltar. Plato placed the lost continent of Atlantis beyond the Pillars of Hercules.

He looked too young to be Queen Victoria's agent, but he spoke with a monumental cock-assuredness. I decided it would not do to set her nose out of joint. The sun was nearly out, leaving behind brilliant blood-gold bands. It'll be pitch-black soon. I put my notebook away.

"No," I told Mycroft. "I won't tell it. It wouldn't suit the tone. This is a travel book, not a damned dime novel. Not like anyone'd believe it anyway."

He nodded. "Well done. As for myself, I am determined to stay put from now on. London is my home. Let the adventurers go out into the world. My talents lay at home." He gazed not at the sunset, but northwards to England. "You must come and visit."

"Not if I can help it," I said bitterly.

Afterward

Looking through the electronic folder containing my collection of notes, images, PDF books and other ephemera, I find it hard to believe that writing this story took two years. But there it is, in the dates when files were created, and the date when the "Great War I" volume in the 223B Casebook series was published.

What's also odd is that this story came up out of nowhere. It's not on the list of possible stories I created at the start of the project. It must have arisen spontaneously and gotten its hooks into me.

The inspiration came from Twain himself. His chapter on Tangier in *The Innocents Abroad* is remarkably incomplete. Much of it consists of stuff he pulled from guidebooks and histories, and he ends the chapter with a long piece about the time he spent with the American consul's family. It was as if he did things there that he couldn't tell his readers. I decided that this story would provide the answer.

By this time, I was inspired by the appearance of Irene Adler in the "Jersey Girl" story to consider who else from Holmes' world could crop up. That naturally led to Mycroft, and as I did with a young Watson in "Dancing Man," I decided to introduce a young Mycroft to Twain in Morocco.

What I didn't expect was to do a lot of homework. I read up on what little Conan Doyle had to say about the man in the stories, figured out how old he'd be in 1867, and why he go there in the first place. I consulted Mark Gatiss' comments on Mycroft at a Sherlocked event. I confess that I even found photos of a university-age Gatiss to use as an inspiration.

That led to numerous books about Morocco, many of them travel books by intrepid visitors. Fortunately, I live in the age of Google Books and Internet Archive. Except for one book on Moroccan cooking, all my research was performed online. There's a list of them in the bibliography. I confess I didn't read every word of these books, except Edith Wharton's *In Morocco* and the pulpish *King of the Air: To Morocco by Plane*. I looked for chapters on Tangier and used keyword searches for certain subjects. From them, I compiled a 7,000-word file on 40 subjects, from animals to women, including the races, their attitudes, and the country's relations with Spain (poor), Britain (excellent), and Germany (just beginning).

As for the story, the basic thread was there, but the twists and turns it takes took a long time to sort out. Who did the kidnappings and why? How would they escape? Why would Mycroft go there and how would he get along with Twain? Lots of heavy thinking went into the process, and a file of text cut from the MS shows the different directions it could have taken.

The Adventure of the
Dancing Man

The Adventure
of the Dancing Man (1868)

———◆———

HARRIET BEECHER STOWE CROSSED the river a decade ago this week. An article in a Cape Town newspaper reminded us of her passing, and that started a train of thought in my head. She lived next door to us in Hartford. I knew her well. She was an eccentric lady, and as she grew older her mind began to slip its moorings, when she would wander and talk nonsense. If she caught you unawares, she'd let out a war whoop just to see you leap. Seeing her then, you wouldn't believe that this was the woman credited with starting the late, lamented conflict. But she always had a kind word for people. Once, she stopped me on the street and held my hand in her shaky, firm grip. She told me that the Pauper book was the finest story for children she had ever read. I about busted into tears. She was so sincere and so powerful in her opinion, that you knew it had to be true. This, you knew, was the woman capable of making you care about Eliza and Eva and Uncle Tom and what happened to them and to hate with a passion the men and society who put them there. To her, the argument over slavery was simple. Men and women should be free. Everything else in her philosophy flowed from it, and we became a better nation for it.

I watched the storm that grew and broke over that book of hers, and I wondered what she did with her words that caused it. The difference between lightning and the lightning-bug. That's the difference, as I've said elsewhere, between myself and the humorists, acclaimed in their time and forgotten today. The humorist who gauges his success by the number of laughs he elicits is damned to obscurity. He tells jokes; I preached. I made the audience laugh, and that gave me the opening to slip in my sermon. But did anyone really listen? Mrs. Stowe did not tell jokes, yet her words carried all before her, like an avenging army of angels.

It brings to mind another writer whose stories are popular, and I wonder what'll happen to them when he's gone. They're all the rage nowadays, and I blush to say now that I knew him before he wrote those stories. But this is my autobiography, set down now and not to be published until long after I have slid into my grave. So I will tell this story, because I knew John H. Watson, and I knew Sherlock Holmes. I will not see them anymore on this side of the earth. Watson's retired and Holmes, we're told, has fled to his farm on the coast. They are in my past, and as long as I'm telling my story I might as add my times with them as well. I don't know if I want them read. I'll decide that afterwards. If I don't, I'll have Katy use the manuscripts to light her fires.

The story takes place in San Francisco back in 1868. It is a mighty metropolis today, a crown jewel in the coronet of this nation. Back in my day, it was a roaring, brawling mining town. The first wave of '49ers had crashed into the California hills and receded, leaving 50,000 souls, half of them miners from the hills, the rich and the busted, and the other half tending to their needs. Inland, there were thousands more in the mining camps from Rich Bar to Mariposa, scratching and digging for their lives.

I had spent several years out West, failing as a miner and day laborer until finding my niche in a Virginia City newspaper. Then I moved to San Francisco, stayed a few years, and then rambled about the Sandwich Islands. I had made some noise in the East with a villainous backwoods sketch about a jumping frog, and saw the wonders of the Holy Land with a pack of pilgrims aboard the *Quaker City*. My letters to the *Daily Alta* newspaper created a boom in my stock, and the publishers were asking me to make it into a book. At the time, I was working for Senator Stewart in Washington and heard that the *Alta* was planning to do the same with my letters. There might be a call in the market for one book, but two would be more than it could bear. I had to throw up my position, take a steamer via Panama, and land in San Francisco to resolve the matter.

When that was settled to my satisfaction, I resumed work on the manuscript for *The Innocents Abroad.* I lectured in town, then wandered to Sacramento, Virginia City and Carson City. That kept my pockets full without descending into newspaper work. I finished the book and the lecturing before the Fourth of July. That left me two days before the 6th, when the steamer *Montana* would carry my carcass back to the East.

Nowhere else could the Fourth of July be celebrated with as much spirit as in San Francisco. The town dressed itself up in bunting and flags so elaborate that some buildings acquired a second skin. If that wasn't enough to remind you of the founding of the country, there were the parades, literary exercises, bands a-playing, speechifying, parties, and balls to remind you. The day had begun chilly and windy. The breeze came in off the bay, turning a ton of Pacific water to mist that hazed the streets. The field batteries at Fort Point and Alcatraz raised the dawn, and the vessels in the harbor responded with full-throated roars of their own. That's the signal for people to set off their fireworks, and the racket did not stop. When one group faded, another picked up the job. I was enjoying the riot with Bret Harte. He had been working like a fiend, overseeing the *Overland Monthly* and reading the *Innocents* manuscript, and was ready to play. We cheered the procession, looking in on the speechifying, and drank the health of the country at lunch. The tide turned in the afternoon, and it became sunnier and warmer, adding to the cheerfulness of the day. We observed the regatta during the afternoon, and walked the crowded streets, dodging the Chinese fireworks and soaked up the happiness.

We landed on the grounds behind the old Mission Church, watching the cricket match between the Pioneers and St. George clubs when we heard an English voice explaining the leg-before-wicket rule.

"It's quite simple, really. A batsman who uses his pads to

stop the ball from hitting the wicket can be declared lbw by the umpire after an appeal by the opposing team. But only if the ball is in line with the wickets and its trajectory is such that it would have hit the wickets if the batsman did not stop it. But not if it hits him outside the line of off stump — oh! well played! Did you see that googly?"

He was a young lad, barely old enough to shave, but already he was bluff and hearty in that English fashion. He seemed animated by springs, and his voice carried in great gusts across the field. Despite his ancestors being on the losing side nearly a century before, he was in love with the world and wanted everyone to appreciate the day as much as he.

He saw us noticing him and asked if that was, indeed, the googliest googly we had ever seen. We agreed heartily.

"Who is the lad bowling for the Pioneers?"

We said it was the captain, Chisholm. This pleased him even though he didn't know the man. We said who we were. That pleased him more.

He told us he was John Watson and pumped our hands as if he were a thirsty man hoping for water. He was bound for Australia. He had developed a powerful curiosity to see the New World. He looked in at New York, then took a steamer via the Isthmus of Panama to San Francisco. The next ship bound for Sydney was the *Day Dawn* on the 15th, but he hoped to find one leaving before that, as he was low on funds.

We were charmed by his accent and his bluff heartiness. He was as boisterous as a puppy. Harte and I knew our duty. I was flush with proceeds from my speaking tour, and Harte knew the freshest entertainments the City offered. We needed to take this child of the Empire under our wing and show him Western hospitality. From that moment, his purse was not to be opened under any circumstance.

After the match was over, we toured young Watson through the town. We walked down Market, passing the wooden stands that were erected to watch the fireworks show. John described the ascension of the flying machine

Gladiator earlier that day, and we speculated on using giant balloons some day to travel across the sea in comfort and complete safety. We stopped for refreshments frequently and at each stop introduced Watson to a new companion. At each encounter, he revealed a mind fired with curiosity. To Doctor Gillespie, he enquired about the diseases he had befriended and the course of his medical training. To Buck Kennedy, who haunted the mining camps since '49, he educated himself about the latest mining processes. With Colonel Warden, the Indian fighter, there was an earnest discussion about the difference between spotting a Comanche and an Apache at a distance — the best way to encounter them.

By sundown, the winds had shifted seaward and a chill infested the air. The streets darkened, and the gaslights illuminated the buildings and cast parades of shadows on the streets. We had enough time before the fireworks exhibition to duck into Martin's. We loaded up on porterhouse steaks and buckwheat cakes, topped with shots of whiskey, and followed the crowd back out into the street. Overhead the fireworks glowed and thundered, some low enough to dust our clothes with stray cinders.

We were nearing the intersection with Montgomery when we realized that we had mislaid a Watson. We scanned the crowds high and low, but neither hide nor scalp could we see. Bret and I retraced our path. The street was wide, so he cast an eye to port and me to starboard. We let our ears set our course. San Francisco is home to many accents. It is Babel of flat American tones, lilting Irish chants, melodic Mexican accents, and the inscrutable Chinese dialects. But speakers of the Queen's English stand out.

I spotted him in earnest discussion with a trio of ruffians down one of the narrow alleys. He was just a few steps off the street, down in the shadows. I looked over his broad back, and saw that one of the men was holding a young Chinese woman dressed in the plain woolen dress common to their race. Her downward stare did not show fear, but her rigid stance, still as a cemetery angel, spoke volumes. What caught my attention, moreover, was her hair. It was streaked with silver, bound with the traditional bun in the back.

As I drew near, the gist of John's talk grew clearer. The three men had been sporting with the girl; her objections had caught John's ear and he was giving them an earful of English invective about their manners and sportsmanship. They were shooting each other sly looks, and it was clear that their steam was rising. Two of them were of a type common in the City. They could have been twins. They wore slouch hats, blue woolen shirts, loose denims crammed into boots. They were clean-shaven, but only a mite dusty, and were expelling fumes like a distillery, so I reckoned they had come in from the mining fields and been civilized only for the day.

The third fellow was leaning with his arms crossed against the far alley wall and showed more intelligence in his eye than the other two combined. His face looked familiar but I could not spare too much time from the conversation in progress.

John became aware of me by his side and said, "Sam! I'm glad you're here. They refuse to let this girl be."

"This is none of your concern," the man holding the girl grumbled, "so why don't you skedaddle before you get hurt, kid." John's Adam's apple was working like a pile driver, but he wasn't going to show yellow. "Excuse me, Clemens," he said, and struck a plucky fighting stance that would have made the Marquis of Queensbury beam with pride for the courage of his countrymen.

When they heard John call to me by my last name, everyone wanted to contribute to the conversation. It's difficult to express in prose, but imagine if you would the following happening at the same time:

"Now John —" [Me, nervous about what could happen.]

"Let the girl go." [John, striking a pose reminiscent of Ivanhoe.]

"Clemens! Clemens of the *Call!*" [Wall-holding fellow deciding to take a part in the proceedings, at least the part that involved me.]

"Bugger off, Limey" [One of the twins, giving the Chinese girl's arm a wrench for emphasis.]

"Fàng kāi wǒ de gēbó." [The Chinese girl, begging to be released.]

"Want us to scrag 'em, Big Jim?" [The other twin, reaching behind him for something that was probably not to our liking.]

"Ching-wah tsao duh liou mahng!"[The Chinese girl, characterizing their parentage and suggesting they're fond of frogs, better left untranslated.]

"Release the girl!" John said. He began bobbing on his toes like an engine piston turning over.

"Oh,—" [Me, realizing with a sinking heart that I had been spotted by Big Jim Crosby, saloon owner and brother of a police official I had regularly torn apart in my columns years before.]

I looked for Bret, but he had vanished in the riot of wagons and crowds. Meanwhile, the twins had a good laugh at John's threat, until he bounded like a kangaroo and popped one of them in the nose. It was the one holding the girl, and he squealed like a lanced pig and clapped his hands to staunch the flood of blood from his nose. The girl was quick-witted enough to push behind him and sprint down the dark alley, but not before turning around and giving him a kick.

A blast overhead temporarily deafened the conversation, and that was the last I saw of John. He advanced to engage the enemy. I retreated onto the higher ground of the sidewalk and then streaked into the street. I plunged into the crowd, hit the dirt road, and pumped my legs. The twins followed, leaving John and Big Jim to settle the debate between them. Any guilty emotions that I felt for abandoning him were tabled unanimously in favor of saving my skin from a hiding.

At the cross street, I dodged under a slow-moving wagon and turned right. I pounded down the sidewalk, dodging the strolling citizens and hunting for a bolt-hole. I ducked down an alley, blindly scattering the trash and gasping for breath. My thoughts caught up with me and I began to put the pieces together. Big Jim Crosby was noted for never straying far from his saloon. That meant that I was running around Big Jim's building. I was in the alley behind his place, so one more right turn, and I would run into him.

I was planning on streaking straight, but my arm had other plans. Something hooked my elbow at the intersection. Most of me wanted to turn. My feet debated carrying on straight, but changed their vote at the last minute and that carried the motion unanimously. I faced the rough wooden wall and the blow scattered my wits. The wind was fair knocked out of me, and I was helped down to the ground near some crates. Before I could ask who was to lead this dance, a soft feminine hand clamped over my mouth. She was none too careful about it, because she closed my nose as well. Suffocation became a consideration.

The alley had grown crowded. There seemed to be a convention in progress, but I wasn't in any hurry to stumble away, so I held my peace. In the dark, the pounding footsteps grew louder and louder. I heard boots scraping the dirt near us as they skidded to a halt.

"Where'd he turn?"

"I don't know. I was following you!"

"You were 'posed to keep track of him."

"How was I 'sposed to do that when you were in front? Where were you looking?"

"I was making sure you were following me! You're as slow as a sway-back mule."

They continued to discuss the matter some until Big Jim showed up. He cursed them. He cursed John. He cursed me in particular and most of all the missing Chinawoman. He added a few words blistering the thunder of fireworks, too, just to let off some of the pressure. When he ran low on steam, he ordered his men back to the tavern. That was followed by thundering knocks on a door: *Bam! Bam! Bam!* followed after a pause by another *Bam!* A voice from inside cursed the knocker, not realizing it was his boss until, judging by the exhalation of air, he took a kick in the gut. The door slammed behind the crew, and all we could hear was the riot in the streets and the hammering of my heart.

John's voice said my name, soft and hoarse and scented with whiskey. The hand vanished from my mouth, and I stood up and leaned against the boxes to catch my breath. I suggested that we caucus elsewhere that didn't remind one of the bottom of a mineshaft. John agreed, and he took my arm and we continued down the alley toward the main street.

"Let's head to the Occidental Hotel," I said. "I have a powerful hankering for oysters. Evading a thrashing from Big Jim works up a powerful hunger."

"I don't think that will be possible," John said.

"Nonsense. After that scare, not even the devil and his legions will keep me away—"

"It won't be the devil, Sam, but our company that will keep us out."

We had reached the end of the street. John turned me around to introduce me to his new companion, and I had seen what he meant.

Because our companion was the Chinawoman.

We ate in Chinatown instead. She led us up Montgomery and west on California until the streets grew close enough to meet overhead, and the signs changed from English letters to the bars and broad stokes familiar to that race. The English signs we saw were those intended to attract custom, such as laundries, opium dens and disorderly houses.

She led us up another alley and down a set of stairs and into a large, well-lit basement. The familiar smells of cooked noodles, chicken and ducks swarmed over us. Through the door, and a wave of human heat followed. The room was packed with Chinamen, as alike in their grey suit jackets as eggs in a basket. They were hunched over their bowls of rice and noodles, jammed so tight we shuffled sideways behind our guide. The tables were packed with bowls of rice, soups and meats. The only offerings to Western tastes were the bottles of whiskey and shot glasses.

Silence spread from near us outward as they realized our presence. I had heard silence before, but this was thick enough to stop us in our places. A kitchen door opposite us opened, steam rolled out, and a short, bland-faced Chinaman crept into the room. He stood as high as the Chinawoman and his face was shining in sweat. In one ham hock hand he held his cleaver up near his shoulder, hefting it gently as if calculating his range.

The girl pushed herself forward and locked Mr. Cleaver in a violent argument. We stood in silence and looked around. I had known Chinamen and their ways from my years in the city. They work hard, cause little trouble and in return are subject to harassment, beatings and the occasional light murder, all of which goes unpunished. They move about with their heads down, trying to cause no trouble. Here, they gazed at John and me with poker faces that were still unnerving. You never know what they were thinking outside, in the street or in the mines. You still don't know here, but you know they're thinking different thoughts.

I felt a close presence behind me and a voice in my ear:— "Sam, where are we?"

I took stock of my inner map and gauged the direction of the sun:— "Chinatown."

"Could ye be a wee more specific?" he said. "Could we, say, find our way out if the fellow with the cutlery objects to our presence?"

"Oh, sure, if the sons and daughters of the Celestial Empire here will let us leave. This neighborhood's no larger than seven blocks by three."

The argument was nearing a crescendo and it appeared

that our champion was scoring points and about to carry the debate. Judging by the nods of the Chinamen who were paying attention, it might be by acclamation.

"Going by the number packed in this room," John said. "How many do you think are living in these 21 blocks, you think?"

"Oh, about thirty thousand or so."

"My God—" he breathed, cut off when Mr. Cleaver planted his chopper into the table. Fortunately, no one's arm or neck was in the way. He waved the diners near him to clear a space, and the Chinawoman turned to us, bowed, and directed us to sit among her compatriots.

We squeezed into the pack. Fresh bowls of fish and noodles were placed in front of us, along with shots of whiskey, and we set to as we listened to her story.

She told us she was Chen Yin, which produced a chuckle from me, a smile from her and confusion from John.

"Yin means silver in her language," I told him.

Her story was familiar to me. She and her husband were going hungry in Hunan province when they agreed to come to this country with the help of the Sam Yup Company. "One of the six merchant trading companies that run Chinatown," I said to John. "They import laborers, for a fee, which the worker pays back."

She nodded. "It is our way. But Chen Fu was a gambler. He fell into debt. He went to Big Jim for a loan. When he fell behind on that, Big Jim held him in his music hall and took it out in work. I worked to pay off his debt to Big Jim. Tonight was to be last payment. But he said Chen Fu owed the interest on the loan, bigger than what he borrowed. I argued."

"Is this true?" John asked me.

"He's lying, of course. I wrote about it when I was at the *Call*, along with the other abuses that have been heaped on the Chinese here. They didn't endear me to Big Jim." I finished the bowl and drank off the remains and thought. "To be remembered like that's quite a compliment, if I say so."

"Well then," John said. His face had grown redder and redder as he came to understand the injustice. "We'll go to the police about this. Won't we, Sam?"

"Can't say that'll help. The police here tend not to bother about a Chinaman unless they need one to arrest for something."

Then the damn fool puffed himself up like a peacock and said something that sent the shivers rocketing down my spine and turned my guts to water.

"Then we'll just have to free him ourselves, right Sam?"

I heard his mad scheme as the horror bubbled up inside me. We were to use the coded knock to gain entry by the back door. We temporarily inconvenience the custodian of the portal, free Chen Fu and any other Chinamen who was being held there, and leave.

Chen Yin said, — "I'll take him to Sam Yup. The company will get him out of San Francisco. Send him to work the mines in Chinese Camp. That teach him to gamble."

I said I wasn't of a mind to care about his future more than my own. I confessed that I wasn't much in a fight.

"But you think fast," John said, beaming at me like sunshine. "That was a brilliant plan, drawing off those scoundrels and giving me time to run after Chen Yin. How did you deduce that they'd chase you?"

I blushed and looked away. I felt like a fraud, but I didn't want to disappoint the lad. "They're miners," I said. "Their kind always give chase, if only for the sport of it. They're like cats in that way."

And then, God helped me, he clapped his hand on my shoulder (leaving me with a distinct crick that I can feel to this day) and said, "I owe you my life."

Even in the dim candlelight of the cellar, I wondered if he saw my face burning bright. Especially since Chen Yin, leaning back so John couldn't see her, buried her face in her hand, silently laughing.

An hour later, we had returned to the old homestead. We were delayed by an argument over what we needed. My suggestion of a sledgehammer and saw was raised by a rope and wedges. John pumped for a revolver, but I told him that those that had them provided undertakers with too much business. We realized that neither of us had experience at breaking and entering and rescuing males in distress. We decided to take ourselves there and improvise. Chen Yin gave us a hank of rope, reasonably pointing out that we needed to do something with the fellow at the back door.

We reached the back of Big Jim's saloon. It was pitch-black, with the only light coming from where the alley met the street, and the flash from the occasional blast overhead. We paused awhile to build up our nerve and let our eyes adjust to the gloom. My heart, which had done enough back springs for the day, was pounding again to beat the band. My knees were weak, and I leaned against the building to keep from going faint.

Soon we could dimly see each other. "Are we ready?" John said. I could see the worry in his face. The alcohol had worn off and the thought *What were we doing?* hammered me. The scheme was sheer madness. Big Jim had it in for me. To be caught stealing a Chinaman from him was tantamount to the Christians entering the lion's den and laying down in front of them with a sprig of parsley as an appetizer. Chen Yin had stayed behind; this was clearly the time to retreat gracefully before the worst thing that could happen, happened.

Then the door opened. I could tell because I had unwittingly leaned against it. Instead of the floor, I hit solid flesh. Strange hands grabbed me and whirled me around in a do-si-do. It was one of the alley rascals I had evaded, and judging by the swollen nose, the one John had punched. He had been wary that it was Big Jim returning to pummel him again. But once he saw me, a grin split his face. Here was an opportunity to get his own back, and he raised his fist. John grabbed his arm, spun him around and head-butted him. He went down.

"Aren't you going to knock him out?" I said.

"That only happens in the penny dreadful," he said. In a trice we trussed him with the rope like a Christmas goose and stuffed a rag in his mouth to stifle his objections to the quality of our work. There was a staircase nearby and we hoisted him down with us for company. At the bottom was a dark, dank basement stuffed with boxes and barrels, and we left him there to rest awhile, with his legs tied up to encourage him to stay.

Upstairs in the hall, we could hear the party going on in the saloon, so we paid no never mind to making noise. We followed Chen Yin's directions and went down the snaking hall a ways until we found where the Chinamen were kept. It was a heavy door from a medieval dungeon, made of stout oak with bars set in it. There was no knob, just a keyhole for a lock.

John looked in the barred window and called out for Chen Fu. He responded, and appeared at the window. We held a confab, and he agreed to come with us if we could spring him. We hunted around for a key, hoping it was hung up nearby, but there was nothing.

I stared at the door like it was my most hated enemy and said. "Pity our success hinges on having the right tool."

At that, John laughed and clapped my other shoulder, fracturing it as well. "Clemens, you're a genius! The hinges!"

I had ignored the obvious. A door meant to keep someone in the room had to be turned so that the hinges were on the outside. In the hall. With us.

We found a box of hand tools in one of the rooms we had passed. We hammered out the hinges. We lifted the door from its hinges, and we were flooded by Chinamen. Big Jim had built up a significant bank of them to run his business, and now many of them were advantage of the opportunity. The rest, perhaps out of loyalty, perhaps out of fear, stayed in their bunks.

Then a hand clamped again on my shoulder. I turned, expecting another burst of admiration from John, and caught a blow on my ear that created a sudden darkness. I should never have minded John. It turns out that a punch can knock you out.

When I awoke, I was staring at the ceiling. This is my natural posture upon awakening, but I'm not usually behind the bar. Nor did I usually smell of rotgut whiskey and cigar butts. Not lately. The roar had not abated, and my head ached abominably, so I chose to stake my claim to the floor and learn as much as I could with moving anything, including my eyes.

Above me, a bartender puffing on a stogie busied himself with pouring whiskeys next to two men standing on the bar. One of them was Big Jim. He busied himself giving a speech to the crowd and being rewarded with huzzahs in return. Standing comfortably next to him was John. His hands were bound. He was the silent partner in the act, because he had a gag around his mouth. I blinked away the fuzziness in my head and realized, to my growing horror, that he also had a noose around his neck, with the rope rising up to the balcony that ringed the room.

Big Jim was apparently making a fine speech to the crowd, judging by the roaring response. He was pointing out that it was the Fourth of July, the day that marked our separation from the Mother Country. He reminded them of the many atrocities the British troops and the Loyalists who still backed them inflicted on all right-thinking Americans. How they burned our farms and hung the men who fought under Washington, and how they came back in the year 18 and 12 and burned the White House, and how we beat them back and how we're still fighting them. And now, to mark the solemn occasion, they were going to hold a mock lynching to show how they feel about the English, using a live Englishman who he caught breaking into his building!

"But first," Big Jim yelled. "He's going to sing for us! Who wants to hear 'Yankee Doodle'?"

I had heard enough to scare my hair white. I didn't know what to do about it, but I did know that I didn't want to hear anymore about it. The barkeep finished his work above me and stepped away, leaving me stained with vile whiskey and cigar ash. I saw my chance and I took it; I rolled over and crawled like a baby for the end of the bar, and ducked through the closest door before anyone noticed.

I found myself back in the hall that we had abandoned. I did not stop to take stock of my situation. I did not stop, period. I ran for the back door (now left unguarded; no one taking notice in the confusion that the man had abandoned his post and was, I hope, being nibbled on by rats in the basement. I unhoisted the bar from the door frame and opened up.

I took three steps into the dark alley. Before I could build up a head of steam, I was grabbed again and made to eat the wall. My protests were silenced when I felt the blade of a knife rubbing up against my jugular.

"Hold still!" I heard Chen Yin's voice. "It's my husband's rescuer." I turned and saw in the light from inside a horde of Oriental faces grimly assessing my skin, led by my silver-haired rescuer, with Chen Fu next to her. I could have kissed them all, even the uglier ones.

"We heard that you had been caught," she said.

I admitted the fact and explained the uproar that was about to commence. She turned to her countrymen and blasted them with Cantonese until they fled. Some vanished in the darkness of the alley. Four of them, including Chen Fu, pulled out short cloth bags filled with buckshot and went inside.

She took my head in her hands. "Walk to the entrance and go in, but stay by the door. I will follow behind. Quickly!"

I obeyed. I still had no idea what to do, but obviously something was about to happen. And since she and I were going to be in public, she needed to walk behind me. Not ahead, leading me. Not by my side, but two steps back, her head down. Such were the ways of that time.

I hurried down the alley to the street, turned, and hustled passed the row of Big Jim's curtained windows to the door.

John was still on the bar, but he had been colored up some. He had been used for target practices, for he was covered with flour and struck with reds and browns, the sources of which I'd rather not consider. But he looked proud and angry, and glared at the crowd of sozzled miners, grafters, bums, blacklegs, thieves and other scum of the Barbary Coast. The noose was still around his neck, the rope disappearing through the railings on the second floor.

Big Jim had reached the heights of his peroration and called for the rope to be hauled up. The rope tightened and John was launched. I must have cried out in horror, my screams lost in the general cheering.

John was only supposed to be suspended a few feet, but for some reason the rope kept pulling and pulling. Big Jim, a look of panic spreading over his map, gave a yell to the haulers to avast. Something was going wrong, but any thoughts in that direction were interrupted by an even bigger noise that filled the room and the heads of everyone present.

As John was being pulled heavenward, the saloon exploded in fireworks. Multiple rockets crashed through the windows, trailing broken glass and fire and smoke. The explosions sent everyone to the floor, including myself and Chen Yin. But I kept my eyes on John, unlike everyone else, and so I saw that the Chinamen on the balcony received him, hauled him over the railing, and disappeared in the smoke and confusion. It was done as neat and quick as a magic act.

Reasoning that I should do the same, I took Chen Yin's hand and followed their example, helped along by the audience moving as one in the same direction. She led me back into Chinatown, where we ducked down one of the twisty alleys and up a set of back stairs to the roof. There, to my joy, was John, freed from his shackles, slamming the filth from his clothes and hallooing to beat the band.

"What an adventure!" his voice had acquired a rasp from

the rope, but he gripped my hand like a vise. "I was confident that you wouldn't let me down, and you didn't! Did you see those explosions? I was occupied at the time trying to breathe, but you should have seen it! Imagine rockets flying at the bar, trailing clouds of sparks and smoke and blowing up as they crashed into the wall behind it! Big Jim's will have to undergo serious repairs before he can reopen."

I agreed, but pointed out that he might be more occupied in finding out who freed his Chinamen. I urged him to find a place to hide for a few days before his ship left.

"That will be no problem," Chen Yin said. "Our hospitality to him will be limitless, and to you as well."

I thanked her as prettily as I could but said I should be able to shift for myself. I'd return to the Occidental and check aboard my ship tonight.

And that's the end of this story. John made it to Australia, and then back to England, where he fell in with a ruffian named Holmes. He must have told him about me, because at every opportunity, when the great detective needed someone he trusted in some desperate situation, he would turn to me, which led me into more hair-raising scrapes than I'd care to confess. No matter how many times I resisted, no matter how many times I told him of my cowardice, he refused to accept it. Apparently, people will believe everything they hear, but the truth. Such is the curse of the humorist.

Afterward

Of course, when it was time to write the second story in the series after "The Adventure of the Whyos," I dumped Holmes.

But let me back up first. Once I had decided to write a series of stories, I had to research Twain, his life, his works, how he spoke, how he told stories, and what he did where.

I did this in my usual fashion: erratic and harum-scarum.

I gathered books and tore through them in an irregular fashion. I made lists of the words Twain used, and examples of how he talked. A volume of his speeches as recorded in contemporary newspapers described how he dressed, walked, and spoke. A friend published his memories of Twain in Europe, including his table talk. His maid, Katie Leary, published a small book of her memories serving the family.

At the same time, I gathered digital copies of the Holmes stories, even those in the *Casebook*, some of which are still copyright protected (but not in Australia, ahem). I read them on my ereader, highlighting significant passages that showed how Holmes deduced, how Watson spoke, and other details worthy of sticking into the stories.

From this collection, I built up a pile of information, and from them, certain combinations would spark ideas for stories. One of them was to examine the dynamics among Twain, Holmes, and Watson. Watson was a writer, like Twain, and even though he was more a Boswell with one subject, would it be plausible that he would be jealous of Twain occupying Holmes' time? Would Twain write up his adventures with Holmes? What did Twain think of Holmes anyway?

Then a new idea came up. Watson had traveled before heading off to Afghanistan; Holmes mentioned his experience with women on three continents. There was even a suggestion that he was familiar with the mines of Ballarat in Australia. Several scholars have put forth their favorite theories. For my purposes, I was more interested in the story. What if Twain and Watson met before they knew Holmes? What would *that* look like? How would they get along? The idea excited me.

I knew that Sam Clemens headed for the frontier with his brother, Orion, in 1861, avoiding the Civil War and embracing the still-Wild West. He was in his mid-20s, a young man full of energy and oats, and judging from the few stories that have come down to us, he had no problems drinking, carousing, and, if one comment from him was true, bedding hotel maids. There was mischief to be made, and he wanted to get started.

His writing also got him into trouble at that time. He had written fearlessly about police corruption and abuses of Chinese immigrants. Some of his hoax articles bent more than a few noses out of shape; one, in fact, raised such a ruckus that it was thought best that he head out of town and stayed away until tempers cooled.

That left finding an ideal time for Twain and Watson to meet. I chose 1868. The year before, Twain had gone on the European cruise that would inspire his first best-selling book *The Innocents Abroad*. With a publisher's offer in hand, he had learned that the Sacramento newspaper he had sold the letters to (and that financed his trip) was planning to publish them. He returned to San Francisco in April, resolved his business with the newspaper, then visited friends and lectured before leaving in late July.

Watson, born in 1852 (according to Les Klinger's timeline) would be about 16 at that time. Admittedly early for a young man, but not necessarily impossible for a young man of high spirits to go off and see the world. Watson's energy, impulsiveness, desire to see everything and courage mirrors Conan Doyle, so it was clear that the story was going to be about two young men looking for fun and finding it.

Next came the historical research. The celebration on July 4th offered a vivid setting, with the town bedecked in bunting, cannons and fireworks going off, and people in a celebratory mood. A search of digitized newspapers at The Library of Congress' Chronicling America and the California Digital Newspaper Collection showed what Clemens and Watson would experience during the day: patriotic speeches, a baseball game, fireworks, and plenty of alcohol.

As for the story, the details of how it all came together have vanished from my memory. I don't recall it being difficult to write. I had so many cards in my hand that it was just a matter of playing them in the right order. Rereading it for publication in this book, I find myself still pleased with it. I hope you'll agree.

The Adventure of the Jersey Girl

The Adventure of the Jersey Girl (1878)

————◆————

"To Sherlock Holmes she is always *the* woman." When I read that passage in *A Scandal in Bohemia*, I blushed for him. He must have met many women in Baker Street, in as many shades of color and morality. If he paid attention to them as people instead of puzzles to solve, he would not have made such an extraordinary statement. Or maybe Watson got it wrong, which wouldn't surprise me. He was an impetuous and decisive lad when I knew him back in '67, always haring off on a new line by instinct and without thinking.

I can speak as an authority on Irene Adler because I knew the woman, and while I am not ass enough to call her *the* woman, she certainly was *a* woman. More so than most, even. She was — but now I see I have plunged too deep into my story, so let me back out, recover my breath, and try again.

I met Miss Adler in Heidelberg. I had taken the family to Europe to gather material for a travel book that would become *A Tramp Abroad*. Don't go ciphering through it for her. Read as hard as you can, but not a ghost of her you will find unless you know the whole story of the count, the no-account, the castle, the duel, the — but there I go, getting ahead of myself. I have never told this story. I was afraid even to confine it to my notebooks. It would not bring credit to anyone, least of all to myself. If I were not writing my autobiography for posterity, to be read a century in the future when no one alive today will care, I would remain as silent as the grave.

It occurs to me now that the times I have found myself in improbable and dangerous situations have been at the hands of Holmes. If ever a person was marked for trouble, it was him, even when he was not at his post ferreting out wrongdoers. When I add up the suppressible parts of my life that involve him, Watson, Mycroft, Miss Adler, and his other associates, it inspires me to wonder about the morals of the deity who cursed them.

I see that now I've gone sideways in my story, so let me start again. As I said, I had brought my family and servants to stay for several months in Heidelberg. We lived in the Hotel Schloss, on a hill above the noble ruin of Heidelberg Castle, which itself overlooked the town that nestled alongside the swift Neckar River. It was a pretty location. The river had spent millennia cutting a gorge with steep ridges and sweeps of wooded foliage stretched unbroken all the way to the summit.

Our hotel had a peculiar feature that in a just world would be recreated in any building which held a commanding view. This was the presence of long, narrow parlors clinging to the outside of the building. We had two of these bird-cages attached to our corner room. One looked downriver over the castle and town, and the other looked upriver. It was a peaceful feeling to stand there on a summer night, smoking a cigar, feeling the warm breeze, and hearing the rumble of the Neckar over her dikes and dams. At your feet the massive block of the Castle rose from the trees, broken and beaten-down in places, functioning in others, but always bearing proudly its mantle of royal authority. Beyond it the intricate cobweb of streets were lit by the twinkling of gas lamps and the row of lights on the bridges flung shimmering lances across the water. The effect made it appear as if the land was shaped by stars scattered by the creator's hand.

How the days faded from one to the next! I had rented a room across the river for my study and I would stay there until 4 p.m., scribbling at the story or translating one of the German fairy tales to drop in where needed, then walk back across the bridge, through the narrow streets and up past the Castle to the hotel. I was not lionized as I was in London. I could walk the town like a Parisian *flâneur* marveling at the charming views and taking notes for the next day's writing. The evenings were spent in my glassed-in bird-cage, smoking my cigars in the company of Livy and the children and watching Heidelberg shift its coat from auburn to gold to copper, fading to night, as comforting a feeling as Adam and Eve must have experienced in the garden.

My downfall began with an errand. My longtime friend from Hartford, the Rev. Joe Twichell, was expected in Heidelberg in a few days. We intended to spend several days tramping about the Black Forest region in pursuit of the book and meet up with the family in Lausanne, Switzerland. But Livy had heard rumors in town that an opera was about to break out, and I was dispatched to seek news of the riot and, if true, to procure tickets to it. The family has a passion for theatre. They would probably enjoy it more if I were not in attendance. I can appreciate a show if my subconscious would let me. I had a surfeit of theatres when I was a reporter for the *San Francisco Call.* I would have a full day's work, and always finish up by going to seven theatres every evening. I had to write something about each of them, and I could only afford ten minutes here, a quarter of an hour there. The result is when I go to a playhouse now and I have been there about fifteen minutes or half an hour, I fidget around, thinking, "I shall get all behind if I stay here any longer."

Then there's opera, which I would enjoy more if there were less singing. An opera performed with a total absence of singing would represent the acme of the art.

I abandoned my desk early the next day and ambled down the road and into town, prepared to exercise my German to find the opera house. My ability with the language is perfect: I always understand what it is about, and it always does not understand me. I've aired my views on the awful German language before and the intervening years have not altered my opinions. I learned well enough to read the newspapers but ciphering speech required more time than I could devote. The language has a perverse sense of humor. It delights in making females out of words that are without dispute male and the reverse. It agreeably considers a woman to be female until she becomes a wife, when she is neutered. A fish is always a male, no matter how it conducts itself to another fish. The language also enjoys creating new words by slamming together the words that make up its constituent parts, turning them into mountain ranges of letters that fence off part of the page. And when two words of different genders collide for the first time, only heaven will know which will dominate.

It took numerous questions to passers-by and an impromptu aria to demonstrate to one mutton-headed Heidelberger what I sought, and I was directed to a building at Theaterstrasse 10.

Compared to the grand houses I've seen, the opera house in Heidelberg was but a town hall with ambitions. It was a modest brick structure of three stories. The only sign it gave of its occupation was through the generous installation of doors and steps in the front. Inside there was a row of ticket cages, one of which was occupied by a man. I directed my inquiry to him. My luck was bad: There were tickets available for the last performance of *Tristan and Isolde,* two nights hence. If Twichell was on schedule, I would see him that afternoon, take in the noise, and leave for the Black Forest the next day. I secured the box and palmed my change when a door from the auditorium crashed opened followed by a whirlwind.

Walking backwards was a young woman who was very tastefully dressed and very beautiful except for the anger than inflamed her cheeks. She was softly hissing a stream of German toward the finely dressed tall gentleman pursuing her. She had her arms open to him; clearly she was pleading, and he was angrily denying her words with vigorous chops of his hand. He also stabbed the ground with his cane, giving him the air of an elegant stick insect. I could only grasp a few words, but none that made any sense of the source of the troubles, before she turned to flee him and crashed into me.

My pfennigs and marks scattered like grain seeds in a whirlwind, and to keep myself from falling I held her tightly. She repaid the clutch with interest, and the heavy folds of her dress provided an admirable counterweight that kept me from conferring with the floor. I was close enough to smell her jasmine, and as she was my height I could see into her rich alluring brown eyes.

It was then I realized that silence had descended on the tableau and that our clinch had progressed from the functional to the pleasurable. The finely dressed gentleman looked bug-eyed at me from underneath his smokestack topper. The force of his glare encouraged me to disengage from the woman, who looked at me now with a puzzled have-we-met-before aspect, and I composed an apology in German to the company. I bowed to the gentleman and turned to her to begin my little speech when she cried out in French-tinged English:

"Of course, it *is* you. Mark *Twain!* Oh, you darling man!" and she cradled my face in her hands and kissed me soundly.

I could feel myself blushing furiously but kept my counsel. It was a pleasant feeling, being bussed by a beautiful female. That she was unknown to me lent a piquant flavor to the moment. On the street I would have had to discourage her attentions, but we were secluded and I reasoned that foreigners did greet each other differently overseas, and it would have been rude to suggest that I found her action distasteful.

She receded, still keeping a caressing hand on my cheek and murmuring my name. I struggled to restore a semblance of equanimity to my features. I acted as if this sort of thing happened quite a bit in my line. That I didn't succeed — that I must have looked pretty pleased with myself — was seen in the gentleman's face. He barked a question at the woman and she replied in her imitation of a soft-spoken steam kettle. He cried, "Bah!" and stalked out the door, slamming it behind him. She went on talking to me as if she hadn't been interrupted:

"I *knew* I wasn't mistaken! If Dietrich wasn't in *such* a state I would have introduced you to him. Excuse me, I must keep my voice down to preserve it" — and she reverted to her soft hiss — "Are you coming to *Isolde?* You *must* have a box, oh, I see you have one. Then you must come back afterwards so you can meet the company. Dear me! You dropped your money. Let me help you collect them."

We scrambled about the carpet, picking up the coins, until we both ended up on our knees to find the small pfennigs. A glitter of light from around her throat caught my eye. It was a confection made up of a band of diamonds worn around the throat, with alternating loops of pearls and rubies that had fallen from the recesses of her most un-morning-like dress.

She then caught me staring — at her necklace. She blushed, and I stammered that we should suspend our pursuit; my family would not be impoverished by the few coins we had missed. I raised her to her feet and she caressed her necklace back into place and replied:

"This is one of Dietrich's baubles. He wanted me to wear it during the performances but we — never mind. What are *you* doing in Heidelberg?"

I explained my mission, and she clapped her hands in delight and rose up on the balls of her feet.

"That's marvelous! I have your *Sketches* and *Roughing It* but *Innocents* is still the tip-top. I *laugh* when I see the American excursionists; they act just as you portray them. And you saved my life with *Gilded Age*. I was starving in Paris when I landed the role of Laura Sellers in the production, and that's where I met Dietrich and that got me the part in *Isolde*."

I must confess that this gushing pleased me, even if it was for my early works. She was amiable, cheerful, and spirited, and unencumbered in places by clothes usually worn at this time of day. I even forgave her participation in a pirate production of my play, from which I never saw a penny. I asked for her name, and her mouth formed a pretty little "oh" that she covered with her gloved hand.

"What you must think of me? I did forget my manners, didn't I? Please forgive me. We creatures of the stage should not mix with genteel company without plenty of preparation. I am Irene Adler, of the New Jersey Adlers." I laughed at her comic imitation of the way Americans simpered abroad. She had even copied our nasal drawl that set us apart.

I said I found this surprising; not just to meet a fellow

American, but one who spoke English like a Frenchwoman.

"That comes from living in Europe for too long. French was the first foreign language I learned, and whether I'm in Paris, or Rome, or Vienna, or Heidelberg, my voice *still* believes it is in France. If I lived in England or back in America, I should lose my affectation. But lately I have spent so much time rehearsing Brangane — she's Isolde's maid — I swear I'll be speaking only German from now on." She expelled a small cough and added, "I'm famished. I simply must have coffee. Would you care for a cup?"

When I agreed, she replied, "Hook in, then!" and arm in arm she led me to the dense atmosphere of the beer-hall down the street. There, we saw a singular sight. A group of students were swilling lager, smoking their long pipes, and singing, when a professor appeared at their table. The students, as a group, rose politely and doffed their caps, and the professor responded with a bow. He seated himself at the table, was quickly served, and engaged in spirited conversation with the young men.

I hauled out my notebook to record my impressions. Miss Adler said, "So *this* is how a writer composes. Do you take your notebook everywhere? Do you record everything?"

"Only what I have a mind to record. How long have you lived in Heidelberg?"

"Am I material for your notebook?"

"Depends on what you say."

"I should answer charmingly, but that would require lying. Since I cannot be charming and honest at the same time, for you I shall be honest and say only for the summer."

"And before?"

"Everywhere. I was fourteen when my mother brought me to Paris from Red Bank to learn singing under Madame Marchesi. I always liked to sing, and my mother encouraged me. My father was a glove-maker. He would take the steamship down the Navasink to Manhattan to sell his stock. After he died, she decided I needed to come to Europe. I have been on my own since I was seventeen." A shadow passed over her face momentarily, and then she brightened. "But you must still consider me a Jersey girl, even if I do sound like a Parisian." Then she said something I have rarely heard anyone utter: "But enough about me, what can I do for *you?*"

I paused before answering, struck by the notion that Miss Adler was a woman who listened. That is a rare trait. Most animals don't listen to us; it would not be to their benefit or pleasure. Cats, rarely; dogs, always; men and women, only occasionally. If we listened more than we talked, we would say less and learn more.

I detailed for her my wanderings about the town, seeing the Castle with its extensive grounds and its buildings both ruined and functional. I described the Tun, the giant barrel displayed there, built hundreds of years before to store wine, now empty but still a startling sight. I had visited the university and glimpsed student life and how they conducted classes. I had tramped through the forests and collected folk tales. I only expressed regret not learning more about the duels that the student clubs indulged in.

"Then I shall be your guide. You *must* see a duel. I know just the boy. Gunter is a student in the White Corps, and he would be happy to demonstrate how they train and fight. He has been in two duels already and is considered one of the best swordsmen in the university."

We set a time to meet on the morrow and parted. I walked slowly back to the hotel with my notepad out and jotting down the particulars of the day. It had been a fine afternoon, and tomorrow promised to be better. There is nothing like the approval of a pretty woman to set a man up. It is a balm to the soul. It was also this self-satisfaction that led to the trouble.

I was so taken up with thoughts of Miss Adler and the details of the day that I didn't see the man jostling me. I looked up, and before I could react further, several men grappled me off the street and into an alley, where they could attend to my business in private. I was startled and became as limp as three-day-old celery. They were working men, in white shirts, vests and cloth caps. They muttered in German something that sounded like demands for information, but what they wanted I could not fathom. They'd launch a sentence at me, and I would set to untangle the genders of the words and transplant the verb from the end of the sentence to its proper place. I would get halfway through the process when they'd fire another barrage at me, only louder. They had apparently learned this trick from our tourists; if you don't get an answer, shout. In frustration, they flung me against the wall, and my head fetched with a crack, so I decided to stay there awhile.

The lead tough had a face like well-used leather, dark and sagging. He thrust his hand inside my coat and borrowed my identification papers. He muttered something in his guttural dialect and I heard my name here and there. That started a roundelay in which the other two men contributed in the form of questions and assertions. Considerable language not fit for print was used to describe me, and then they resumed seeking my opinion.

We were interrupted. An officer of the law stood in the head of the alley, hands on his hips, and barked orders at them. He was not interested in anyone's questions. He was not interested in what we were doing there. He did not approve of us and wanted us out of his sight. *Raus!* Leatherface tossed my papers to the ground, gave me the evil eye, and sauntered down the alley and out of sight. This left me alone with the police officer, who picked up my papers, examined them with a critical eye, and launched an intense discussion about my choice of companions before sending me home.

The next day, I breakfasted with a troubled conscience and sauntered to the opera house. It was a fine, warm day to view the town, and the rustle of leaves followed my steps down the hotel and past the Castle. Miss Adler was in excellent spirits, and my worries eased as we spent the morning strolling about Heidelberg. She was a fountain of facts and I rapidly filled the pages in my notebook. I also kept a weather eye out for the myrmidons. This was easy because loafers were thin on the ground in German towns. Doing nothing was considered a civil offense and subject to interrogation by the police. Everyone went about their business as efficiently as a machine.

She led us down a passage too narrow to admit wagons to an undistinguished building of brown stone. This was the home of one of the student corps. The door was opened to her knock by a cheerful chubby student. I was surprised. From Miss Adler's description of her friend's prowess at dueling, I had expected an Adonis, a Scaramouche, a d'Artagnan; not what appeared to be the son of a beer-garden owner who was groomed to inherit the family business. But the decoration on his cheek, a horizontal slash that was healing nicely, represented his membership card in the fraternity.

Gunter clearly did not expect to see her there. From the few words I picked up and his gestures and nods, I could tell he asked who I was and what I wanted. Adler settled him with a kiss on both cheeks and reassured him that the silverware and plate were safe from me.

The building had that air common to student clubs. The atmosphere was infused with a faint cheesy smell of stale beer and unwashed men. Gunter led us through the rooms and described — in some English and with Miss Adler translating the rest — the corps system in Heidelberg, the students with the different-colored caps, and the etiquette that determined when to ignore each others' presence and when not to. Members of the corps gathered in the main hall for drinking and revelry, and there were rooms devoted to meetings, study, and treating the wounded. He led us downstairs, where there was an extensive gymnasium devoted to practicing swordsmanship. Three students were present in their padded practice armor. Two stood face to face at sword length, slowly rehearsing their movements, while the third boy stood by and offered advice. The presence of three scars on his face, including a deep cut in the jaw, denoted his status as Senior Boy.

As I explained in *Tramp*, a dueling scar was a sign of honor and courage, and every member of the club was expected to earn one. To duel, you had to be insulted. For most students, that is not a problem; they're capable of insulting someone merely by the way they said *"Guten Morgan."* But there were the well-behaved boys who never get into a contretemps. Gunter explained that a mock reason had to be devised for their challenge to be issued and accepted.

Gunter led us to a long tall wooden rack where the weapons were displayed. He took them down and explained their purpose. The students used long swords with a basket hilt that shielded the hand from cuts. He handed me a mask the duelers used, with large leather pieces that protected the forehead, eyes, and nose, but left the cheeks and chin exposed. They were held to the face with leather straps that buckled behind the head. He put on the leather apron that shielded the torso and legs, slid on a glove with padding all the way to the shoulder and asked us to strap him in. Thus shielded, he approached a tall pole with a padded top about the size of a human head and began slashing vigorously. I winced at the rapid thwacks inflicted on it. I had seen and heard of plenty of duels out West, but I had never felt the need to experience one myself, even when I was invited. I glanced over at Miss Adler to see how she was taking this violence. She had cocked her head like an art connoisseur judging a new oil painting.

He had me put on the heavy leather clothing next. I whaled away at the head for several minutes. Gunter was encouraging; stopping me several times to show the right angle at which to slice open a cheek, or split the chin. At his invitation, Miss Adler attempted a bout, but without the leather equipment. Since she was my height, Gunter didn't need to lower the post. She attacked with vigor and was breathing hard after a dozen strokes. She fatigued visibly, for after the last swing she missed the head by a large margin.

I said to Gunter, "In a real bout, she would be a deadly opponent — to herself." He looked puzzled, whether at Miss

Adler's behavior or my own I couldn't tell, but he translated my sally to his fellow club members, and I was gratified to hear their laughter.

Miss Adler sat down to recover her breath and she fanned herself with her hand. There were rivulets of perspiration running down her flushed cheeks that were charming to the eye. She said:—

"Perhaps Mr. Twain should try a bout with Gunter. I'd love to see if you fight as well as you talk." I was taken aback at the suggestion, although in retrospect I should have expected it. If I had known where this demonstration would lead to, I should have turned tail and ran until I reached the Neckar, jumped in, and swam for the Rhine. But beauty has powers that women only suspect but never truly understand. A suggestion from a man that would be rejected outright would be seen as charming from a pretty woman.

We reupholstered ourselves and squared off. Gunter set his pace according to my moves. A good attack drew appreciative cries from the students, interspersed with encouragements and compliments in German. I am not a fighter. I'm sure it showed. But my blood warmed, and I puffed and preened.

Then he clipped me on my side under my arm, hard enough that I felt it through the thick cloth. He stirred a most righteous anger in me. I swiped at his head. He ducked and thrust. I whipped my blade in front of me and brushed his sword-point aside like a fly and swiped again. We crossed blades and our steel rang as if we were stage-fighting, and the cheering filled my heart with joy.

He could have launched a killing attack, but stepped back and peeled off his mask, grinning like a fool. "*Gut!* You have the instinct for the duel. You must have fought. I'm sure of it!"

I was breathing too hard to respond. I got my mask off with Miss Adler's help. She kissed me prettily on the cheek. "So brave. You fought like Tristan!" She was a distraction with her hands on my chest and her bright shining eyes staring into my own. The truth never comes out in these situations. I said to Gunter, "One or two."

"And no scars. Tsk, tsk," he said to general laughter.

We said our goodbyes to Gunter and stopped at a beer garden where we supped on sausages, radishes and steins of pilsner. We walked outside and down the street toward the Castle. I lit a cigar, and Miss Adler hung onto my arm and chattered about my prowess in swordplay. A man turned the corner and approached us. He moved slowly, giving me time to give him an eyeful. It was the leather-faced man. My blood froze along with my breath. He had displayed himself to me and without a word or any other sign of recognition, he passed us and we separated.

Miss Adler had to have seen him, but if she recognized him she gave no sign. I pointed him out to her and described yesterday's meeting with him. Did she, by chance, know him?

She hesitated. Her cheeks colored prettily from the memory, but her attitude was that of a fearful woman. I pressed the issue, and she confessed that the leather-faced fellow was Dietrich's servant.

The dam burst, and the story flowed from her. Count Dietrich von Nordmark was the younger son of Heidelberg nobility, a distant relation to the family that rules the Grand Duchy of Hesse. He had seen Miss Adler on stage and fallen madly in love with her. She had returned his affections, for awhile, but she had grown tired of him. She was trying to end the attachment, and was looking forward to the last performance, when she would be free to go.

"I had hoped that he would be a gentleman, but German men tend to not see the withdrawal of one's affections as French men do. He has become more demanding. More insistent. I refused, of course, but it is becoming more . . . difficult. He sets his spies on me. There are jealous scenes. I would leave, but I need money to do so, and I won't get paid until the end of the run. I owe so much already! I'm sorry to tell you all this," and she brushed closer to me, purely by accident, I'm sure, and I could catch a whiff of her perfume. "I will talk to him about it. You need fear nothing from him."

"And what about young Gunter?"

Her blushes were all the words I needed. We moved on to her plans for showing me the rest of Heidelberg tomorrow, but I listened with half a mind. I have heard this song before; a young, comely woman entangled in an affair, seeking a sympathetic ear. Not that I'm a prude. I had lived in the mining camps of Nevada and caroused in the streets of San Francisco. I dined with the notorious actress Adah Menken, who rode a horse in a sheer body-stocking so enticingly in *Mazeppa*. Age begets wisdom that when heeded keeps one out of trouble, especially enticing, adventurous trouble. I had a good nose for trouble, and this reeked with it.

We parted, and I walked across the river to my rented room. Rev. Twichell was coming on this afternoon's train and I didn't want to miss my friend. I resolved that the closest I would come to Miss Irene Adler after this was the distance from the stage to my seat. Drawing a half-sheet of paper from the desk, I wrote a note and sent it to her by messenger:

> Dear Miss Adler,
>
> My hide is precious to me, so I mustn't see you again. I shall abandon Dietrich and you, leave Heidelberg and head for Bavaria.
>
> Clemens

That evening, Livy and I saw *Tristan and Isolde* with Twichell, who occupied his time in a long, refreshing nap. The show was a roaring success, and Miss Adler appeared on stage with the other cast members bearing two large bouquets of roses, her jeweled necklace glittering like the gas-lit waters of the Neckar.

I led the party toward the rear of the auditorium. I anticipated no further troubles until Livy laid a gloved hand on my arm.

"We *must* go backstage and thank Miss Adler."

I felt the room sway, like I did when the temblor hit San Francisco back in '65. "You know her?"

"She sent me a lovely note thanking me for letting you accompany her, and I must do my duty in replying."

There was nothing I could say to that but, "Yes, dear."

It was crowded and hot in the narrow backstage area. We found Miss Adler talking to Dietrich. She introduced us, and he nodded knowingly at the sound of my name. Miss Adler turned to Livy who was exclaiming over the jewelry she was wearing, particularly the necklace of diamonds, pearls, and rubies that had caught my eye at the box office. They entered into a deep discussion over the composition and provenance of the necklace, and Dietrich turned to me, bowed with a broad smile and said in perfect English:—

"I must apologize on behalf of the behavior of myself and my servant. Miss Adler explained everything to me. You'll find that I have a great fondness for Americans. She is a young country, a vigorous country. If she were more German, America would become a great nation."

"America," I said it the way he pronounced it, "Ah-MER-i-kan."

When Livy and Miss Adler joined us, Dietrich became more expansive. "She has told me that you are writing about Heidelberg. If you like, and if your lovely wife will permit, I can show you my home. I was planning a late supper with friends, and there we will drink and smoke and I will tell you stories about the Grand Duchy of Baden for your book. And," he bowed to Livy, "if your wife would like to accompany us . . ."

Livy said she would be pleased to come, but that it had been a long day and she needed to retire. It was decided that Miss Adler would dress quickly and convey Twichell and myself in her carriage. Free grub and good cigars always find a home with me. I should have realized that Dietrich, like any good fisherman, knew the right bait to use to catch the fish he wanted.

Miss Adler reappeared in a simple black dress. I saw Livy off to the hotel in our carriage — she whispered in my ear not to stay out too late — and Twichell and I accompanied Miss Adler to hers. I positioned myself alongside Twichell on the bench and lit a cigar. She called to her driver, and with a crack of the whip we were off.

We smoked our cigars contentedly in silence. The passing gas lamps highlighted Miss Adler in bands of gold and black. She was in a brown study. I spoke, if only for the look of the thing, "Dietrich seems like a bully fellow."

She did not respond.

"Are you concerned about seeing him again?"

"No . . . no," she sounded weary and I said so.

"It has been a long day. I am absolutely beaten."

I yawned. "You should go on home then. Drop Twichell and me off, and we'll find our way back to the hotel."

"No. Dietrich expects me and—" she was considering me carefully.

I yawned and slumped into the seat, and as the carriage turned a corner I found myself in one as well. The only sounds were the creaking of the vehicle and the rattle of the wheels on the cobblestones. They were soothing sounds, and an idle fancy arose that Miss Adler, Twichell, and I were sailing the stars in a gondola. Travel has effect. We're unmoored from the familiar, detached from our language, friends, the foods we eat and everything else that reflects who we are. When they go, what is left behind?

The thought amused me. Seeing Miss Adler's handsome face reminded me of Livy, and how much I missed her. At that moment I would have told everyone to go to the devil if I could be in the same room with her again. I felt a pang in my chest and an emptiness of spirit at the thought of never seeing her again. I felt tired; so tired that I nodded off, cigar in my hand.

We shuddered to a stop and I found myself on the floor of the wagon before Miss Adler and Twichell next to her. She squealed in surprise, but no more so than I when my hand found the burning end of my cigar. I thrashed about on my knees, hunting for the handle of the cigar and knocking about my top hat. I unloosened a barrage of curses, and then the carriage door opened and by the light spilling from the open front door I could see Dietrich and his friends ready to welcome us.

In most places in America, my behavior would have been the object of much fun, none of it genteel, before I would be slapped on the back, and forgiveness for my behavior shouted to the heavens. But they do things different in Europe. Dietrich ignored my undignified position and profanity and helped me from the carriage as if he were my manservant. He conducted me inside with gentle enquiries of what I thought of the opera, and provided explanations in response to my inquiries about the décor and the paintings.

He led the party to a long table. Around us the portraits of bewhiskered and bejeweled ancestors judged us. The champagne had been uncrated for the first course of the bacchanals and the bottles soon were circulating along with plates of dried fruits and nuts, while the servants moved in and out, setting out on a sideboard plates of chicken, sausages, sauerbraten and other delicacies.

Miss Adler had left the room, leaving the men. I had intended to ask after her, but I became occupied with the talk that flowed around and about me. True to his word, Dietrich told me tales of those portrayed on the walls and the ways they distinguished themselves during the multitude of wars the German kingdoms indulged in. I saw my friend from the alley among the servants, looking like a stinkweed among the roses. As he will be with us for the rest of the story, he'll need a name. I'll christen him Leatherface.

Leatherface refused to meet my eye, and I meant to do the same. Fortunately, he was among those responsible for fetching and carrying instead of serving, so I saw him rarely.

Several of the men had read my books, so there were questions about San Francisco. They had read Karl May's stories about the Apache chief Winnetou that were inflaming the German imagination at the time and were intrigued about the West. Was it as barren as he had painted it? Was it really as large? The German mind, unlike that of the French and English, was captivated with the concept of the West's near-unlimited space. They hungered for it, and for the freedom to move about and talk as freely as they wished, gifts we Americans take as our birthright and therefore for granted.

We ran through several bottles of champagne, then the cognac was broken out and someone suggested a card game. Draw poker was chosen in honor of my presence. Dietrich directed me to the sideboard on which lay a leather case: "Open it, please. It contains the cards and chips. Make sure everything is there."

I unlatched the case, and handled the lacquered chips bearing the Dietrich family crest with a heft that felt as solid as English guineas. The cards, too, bore the crest on their backs, and were stiff enough to slice cheese. It was a handsome set. I brought it to the table. Five of us took a seat, with Dietrich at the head, and the rest of the mob divided their attention between our play and the buffet. The stakes were moderate, too small to matter to the nobility, too high for the peasants. The play was one of the most professional I've seen outside the doors of a casino. Leatherface was called to the table to act as banker and dealer.

Dietrich seemed to become more American as we played.

He roared at my stories and joshed his friends at their card play. As hand passed hand, he seemed to get more excited. I also noticed after awhile that he drank much less than anyone at the table, while his friends encouraged me in, as they expressed in English, "drinking a bumper" with them. The atmosphere was formal but relaxed, and breaks were taken by the gentlemen for smokes and other purposes.

It was during one of them that an odd encounter occurred. I was on the balcony taking the air when there was a presence beside me. He was a small man with the formal attitude of an undertaker. His hair was slick and parted in the center. It looked like the blunt end of a pencil. He was smoking a large cigar from which he inhaled and expelled chimneys of smoke.

He seemed to ignore me for several minutes, even though he was so close I could feel the nap of his coat. I performed the same service for him. He rolled the end of the stogie on the balustrade to shape the ash and said in quiet German-inflected English:—

"You need take care, Mr. Twain."

I nearly bit through my cigar. I said nothing to that extraordinary statement. I expected him to flesh out his argument, and he did so.

"I suspect that there is cheating at the table." He turned to me and opened his mouth as if to say more, but instead brushed his hand against the lapels of my coat and said, "You have spilled ash on your jacket. I see I have upset you."

"Not at all," I lied.

"Perhaps it is nothing. Forget I said anything."

But he was right; there was cheating. We played only for another ten minutes. His warning had grown in my mind until I could think of nothing else. I had resolved to back out of the game and take my leave, and intimated as such. Dietrich heartily agreed and called for one last hand.

It had been a difficult hand to play, and we had gone through several rounds of betting. Everyone had dropped out but Dietrich and me. He asked for three cards. I had a pair of kings, so I did as well.

Leatherface dealt me two more kings.

This cheered me up immensely and drove from my head my fears of being cheated. Dietrich had been pleased with his hand as well, and we raised each other. Several hundred marks were on the table, and I saw the possibility of pocketing it all. My luck had been good thus far, and I saw no reason for it to change.

We displayed our cards, and my four kings beat his pairs of aces and eights.

In the general clamor after the revelations, Leatherface expelled a grunt like a pig knocked with a pole.

Dietrich asked Leatherface for elaboration.

"Herr Twain, he is cheating. He has cards in his pocket."

The table went dead silent. I plunged my hand into my coat pocket and pulled it out. Empty. I checked the other one where I kept my matches —

— And pulled out three cards.

I was as startled as if I had performed a magic trick without realizing it. They were useless cards — a trey, a deuce and a five — but they were from the deck, and that implied that I had swapped them for better cards.

I threw them as if stung. I protested, but for a moment. Dietrich snapped orders and I was pinioned and dragged before him. Joe Twichell added his voice, "This is an outrage. I've known—"

"Silence!" Dietrich said. "Herr Twain and I must talk." He turned and left the room, leaving Leatherface and his comrade to escort me behind him. We stopped when we reached the library, lit by the dim light of a gas jet. They tossed me into a chair as Dietrich turned up the lamp on his desk. Leatherface stood behind me while his pal closed the door on his way out.

"I will not mince words with you. You have publicly insulted me. You have been caught cheating."

"I have not!"

"You have. I accuse you of cheating. This is a matter of honor, and there is only one way to resolve this."

It was a good thing I was seated. My legs clearly were in no mood to perform their duty. But at least my mouth was in working order. "I will not! I am a writer. I have been a reporter, even an editor! I have no honor to dishonor."

"That is a sorrow. Your exhibition at the student club gave me hope you would be a challenging opponent. I will have to be content with thrashing you."

My heart was hammering, but my head was thinking. Dietrich's anger was too calm, too focused. Catching a gambler with the wrong cards created chaos that was short-lived, at least for the cheater. *I* know that I didn't pocket those cards; so someone planted them on me. In a flash, I realized it happened on the balcony, as pencil-head was warning me against being cheated. Only Leatherface might have something against me, but he only acted on his master's orders, which meant —

"Adler?" I didn't have enough facts to touch on any particular point. It just seemed as if she were involved in this somewhere.

"I tend to take her suitors seriously."

"I don't! I'm — you ass! You ninny! You politician! Do you really think — ?"

He waved my words aside like smoke. "Save your words, Herr Twain, they'll do you no good here."

"Ask her!"

"I did, after I found this in her fireplace grate." He pulled from his coat pocket a slip of paper, one side burned, and handed it to me.

It was the note I had sent her. Much of it was burned away, but what was left told me why he thought the way he did:

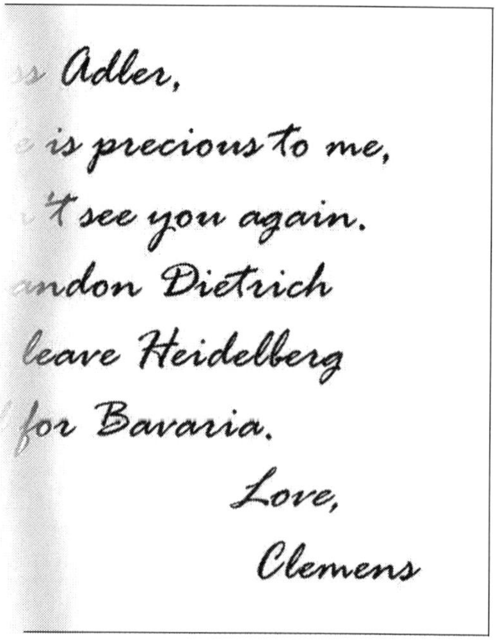

s Adler,

is precious to me,

t see you again.

ndon Dietrich

leave Heidelberg

for Bavaria.

Love,

Clemens

I groaned. My head swam with too many questions to nail one down long enough to ask. Not a word could I say that wouldn't ring like a counterfeit silver eagle. He took my silence for assent. He stood, smoothed his coat-front and snapped his fingers at Leatherface. "We go now."

At least there's one question I could ask.

"Where?"

"To the Castle. To the dueling grounds."

Dietrich had organized everything with typical German efficiency. Our carriages were waiting for us at the front door. The seating had been arranged, with Leatherface and Twichell, who agreed to act as my second, in Adler's carriage, and everyone else distributed among the rest.

We rode mostly in silence. Leatherface preferred to put all of his energies into glaring at me. I resolved to contribute nothing to the atmosphere. Only Twichell leaned over and patted me on the arm.

"Be brave, Sam. Everything will work out."

I relieved myself with a few chosen words and he stopped

elaborating on his sermon.

The scene passed before me like a dream. We arrived at the field outside the castle walls. Dietrich hopped out, went to the back of his coach and opened a trunk. The servants lit torches and formed a ring where the battle would take place. When Twichell dragged me out and to the rear of our carriage, I saw that we were on the opposite side of the circle.

Twichell said to Leatherface, "Go see your master. My friend needs to compose himself before the thrashing begins."

Leatherface spat and said something insulting, but he did leave.

In the trunk of Adler's carriage were the mask and sword similar to what we had seen at the club. He applied the mask to my face and belted it behind. He pulled out a long, heavy cape which he draped around my neck.

"Twichell, it's customary to decorate the corpse after he's perished."

He attached the cape at the neck, and set a wide-brimmed hat on my head. I snatched it off.

"If you're trying to blind me you're doing an excellent —"

Twichell snatched it back and jammed it on my head.

"If anyone asks, Sam, it's the way you fight in America. Don't let them tell you otherwise. Hear me? *You fight in this.*"

"You know I don't fight."

"Yeah, but they don't. Keep that in mind. They think you're Rudolf Rassendyll." He handed me the dueling sword. I looked across the field, Dietrich was nearly finished dressing. When Twichell let me go, I fled into the carriage with him hot on my heels.

"You need to step out, Sam. Now."

"Twichell! How can you say that? Get topside. Tell the driver to get me out of here, damn you, or —" I battered the ceiling with my gloved fist in an attempt to get the driver moving. The blade was in that hand, and it was whipping around, threatening to lop off an ear or worse.

Twichell threw himself on the floor before me and

gripped my shaking arms.

"Sam! Trust me! Get aholt of yourself." He gave my chest a hard thump with his palm and talked to me like he was soothing a skittish pony. "This is the hand you're dealt, don't you see? If you run, he'll track you to the hotel and thrash you there. You want Livy to see that? Your daughters? So here's how you're going to play it. You step out. You meet Dietrich face to face. You'll show brave. You'll step back six paces. The command will be given, and you will fight. D'ya hear me? Walk out there like a man, or so help me, I'll drag you to the field by your collar and throw you at him."

Twichell managed to silence me; something I swore no man would ever do. I had known him for nearly a decade then. He was a Congregationalist minister who helped officiate at my marriage. He had never, ever, talked to me like that. He had always been the most amiable companion. He had been an Irish setter, who suddenly bared his fangs at his master.

He reached into his pocket and brought out a silver flask. He uncorked it and lifted it to my lips, and I tasted the foulest stuff in my life. It must have been distilled in tar barrels. My lungs took in a pint as well, and I ejected the surplus onto the floor.

There was a knock on the carriage door. It opened to reveal Leatherface. He and Twichell exchanged views in German while I sputtered and choked and ran my fingers underneath the leather mask to clear my eyes. Despite the treatment, I was much calmer. An immediate discomfort distracts the mind from the larger horror.

I stumbled from the dim light inside the carriage into the darkness. I can still remember every second of my walk to the scene of the tragedy. It's still capable of making me leap up at night in a cold sweat: the sound of my boots brushing the short grass; the feel of my cloak over my shoulders and the closeness of the hat over my forehead; the keen smell of the evening mountain air and the lingering fumes of the brandy decorating my shirtfront. We walked and Twichell adjusted the straps in the back of my mask.

We walked into the circle of torchlight where gathered the surgeons in their black coats and tall hats, their leather bags with their saws and lancets at their feet. There was one of Dietrich's gentleman friends, solemn as an owl. His eyebrows shot up at my costume, and so shocked was he that he lapsed into German.

"*Was zur Hölle ist das?*" I opened my mouth but Twichell stepped in.

"It's how we do it in Nevada. Official dueling outfit."

Everyone looked to Dietrich von Nordmark. He was too polished to react, but coolly nodded. A faint contemptuous smile played on his lips. To my surprise, I chuckled. My brandy-fueled courage flared up, and my hands itched to carve his smile off his face. The rest of my corpse-to-be disagreed. My legs shivered like a wet dog, and my bowels turned to water. All the while a steady drone of words filled my ears. A referee was announcing the rules of the bout, and asking the traditional questions about the sanity of the participants and their desire to fight. Dietrich made his declarations loudly and proudly; I nodded. I paid it all no mind. He was going to disregard the rules and kill me anyway, and then shrug it off as an accident.

My temper did not improve with Twichell's continued fiddling with my mask. His fingers dug into the back of my head as if he was finding nits.

"Pace off!" the judge declared. The suddenness of his words shocked me into action. My legs had been given permission to move, and they did not need encouragement. I jerked back, nearly knocking over Twichell, and stepped off the six paces, little heeding if it were the right direction or not. Let Dietrich adjust himself to match me was my opinion on the matter.

"Ready?" I took one last look around at life. The torches. The circle of light. The eternal darkness beyond. The few witnesses to the slaughter. Dietrich made preliminary waves with his sword, and the sharpened blade caught the light and spread it against the dark like butter.

"Fight!"

I shook my head to clear the remains of the brandy, and as I did I went blind. I panicked. I could hear Dietrich's approach in the grass, and I leaped back, waving my sword to ward him off.

"Halt! Halt! His mask's off," Twichell cried. I adjusted the leather and my vision returned. Twichell had leaped between us, risking impalement. "The strap broke!"

Dietrich uttered a growl from deep in his throat. You could feel his frustration at being denied his execution.

Twichell grabbed my elbow and hustled me toward the carriage. I could hear a gentlemen offer a replacement mask from the count's supply, but he ignored them. "Won't be a minute. We have another one."

"Let's take several minutes," I said to him in a low voice. My legs were shaking so much that if we stopped moving I could collapse to the ground. "In fact, make it a couple hours. Or a year? I'm not in a hurry. Don't hustle on my account." But he seemed eager to repair the damage, because with his iron grip on my arm he nearly frog-marched me to the carriage. He opened the door and thrust me in. In the dim light I could see a hooded and cloaked figure bent over and working his pants into his boots.

Twichell pulled the door shut behind him and tugged aside the curtains. "They're milling about on the field," Twichell said. "You got time. Sam, give me your hat and coat. My God, that was close! I didn't know which of you was going to stick it to me first. Did you have to wave your sword around like a blind man?" He was jubilant at my discomfort.

"That's because I was, you idiot!" I ripped off the mask and threw it on the floor.

Then I got the shock of my life, for the stranger finished with the boots and said:—

"Keep your eyes peeled, Twichell. Like what you see, Mark?" The stranger pulled back the hood and brushed back the cloak.

"Irene?"

Twichell chuckled and handed her my outfit. She was wearing a dueling mask, from which peeped a moustache just like mine. A thousand questions flooded my brain, but all I could say was, "What are you doing here?"

"Saving your life," she took my hat and adjusted the cloak over her shoulders.

"That pleases me mightily. It's well worth preserving." With the immediate threat of oblivion receding, I was feeling more my old self. "He'll see right through you."

"He'll see you. He already got a close look at you. I'll take your position and between his expectations and the torchlight I'll pass long enough to get what I want. See?" She tilted her head this way and that. Now that she was completely clothed, I thought she could pass. Only the shape of her chin gave the game away.

A suspicion tickled me. I grabbed the mask and held it up to the light. I could dimly make out the neat cut in the strap. The cooler I got, the more I thought, and that's when the penny fell. I reached into Twichell's pocket and pulled out his flask. "You're slicker than greased lightning; you planned this, didn't you?" The brandy burned, but not so much. Must have taken off a layer last time.

Twichell laughed and slapped his knee. "Hear that, Miss Adler? I said he isn't as dumb as you thought." He took the flask back, gave it a pull, and handed it back. "You get yourself into the oddest scrapes. She told me what this was about while you nodded off. Didn't have much choice except to trust her and do as she asked."

"Are they doing anything out there?" she said.

"Still waiting, but looking at us. We'd best get going." She picked up her sword.

"Why?" I said, although I thought I knew the answer.

"Dietrich thinks he can do what he wants with me. With impunity." She adjusted the cape to cover her shoulders. I noticed that her bosoms did not show as prominently as before, and I suspected tighter bandages or the removal of whatever illusions she'd used. "I'm no child. I knew there would be an end to the affair. He's about to be married, did you know that?"

I confess I hadn't.

"That hurt, but he expected me to become his mistress. 'Aren't you American girls all like that?'" Her impression of Dietrich would have made a dog laugh, but for her seriousness. She was about to risk her life, and that scared me.

She took a deep breath to steady her nerves. "He's about to learn the difference between an 'Ah-MER-i-kan' girl and a Jersey girl."

Twichell said: "They're coming."

"Stay hidden," she ordered me. "Douse the light."

Twichell turned down the lamp, leaving us in darkness. I jumped onto the seat next to the door, which opened and they got out.

"*Sind Sie bereit?*" I heard.

"He is," Twichell said. "We had to adjust the new mask to get it to fit."

"Good! Herr Dietrich was concerned . . ." their conversation faded as they marched away.

I jumped down, tugged the curtain a crack, and received another shock. Walking away from the coach was Twichell and Clemens. Adler strutted, but as Clemens she shambled and weaved. Watching me walk away to my assumed death was one of the more peculiar experiences in my life.

The torches had burned for awhile so the light was beginning to dim. Dietrich was impatient, marching back and forth, sweeping the grass with his blade. He gave "me" a curt nod as Adler took my position ten yards away from him. The duel resumed. The field was silent but for the sound of the torches rippling in the breeze. Adler was still playing me, slump-shouldered, her head down and trembling like a horse in a thunderstorm. Dietrich was preening. He approached with an insolent stride and without any preliminaries slashed at the face. He intended to lay open my check, and would have if Adler, with not even a glance, parried the blow. The clash of steel on steel carried to the coach.

Dietrich essayed another swipe. Again her blade countered, followed by a step forward and a slash by return mail which he blocked. He had intended to humiliate me with easy attacks. He wouldn't treat me like a real opponent, only a dog to be beaten. She could have taken advantage of this; a lightning riposte would have ended the bout. She wanted to show that he failed. She was saying with her sword, "If you want to score off me, you'll have to do better than that." No attack on a man's body can cut deeper than the one on his pride.

Dietrich stamped. He grunted. He barked as he slashed. He roared as he was defeated. Adler countered each attack, the pace increasing until her blade was in a near-constant motion. From the carriage, I cheered and stamped my approval. I hoped she speared the bastard.

He was in a murderous mood at seeing his stratagems being consistently defeated. They launched into a flurry of blows and counterthrusts and ripostes, moving back and forth with each step marked by chiming blades. The onlookers realized that something was wrong, but they couldn't put their finger on it. They cried out for the duelists to stop, and Dietrich disengaged, his chest heaving for air. He waved his friends into silence, and that was the moment that Adler flung off her hat and pulled up her mask. Her chin was up and her posture, even from a great distance, shouted unconquerable defiance to the man she once loved.

"*Liebchen!*" he said hoarsely.

She said something that even now I blush to recall: "*Fick dich, du miserabler hurensohn.*" She spat and added, "And you fight like a schoolboy, *kurzen Schwanz.*"

Dietrich whipped off his mask. In three long strides, he

re-engaged Adler and in four blows she sliced, and an arc of blood exploded from his face. He screamed and dropped his sword and grabbed his nose.

She backed away, saluted the seconds and the doctors with the élan of a French cavalry officer, picked up her hat and mask and strode for the carriage, her cape billowing behind her. Twichell trailed, looking back cautiously, but never once did she glance back. The doctors ran to Dietrich and tried to work on him, but he shouted defiance at them and tried to rush Adler. Even in the fading torchlight, I shuddered at seeing his face smeared with his blood, his friends holding him back.

Adler entered the carriage, the driver whipped at the horses and we rumbled away. From the window, I saw Dietrich grow smaller and smaller. He tried one last lunge and as the carriage passed through the gate and turned out of sight, the last I saw of him was being borne down to the ground, bellowing in pain and rage.

The next morning I breakfasted with Livy in our glass-enclosed nest. I was a contented man. The ham came from a contented sow, the eggs fresh from excellent hens, and the coffee ground from beans imported from paradise. Last night's horror seemed to be a dream that faded as the summer sun played across the china on the table, the lace curtains carried a cooling breeze and the Neckar burbled off in the distance. I recounted to Livy my adventures of the previous night, telling her everything but the pronouns. I told about the poker game, but not that I played. I told about seeing Miss Adler in the duel, but not that I participated. It was my most brilliant lie, full of incident and color and concealing all that could cause her distress. I was virtuous in my deceit, a flavorful combination.

I was feeling pretty pleased with myself. Twichell and I can begin our walking tour today in the knowledge that Von

Nordmark will be more preoccupied with Miss Adler and healing to bother with me. I had finished my tale when the maid entered to place a wrapped package addressed to me by my plate.

Livy set down her cup and watched as I unwrapped it. She gasped as I opened several small boxes to reveal a beautiful ring inside each. A long case disgorged the diamond, pearl, and ruby necklace. I passed them across to her, and as she cooed over each piece, I read the note that accompanied them.

> Dear Mr. Twain;
> I must leave Heidelberg quickly. Thank you so much for your help. I would have asked Gunter to accompany me last night, but the dear would have fought, and I couldn't risk getting him hurt. Don't worry about him, however; he is with me.
> I must beg a favor. Dietrich insisted that I return his gifts and had been for some time. I was reluctant, but then remembered my lessons in church back in Red Bank that it was better to forgive and to turn the other cheek. Could you see this package mailed to the address below? You can expect this favor to be repaid someday, with interest, from
>
> > Your friend,
>
> > Irene Adler
>
> PS: I apologize for editing the note, but Dietrich needed encouragement. Men can be so obtuse sometimes, wouldn't you agree? I.

That's when the whole of her plan had become clear to me. I read the note to Livy but omitted the PS, and added:—

"Humph! The woman's nerve. Does she consider me her personal postman? I have a mind to drop it in the Neckar. Still, I can't return them to her. She could be on her way to London, St. Petersburg, Paris, or Warsaw. I suppose I should get this taken care of."

"This is curious." Livy was threading the pearls through her fingers.

"You look puzzled, dear. Whatever is the matter?"

"I'm no jeweler, but I could swear these pearls are imitation. They looked so real last night. Do you think the gas lighting could have had something to do with that?"

I rooted through the box and held each piece to the light. Some appeared genuine but some had a feel to them that looked suspicious. It occurred to me that New Jersey girls might forgive, but they never forget. And, when pressed too hard, they make sure to get some of their own back.

I tucked the note in my coat pocket.

"I need to get packing, but I'll make sure to send them along. Maybe from the train station." I reconsidered. "Better still, from Switzerland."

Afterward

Why Irene Adler? Why Heidelberg? Why sword fighting?

It started back in 1977. I was part of a small tour group on a three-week tour of Europe. We blitzed through London, Paris, Belgium, and down the Rhine to Munich. We stood in a crypt where Charlemagne prayed. We smoked pot and drank Algerian wine with students one night by the Seine. We talked about architecture with Albert Speer. We were guided to Anne Boleyn's execution site by a helpful Englishman who could have stepped out of *Kingsmen,* and I was scammed by an unhelpful Englishman in Piccadilly Circus.

One of the highlights was Heidelberg, where one night we

met up with a student in one of the beer halls who took us back to his fraternity house for a demonstration of dueling. He was the lineal descendant of the German army officers whose dueling scars became a villainous trope in Hollywood movies. I'd show you the photos I took that night, but I set the exposure too high on my brother's 35mm camera and they all look like they were processed with bleach.

So I already had Heidelberg in my mind when I came across Twain's account of living there in *A Tramp Abroad.* I had enjoyed throwing Twain and Watson together in San Francisco. It was a natural extension to recruit the most famous and notorious secondary character in the canon.

Writing Irene was great fun. She is manipulative, but she's not malicious unless she's been wronged. She's just a woman making her way in the world, always aware that she needs an equalizer against much stronger foes. This could be another man, her wits, or her skills with a blade. This is not as far-fetched as you might think. Actors, particularly those doing Shakespeare, have to be familiar with bladework, if only to make it look convincing on the stage. It's likely that an actress like Irene would pick up a few skills herself.

The Adventure of the Stomach Club

Perigord ... head-dreſs, in sign of ... hood, a jewel in yᵉ similitude of a man's ███████ wilted and limber, whereat yᵉ Queeⁿᵉ did laugh and say widows in England doe wear ██████ too, but betwixt yᵉ ██████, and not ██████ wilted neither, till ██████ hath done yᵗ office for them. Maſter Shaxpur did likewiſe obſerve how yᵗ yᵉ Sieur de Montaine hath alſo spoken of a certain Emperour of such mighty prowels yᵗ he did take ten ██████ in yᵉ compaſs of a single night, yᵉ while his Empreſs did enter-...in two and twenty [knight:

The Adventure
of the Stomach Club (1879)

T
ODAY'S NEWSPAPER BROUGHT ME JOY in the form of this item from the death notices:

> June 14, at his residence in Mayfair, aged 77, Mr. Stuart MacNaughton, the well-known bookseller and publisher, of 103 Piccadilly. The deceased, the son of a respectable builder, was born at his father's house, in St. John's Square, Edinburgh, and at the age of 14 was placed with the late Mr. Petheram, bookseller, in Holborn, where he acquired a taste for rare and curious books and an all-consuming passion for Scottish history. During his residence in the United States, Mr. MacNaughton appears to have been a keen observer of men and manners, and especially of American humorists such as Mark Twain. He returned to England about 1852, and commenced business in a little slip of a shop in Piccadilly. . . . His remains were interred at Highgate Cemetery, June 21st, and were followed to the grave by many sympathizing friends.

So MacNaughton was dead. Nothing sets up a man so well in the morning than the knowledge that he outlived someone he hated. I have no doubt that there were many in attendance at the revels. A vast, flowing river of humanity followed the hearse to the burying ground, each person in attendance there to ensure that he'd stay down. Do not speak ill of the dead, we are preached, and I shall not. But I do not consider speaking the truth to fall under that rubric. And as the purpose of these autobiographical notes, to be published a century after my passing, is to tell the truth, I would be comfortable in saying that many people were happy that the Scottish laird had breathed his last.

Telling the story properly required some cogitating. I smoked my cigar for awhile and watched from my bed as Sinbad and Danbury vied for a moth fluttering at the window. The kittens gazed at their prey with a stillness and intelligence that men should emulate. As they played, I considered the tale, making sure I had grasped all of the necessary facts.

What happened in London during that damp and miserable summer of 1879 wasn't funny. Not to me anyway. But any tragedy can turn into comedy given enough time. A few years back, that Borden girl over in Falls River picked up her hatchet and passed the time on a sweltering afternoon slaughtering her father and mother. Got away with it, too. I've no doubt that they'll be telling her story again and again, portraying her as a put-upon orphan who was driven to brain her parents. They will praise her piety. They will show that parenticide is a respectable hobby to be indulged in by the young. You may see the fun in it now, long after I have degraded into dust.

Back to MacNaughton.

Livy, the girls and I were spending the season in England. In a London hotel I was furiously writing *A Tramp Abroad*, piling up the pages of manuscript during the day in between sociable interruptions from visitors. Writing can be a tonic when used to relive pleasant memories or act as a safety valve for your anger. Scribbling to meet a deadline, to provide your family with their daily crust, is wearying work. The drudgery was relieved only by attending banquets and dinner parties every night. I was quite the pet then.

One evening, after a particularly strenuous day, Livy wanted to indulge our fondness for the theatre. Henry Irving was finishing his first season at the Lyceum, so we attended a special show in which he performed scenes from *Hamlet*, *Richard III*, *Richelieu*, and others.

We were ushered into a box on the second level, which provided a fine view of the spectacle. We could see the stage and the audience, and the audience could see the stage and the wealthy and celebrated in the boxes. When we tired of each other, we considered the décor. I've never seen so much gold on display outside of a Bavarian church or a California assayer's office. Royal craftsmen must turn to decorating theatres when they run out of palaces to gild.

The circus was a rousing entertainment from start to finish. The actors jumped about the stage as if they had done it before. It was an education to watch Irving command the stage, exerting his personality to the utmost degree to command the audience's attention. After the play, we went backstage to congratulate the players. I was quickly recognized and Livy, bless her, knew that until I was extracted from the mob that she was better off consulting with the other women about the celebrated personages who attended the riot, the females' habiliments, and the shortcomings of their husbands.

All was running as smooth as expected until an interval of quiet. I was left alone, and I took the opportunity to seek solace in a cigar. I had it clipped and in my mouth when the sudden flare of a match in my face blinded me. The scent of sulfur invaded my nose and inflamed a coughing fit.

"Evening, Mr. Twain," the voice said. My sight cleared, and instead of Lucifer I saw a Cockney before me. He was a young man whose face was squashed between his small-brimmed cap and dirty yellow neckerchief. His squint and sallow skin gave him the appearance of being well on his way to becoming a wizened old man, even though he was barely into long pants.

"I'll be brief, sirrah," the gnome leaned in and exhaled a breath composed of beer and onions. "I don't like to discuss business out in public, but seeing it's such an important man as yourself, I'll make an exception. If you call at the home of Mr. Stuart MacNaughton tomorrow at the address on this card, you may hear something to his advantage."

The rout in the room grew louder. Irving led the procession of actors and actresses into the room. He stood by silently, taking in the accolades, while the members of his company were greeting their friends at a volume usually heard in a slaughterhouse. The noise was so great I was forced to lean closer and call into his ear.

"His advantage? Shouldn't it be my advantage?"

"I think you'll take my meaning when you take your meeting. I see your lovely wife coming, so I must go."

"You still haven't said why I should visit," I said.

"Ah," the fraud paused as if he hadn't expected me to ask. "It's to do with your lovely chat at the Stomach Club in Paris. Mr. MacNaughton is by way of a businessman in the book line, and he would like to publish it."

"Absolutely not! You may tell him that for me. I will not give him the speech for all the gold in his vault."

"Oh, don't you worry about his gold," he shied a disgusting leer at me, which unnerved me. "Don't you worry about getting him a copy of your speech, either. He already has it. Greetings, Mrs. Clemens! Lovely play, was it? It's like you said, Mr. Clemens: 'None knows it but to love it; none name it but to praise.'" He tipped his hat and left me with my mouth agape, like a hooked carp.

"Youth?" Livy tugged the crook of my arm. "What's the matter? You look so furious."

I fought to master my emotions, something I fail at frequently. I wanted to bash something. But what? And what for? The scoundrel had quoted those lines in front of my wife, and then vanished in the press of the crowd. I couldn't tell Livy what that was about. Especially over that speech, of which she knew nothing.

"You look heated," she said. She opened her fan and waved it in front of my face. "You've had a long day, perhaps we—"

"Pardon me."

A tall scarecrow of a young man loomed over us. It was one of the actors, still in his costume as the Messenger in "Raising the Wind." He had appeared in several of the scenes, hovering about in the background, but had left no impression on me. That's not meant as criticism. Except for Irving's co-star, Ellen Terry, it was as difficult as climbing the Matterhorn for an actor to shine in the light from Irving's sun.

The Cockney's threat had left me unbalanced, my head spinning with nasty conjectures. But this slender fellow, away from Irving, proved just as commanding of my attention. He solicitously clasped my wife's hand with a slight bow before gripping mine with a startling firmness.

His eyes rapidly darted at my hands and other parts of the corpse, leaving me feeling dissected. Then he said, "You're a writer."

I confessed. He passed over the confirmation as inconsequential and asked what we thought of the performance. We chewed over the play in fine style. Livy took the reins for most of it, giving me a chance to inspect the visitor. He looked quite the gentleman. His accent was polished, but not by any school or class. He relaxed in our company, but inside it was clear that a brain was still at work. He continued to exude this presence, this ability to look in you and see everything. It must be the same feeling a microbe has under a microscope. It was unnerving.

To be honest, I don't remember very much of what was said. They say an execution focuses the mind wonderfully, but so does the sudden realization that your life is heading for the rocks on a lee shore, and decisions must be made immediately.

This was probably apparent to our actor friend. He bowed slightly to get my attention and said, "It is always a pleasure to meet Americans. Especially such eminent visitors as yourself. How did you find Paris, sir?"

I gulped and felt the blood rush from my face. "Fine, sir, fine," I croaked. For an uncomfortable moment, I wondered if he knew of my visit, too? Was he in cahoots with the Cockney?

"And you ma'am? Did you find the fan shop on the Rue di Rivoli delightful?"

"Why, yes," and Livy's mouth formed a perfect circle, "I – but how did you know?"

"Your fan told me so. I'm a great admirer of Madame Caillaux's work," he pulled a card from his waistcoat pocket and handed it to me. "It would be a pleasure to talk with you again. I'm always at home during the day."

He bowed slightly to us and moved on. That was my cue to cut the reins. I told Livy that the air was getting too close for my comfort, so we pressed through the crowd, shielding as much of my face with my top hat as possible, until we reached the street and hailed a hansom.

Livy had much to say about the evening, so I let her carry the weight of the conversation until we reached the hotel. The children were asleep, so we dismissed the servants and prepared for bed ourselves.

Still fully dressed before the chest of drawers, I pulled from my pockets my night's accumulations — money, billfold, notebook, pencil, the usual odds and ends, and the two pasteboard cards. Both were of a piece. Both had the owner's name set in script, twelve point centered, with their address in the lower left corner. Stuart MacNaughton conducted his business in Mayfair, on South Audley Street. He was successful, either in book publishing or blackmail. He worked within a shout of Piccadilly, the Royal Parks and Buckingham Palace.

The other card read simply "Sherlock Holmes" and indicated that he occupied cellar rooms at 24 Montague Street. The address placed him within sight of the British Museum and was more suited to a scholar than an actor. There were mysteries piled on mysteries here, and I shook my head at the roustabout going on in my head.

But Providence had one more trick to play. I tossed the cards in the silver tray, and one of them flipped over to reveal a bit of writing. I took it to the gas jet and tilted it to catch the yellow glow.

For the second time that night, I felt a lurch such as one feels when the steamship you command runs aground, and there will be nasty questions to come. On the reverse of Sherlock Holmes' card — before he had spoken one word to me — he had penciled on the card, in a clear cursive as neat as a schoolmaster's hand, "You are being blackmailed."

The next day, after a hasty toilet and a rushed breakfast, I took a hansom to Montague Street. All of Europe was cursed with a cold rain that summer, so the weather matched my mood. From my rolling throne, I lit my cheroot and watched the buildings roll by, sodden under their grey and black cloaks. The Londoners looked beaten-down under their umbrellas and slickers. I puffed on my cigar and waited impatiently for the curtain to rise on the next act.

At 24 Montague Street, I dashed across the wet pavement into the two-story brick building, descended the fifteen steps to a basement hallway and knocked on his door. He received me with the same courtesy as last night and a cheerfulness that was irritating. Instead of the solemn stick, he bubbled with enthusiasm toward the world in general. It was a shock to see how different he acted backstage. It was almost as if he were another person.

Nowadays, the world is familiar with Sherlock Holmes and welcome his eccentricities. Back then, he was a youth, unknown to all but his family and friends, and his face untraced by Sidney Paget's pen. All the features found in Watson's stories were there, but touched even less by age. The thin face not yet lined with care and concentration, the eyes clear and bright, the voice pitched a semitone high. The last of the boy was fading fast, and inside formed the shape of the man he would become.

I didn't know any of that the moment I crossed his threshold. All that I saw was an unknown actor who knew far more of my business than I was comfortable with. He could be a lunatic — his profession qualified him as a member of that fraternity — and possibly a criminal.

His disposal of my hat and coat gave me ample opportunity to inspect the premises in the grey light filtering through the basement windows. The décor was plentiful and shabby, the furniture used but solid. Two chairs crowded the small fireplace in which a coal fire had been lit. The bookcases that lined one wall of the main room were crowded with manuscripts, scrapbooks and bound volumes. Rough wooden tables were set up for specialized tasks. On one was spread bank notes of various denominations, including one that looked like a work in progress, alongside lenses, bottles of ink and pens. Another table bore the weight of flasks, burners, test tubes, and trays covered with stained clothes. On the breakfast table was a plate under a metal serving cover. I lifted it up, and my stomach revolted at the sight of a dead man's hand. Across its flesh crept tiny flying insects.

Holmes reappeared by my side and took the cover out of my hand. "An observational study. I believe it is possible to determine the time of death according to the state of decomposition. If you will wait a moment—" and he gently manipulated the fingers with a scalpel.

"Did you shake hands with it when he was alive?"

"Yes. He was a generous man," he said.

"Certainly with his flesh," I replied. Under his breath, Holmes calculated the rate of decay and judged the color of the skin. He replaced the dome and swiftly jotted figures into a notebook he kept next to the plate.

"Your guests must find this a charming lunch companion."

"I have very few guests, and they have more concerns than the state of their stomach." He slapped the pencil down with finality. "On to your matter. Please, take a chair. Tobacco? Ah, you have your own. Help yourself to my fire. The gasogene and siphon is beside you."

"Not at dawn, thank you."

"Is it that early? I've been up all night. Perhaps tea?" I shook my head. "Then let us consider your problem. We can start with your name, as we weren't introduced last night."

That brought me up short. "Confound it! What do you mean 'what's my name?' Do you not know who I am?"

"Should I?" I wish I could say he was startled, but he was as calm as a surgeon preparing to operate.

"I! — No, never mind. I'm not used to being a face in the crowd. It gives me the jitters. My name is Sam Clemens, better known as Mark Twain." I waited for a flicker of recognition, or any other sign that he was giving me a hoist. I've been gulled before with absurd questions told with a straight face. Bret Harte made a specialty of asking a question so convoluted in logic that you would not realize that it was composed of 100 percent pure moonshine. He pulled that on me, and I asked three times for clarification before I twigged the trap. If Holmes was bullyragging me he gave no indication. He sat there as if he had never heard of the name that was on the lips of the world.

He folded his hands in a prayerful position beneath his chin and nodded for me to continue. But I wasn't going to be treated like a schoolboy under the master's examining eye. I took out a cigar and reached for the spill vase by the fire.

"See here, how d'you know I was being blackmailed? And what was all that folderol with the fan? What's that about?" I lit the twist of paper and set the cigar alight.

"Handmade objects have a pattern that is unique, and therefore their origin can be determined. Your wife bought her evening dress in Paris; it is of the slimline style favored there but it has not yet been adopted locally. The quality of the workmanship is excellent, as it has to be when the design shows off a figure such as your wife's."

I could feel my face reddening. "Leave my wife out of this."

Holmes went on as if he hadn't heard. "The Parisian connection is redoubled by the fan. There are eight fan makers in Paris whose work is worth noticing." From one of the bookcases he pulled a small scrapbook. He flipped the pages, then turned it toward me. Glued to the page were press cuttings from French newspapers. He tapped a finger on an illustration that was a double of Livy's fan.

"Your wife's fan is made of tortoiseshell with a feather tip, a design that Madame Caillaux favors."

The revelation that he categorized people by their articles of clothing annoyed me. "You have the makings of a fine stock clerk."

"I am merely observant, more so than most people," he said mildly.

"Why bother? What good does it do to tell whether a fan was made in Paris or in China?"

"Because it is my line of work, Clemens. I make my living by consulting with police and private individuals on matters that interest them. To do that, I need tools. I need data. And people dissemble; their clothes, skin, hair, tattoos, everything they carry on them, does not. Their most intimate possessions identify them as clearly as if they shouted it to the world. Learning the language of objects gives us a useful tool for solving crimes." He pointed at his decaying experiment on the table. "Eventually, we will be able to look at a body and tease out all kinds of delicate information; the cause of death, the tools by which it happened. Perhaps—," and then he paused. An idea had struck him and the vacant gaze returned to his eyes. "By examining the blood, even where and how it occurred." He murmured a series of scientific phrases as if forming a hypothesis.

"You can test your little theories after I'm gone," I said irritably. "If you didn't know my name, which I must confess is far greater than yours, then how'd you twig me for an author?"

"The calluses on the edge of your right hand. They are not present on the left. Few professions rely on the sole use of one hand. In addition, your middle finger has the tell-tale dip by the side the nail. You hold your pen there, and it took decades of steady writing to create that imprint."

"I could have been a reporter."

"And still a writer, which proves my point."

"So you don't read books?"

"I read works of use to my profession. Scientific works, the latest monographs by eminent men, and the newspapers. Most literature is a closed book to me. If you had done something notorious, even in America, I would have taken note. You're not a criminal, by any chance?"

"Only on the lecture platform. I am thinking of murdering a publisher, so I may come under your purview before too long. So how did you twig the blackmail? Did that come from my fingers as well?"

He gave me a thin smile. "The answer is so simple that you might think less of me. You were talking to Alf Randall. The police have known him for quite some time. He even served a stretch at Pentonville for forgery. Lately, he's been assisting a publisher of cheap works by the name of MacNaughton. He specializes in pirating books that are popular in the United States and Canada and pocketing the money that normally goes to its creator."

"So you don't know literature but you know copyright law," I grumbled.

"I know crime," Holmes said simply.

"You won't get an argument from me. America and Britain do not respect each other's law on copyright, and unscrupulous publishers have used this loophole to pirate my books. One in Canada even had the temerity to ship their books into my country and undercut the price against my own publisher!"

"Such tactics would not be above MacNaughton," Holmes said. "In addition to pirating works, he also prints and distributes literature of a risqué nature. He also has a reputation, at least among those of a criminal bent, as a blackmailer. Through a network of allies — servants, footmen, spurned mistresses, anyone with information and a desire for money — he acquires letters that he threatens to release if not paid." The thought disturbed his sanguine nature. He gripped the arms of his chair to steady his temper before continuing. "There is probably no crime more heinous in creation."

"Why don't the police arrest him?"

"They need someone willing to come forward with evidence. That's not likely to come from someone with more to lose than the blackmailer. That makes this a crime greater than murder. It forces the victim to cooperate in the commission of a felony. Anyone witnessing your reaction while talking to Alf, would conclude that you had fallen into his hands. What does he have?"

"A talk I gave after dinner in Paris to a group of what I had hoped were discreet painters and writers. The Stomach Club. And never mind the topic. Too many people know about it already."

"So publication of this speech would harm you?"

"It wouldn't circulate openly; the subject matter prevents that."

"But privately?"

"It would seriously damage my reputation." The thought of how Howells, my friend of a decade and editor of *The Atlantic* would take it was particularly unpleasant. "Not bad enough to be cut in the street, but my friends in Boston would maintain a distance from me. Even worse would be the confession I would have to make to my wife! She would be very disappointed and embarrassed. She reads and comments on all of my writings."

"Except for this one."

"Yes . . . yes!" I could take sitting still no longer. I paced the little room. "She would have to endure going out into Hartford society and hear the veiled pity for having a vulgar brute for a husband. Holmes, compared to that my reputation can go hang! I must protect her at all costs!"

"Then the chain of events is clear," Holmes said as I paced. "Someone got a hold of your speech and copied it. It found its way into Alf's hands and from there to his master."

A terrible thought halted me in my tracks. "Good God!

You don't think there is more than one copy out there?"

"No, no, most likely not. It would damage the value of the original, don't you see? If one was already out there, the copy in MacNaughton's hands would be worthless. How much did he ask for?"

"I'll see him later at his home on South Audley. Holmes, can you help?"

"If you do as I say, we'll stand a chance of keeping this scandal quiet."

"That'll be a relief. How do we force MacNaughton's hand and get my papers back?"

"I haven't the faintest idea, Clemens. But all campaigns begin with a first step. Here's what you'll do—"

London is an ancient city. It has had plenty of time to up-end your expectations. There are plenty of palaces, and you might think the wealthiest, most powerful people live there. There are humble dwellings, well-built but not calculated to inspire awe. They appear to belong to the residents who have some money, but are otherwise undistinguished.

And there you would find yourself caught unawares. The aristocracy live in the palaces, but many of them are land-rich and cash-poor. Instead, the wealthiest and most powerful people inhabit buildings that look like they would house the family of a prosperous manufacturer. This is how they brag about the size of their pocketbook; they're so wealthy they can afford to live modestly. Meanwhile, a wealthy factory owner who has bought himself a peerage second-hand will throw up a monstrous pile suitable for a French king. This is to show everybody where he came from.

Stuart MacNaughton was of the former, as I learned when I climbed the steps of his business on South Audley Street. His publishing concern was housed in a modest, two-story structure with two rooms on each floor flanking the landing leading to the staircase.

The butler had the door open before the bell ceased ring-
ing. Despite his uniform, he looked less like a servant and
more like a bare-knuckle fighter filling in on his off-hours. He
was a heavy-set bruiser who had lost all his hair young and
never got over it. His contempt for me appeared to be instant
and eternal. He did deign to accept my hat and coat, presumably to feed the fire when I wasn't looking, and conducted me
to the office just off the front door.

MacNaughton was at his desk writing. He peered through
his gold pince-nez at me and then ignored me while the butler settled me in a chair. This gave me time to take the man's
measure. He was a solemn stick, formally dressed, about as
tall as Napoleon and with as much gravity. He showed plenty
of skull forward, a slate of oily thin hair covered his aft, and
he had civilized his reddish beard into a short and narrow
structure. He looked like a constipated professor. That he was
Scottish was evident by his name and his ancestry, all of
whom were glaring down on him from the walls. They were
bluff and hearty men, dressed in their distinctive family plaids
and sporrans. They looked like they spent much of their time
at the dinner table, raging against the Sassenach when not
leading border raids on rival families. If these men had begat
the likes of Stuart MacNaughton, book publishing has clearly
decayed the family's bloodlines. From their glum attitudes,
they clearly agreed.

When MacNaughton had finished his scratchings, he slot-
ted his pen, patiently blotted his paper, folded it into an enve-
lope and dropped it onto a silver tray. His task done, he took
notice of me. His mood lightened. He greeted me courteously
and offered me a dram of the spirits of his native land. I refused with equal courtesy.

"Ach, weel," his accent burred like a buzz saw. He poured
himself a glass. "I appreciate you seeing me on a matter of business." We traded words, just like many conversations I've had
with book publishers: about the current state of the trade, the
difficulties of getting work finished, the fickle tastes of the pub-

lic. I could feel my steam rising in anticipation of the kick to come, but Holmes had briefed me thoroughly. He wanted details, as many as I could accumulate, and I must above all keep from braining the man. I was not accustomed to acting as someone's camera, so I concentrated on the task at hand, and reminding myself that Livy's fate depended on what happens now.

"You have come about the Work, I reckon," he fixed me with a sharp eye to see if I caught his meaning. "Your name is ranked high by the public, and I should like to acquire anything you might care to offer to the house for publication."

"You already have something of mine in hand," I said. "That's why I'm here."

"Aye," he took a sip, savoring the product of his native land with a smacking of his thin lips. "That there is; there is that. A fine piece it is, and I can see jobbing it with others we've found. Some of them even by you. I was thinking of calling it, 'On the Science of Onanism and Other Sketches' by Mark Twain. Is that a bonny title, ye think?"

"You'll publish no such thing," I roared and leapt to my feet. What followed were detailed descriptions of his character, his appearance and his damnation. How I longed for a tool to smash that smug face! I was angry twice over. Once, for intending to publish the speech, but twice for admitting he would throw in pieces that were not by me.

He took my abuse calmly. "I have heard that before, but I pay it no never mind."

"And I bet you don't even have the speech," I roared. "It's easy to repeat a phrase or two and say you have it. How could anyone have gotten their hands on it when I have the only copy?"

He smiled, and I knew he wasn't afraid of me at all. He positively enjoyed this set-to. "If you will excuse me." He stood and stretched and admired the colors my face was turning into. Then with careful deliberations, he opened a drawer, took out a plain brass key, and left the room.

Quietly, I dogged his steps and paused behind the frame

of the door where he wouldn't see me. He climbed the central staircase and at the head, turned left and entered a room. I poked my head further into the hall, scanning the horizon for the butler. He had vanished. The ticking clock was the only sound in the whole of the house, possibly of all of creation. Keeping cautious and silent, I took the steps two at a time.

My luck was in. The door was ajar. I applied my eye to the crack and saw a large gathering room with a billiard table in the middle. I could see the back of him, kneeling before the central door of a heavy mahogany sideboard against the far wall. A sharp click like a released spring, and he burrowed deep into the cabinet. He seemed to be rooting around for something. I retreated back to the office, my heart hammering in my chest, taking special care that a groaning board would not shout my presence.

When he reappeared with his bruiser butler in his wake, he found me, innocent as a lamb, taking in his collection of mementos from Scottish history. He had quite the bug for it. There were complete sets of Scott, Burns, McGonagall and other literary notables. Among the objects residing in a cabinet of curiosities was a set of medieval chessmen carved from ivory, and a cameo portrait of Mary, Queen of Scots. Had I looked longer, I probably would have spotted the stuffed spider that Robert the Bruce saw spinning its web.

He re-established himself behind his desk, and I moved back to my chair.

"You asked how I acquired the manuscript," he squared the paper on his desk. "From what I was told, there was a moment during the evening when a clumsy waiter spilled wine on your jacket. With your consent, it was taken away for cleaning. While a maid sponged out the stain, two of the waiters rapidly copied the speech. Ten minutes later, all was restored, and you were none the wiser." He waved a sheet before me. "I'm sure you will understand that I did not bring it all. I particularly appreciate this part." He gave a small cough, and I heard my words in his weedy voice:

"Of all the various kinds of sexual intercourse, this has the least to recommend it. As an amusement, it is too fleeting; as an occupation, it is too wearing; as a public exhibition, there is no money in it. It is unsuited to the drawing room, and in the most cultured society it has long been banished from the social board. It has at last, in our day of progress and improvement, been degraded to brotherhood with flatulence. Among the best bred, these two arts are now indulged in only in private — though by consent of the whole company, when only males are present, it is still permissible, in good society, to remove the embargo on the fundamental sigh." He paused. "Do your words embarrass you?"

I writhed in my seat. "It's your performance. You have no cadence, no flow, no rhythm. You read like a boy in short pants."

His chuckle fluttered like dry leaves, and he returned to his torture:

"My illustrious predecessor has taught you that all forms of the 'social evil' are bad. I would teach you that some of these forms are more to be avoided than others. So, in concluding, I say, 'If you must gamble your lives sexually, don't play a lone hand too much.' When you feel a revolutionary uprising in your system, get your Vendome Column down some other way — don't jerk it down."

He set the paper carefully on the desk. I wished with my whole soul that it would burst into flames, and take him and his damnable house with it.

To distract myself, I pulled out a cigar. "How much?"

"It is not money that I want."

I treated the answer with the contempt it deserved. I pulled a match from my vest pocket and scratched it on the sole of my shoe. It failed to catch, and I had to steady my foot and try again.

"You are writing a book. I am a publisher. We can reach an agreement."

A Tramp Abroad?

"Is that the name? Much like *The Innocents Abroad* is it?

That would do well, then. Yes, very well. That would suit the MacNaughton House very much."

I paused to blow smoke at the coffered ceiling and to appear to give the matter some thought. "I'd like some time to consider the matter. This will take some ciphering."

"So long as I get an answer soon. In fact—" he was interrupted by a knock at the door. A housemaid held a brief confab with the butler, who approached the throne with a folded slip of paper. MacNaughton read it, smiled, and asked:—

"Is she here?"

"Her boy is at the door, my lord," said the maid.

"Inform him that she should come tonight when she has the package."

"Very good, my lord."

The butler left, but MacNaughton did not pick up his share of the conversation. He looked at the note again, chuckled as if at some private joke, and slowly hummed a tune as he refolded it and slid it under the blotter.

"I'm giving a dinner party tonight. Just a few authors and company backers. Come and dine. You will greatly add to my credit. You can give me your answer and sign the contract."

"Damn you! That's not enough time."

"What is there to consider?" he waved my speech as if he was fanning himself. "Eight o'clock. White tie."

I returned to Montague Street in a foul mood, which wasn't helped when his landlady said Holmes had gone out. He had left instructions to set out a cold lunch, and that I was to amuse myself as I saw fit until he returned.

Seeing the cold mutton and round of bread next to the domed dish swept away my appetite. I poured off a glass of warm cider, added a dash of whiskey to it, shoveled a double handful of coals onto the fire, lit a cigar and settled in for a long brood.

I was in a fix and I knew it. I would rather burn the *Tramp* manuscript than hand it over to that blatherskite. Would . . . but couldn't. I could see clearly my future with that speech attached to my name. It wasn't pretty. I had given my enemies a weapon. They'd say I hadn't changed. That I was still the crude Westerner carpetbagging my way into the literary East. They would sneer as fools the friends who championed me, like Rev. Joe Twichell. He'd back me to the hilt, but he'd be pitying me as well, and that's a heavy burden for any man to bear. That brought up a fresh head of steam, I relieved myself with fresh damnations of MacNaughton until I felt better.

The door opened. A thin man bundled in a coat and scarf entered and crossed toward the warm fire, his face hidden by his tall hat and coat that marked the undertaker's profession.

"If you came for a body, he's over there," I pointed to the covered hand. "You won't need a coffin to carry him out. A towel would do."

The hat and scarf came off, revealing Holmes' ascetic face.

"Not quite yet, Clemens." He unshucked himself and rubbed his hands briskly. "While you've been comforting yourself by my fire, I have been busy with your problem." He stopped at the table to cut a slice of mutton and a heel of bread before settling opposite me. "While I'm eating, why don't you tell me what happened."

I described MacNaughton's office and repeated as much as I could of our conversation. Between bites, he fired questions to spark my memory. He was an exacting prosecutor, ransacking my brain for the tiniest detail. I've no doubt he would have made an excellent inquisitor, and would have invented a few torture devices as well.

I had no clue what he was gaining from my interrogation, except to test the limits of my tolerance for nonsense. He finally reached it when he asked me to sing the tune that MacNaughton had hummed.

He repeated the phrase. Perfectly, of course. "Is that it?"

"That's right."

He dusted the crumbs from his hands, picked up his violin and plucked the sequence of notes and looked to me for confirmation.

"Right."

"That slow?"

"Yes. Shall I tap it in Morse code?"

"Do you recognize it?"

"Do I? It's 'Camptown Races,' you ninny! Haven't you heard of it?"

"No. Does it come with words?"

"Words? Why — of course it does!" And rather than throttle him, I leaned back and roared:

"De Camptown ladies sing this song, do-dah, do-dah!"

He waved his hand at me to stop. "No, no, just the part he sang! How does it go?"

So I boomed out —

"Somebody bet on the bobtail nag

"Somebody bet on the bay."

That stilled him. He got this look in his eyes like the windows in an abandoned house. I had seen it on the face of an idiot back in Hannibal. With that fellow, it signaled the onset of a fit.

Only Holmes did not flop to the floor and froth at the mouth. He laid his violin on the table, folded his hands under his chin and thought deeply.

I ventured a sally: "I assume this has some meaning to you."

"Of course it does!" Life returned to his eyes, and he waved away his anger. "Never mind. I was concentrating and you interrupted, but, yes, that fits with what I learned at his house. I'm surprised he didn't quote Rabbie Burns, a far more appropriate nationality than your American Stephen Foster."

"I'm grateful he didn't. Associating that wretch with Burns would put me off his poetry permanently. So you visited the house?"

"Yes, in the guise of an undertaker as you guessed. I called at the back door to measure a customer for a coffin. The cook informed me that death had not visited the house, and my charming apologies resulted in an invitation for tea."

"Really?" I said. "I would have thought the undertaker would be the least welcome visitor when not needed."

"To a lonely cook in a small household, any visitor is a fine excuse for a chat over a cuppa," Holmes dipped again into his store of accents. "She took me into the basement kitchen, and soon we were by the fireside, and she was telling me about her life and that, of course, included the master of the house, his little peccadilloes, and his visitors. If I had a few days to spare, and a few nights walking out, I am sure we would have become engaged. Servants are a vastly underused resource, Clemens. They go everywhere, see everything, and will tell everything to the right ear with the right inducement. Remember that when dealing with your staff, Clemens."

The significance he put into that last sentence unnerved me. An uncomfortable memory surfaced of the times I had used profanity to describe my disappointments in the servants. One incident over the missing buttons in my freshly laundered shirts escalated from words into a shower of shirts and profanity from an upstairs window. To cover my shame, I asked:—

"What did you learn?"

"That Mr. MacNaughton uses the house as his place of business, preferring to keep his wife and children in Hampstead. He spends so much of his time there that he keeps only a cook, housemaid and butler, who, as you suspected, had a brief career as a bare-knuckle fighter. This, combined with your information, gives us our plan. If all goes well, we could stop Mr. MacNaughton and protect your reputation."

"And if we fail?"

Holmes opened his hands, palms up, like a Frenchman and said, "We go to prison."

When I returned to the house at eight, I was led to where

the dinner guests were gathered, in the billiard room on the second floor, what the English call the first. This allows you to see who else had been invited and, according to your opinion of them, to fortify yourself accordingly.

Seeing that lovely billiard table nearly broke my heart. There is nothing I like better than spending my afternoons with a cue in my hand, and the thought I shared that interest with my blackmailer saddened me. I turned my attention instead to my co-conspirators at the dinner table. The only consolation I found there was that I would dine among strangers. Over the course of many visits to England, I had been introduced to the cream of the peerage, writers held in high esteem, and people whose company I valued. I would have been mortified if any of them had showed up tonight at that blackmailing scoundrel's behest. And if they had seen me.

The only person I wanted to see there but didn't was Holmes. He had no invitation, of course, but he assured me he would figure out a way inside. His casual reference to prison shocked me into arguing against the scheme. But then he challenged me to come up with a better plan and that took the trick. He even refused my demand for details, except to suggest that I do nothing and leave everything to him.

I was not nearly so confident. This sounds strange now, with Holmes nearly as well-known as myself. But this was when the man had no reputation. He was barely out of the university and believing he was brilliant enough to pioneer a science nobody had ever heard of. He was like many young men I knew. They were building devices to find gold and silver using sound waves, treat diseases with electricity, build airships that can travel the world and machines to reach the bottom of the seas. They were dreamers who believed the rules of science did not apply to them, and many of them found out too late that they were wrong.

If Holmes was as flighty as them, I was sunk. If he didn't show, I would lose my only chance of recovering the speech and be forced to give up a book it had taken two years to write.

While waiting for the call to commence the festivities, I drank my champagne and made small talk. I did not know the other guests, but they made great efforts to know me. A dozen heads had turned upon my entrance. A dozen hands were extended to be shaken. A dozen pairs of ears turned eagerly to catch my sallies. The laughter in response to my remarks was too loud by half, and my heart sank. I was being courted, and I knew what would happen next.

I was drawn like a magnet to the sideboard where MacNaughton had kneeled only hours before. The doors were closed, holding tight their secrets. Some young idiot who claimed to be a humorist was bending my ear. His name was not familiar, of the publications he claimed to have appeared in I was ignorant, and his wit was sad. As expected, he tried to arrange an audience with me after the dinner, to read his work to me and solicit a favorable comment for publicity. I suggested sending it to my hotel, and gave him the wrong name so that his package would not follow me.

When he was fended off, another supplicant took his place. This one was a poetess, thinned and paled no doubt by her devotion to Art, who encouraged me to read some patriotic twaddle on relations between Britain and the United States. She was followed by a printer with a new idea for an automatic typesetter, then an inventor seeking backing for a new coal-mining process.

It was driving me insane. I was standing only feet away from recovering my reputation. If I could, I would rip away the concealing panel, rifle through his papers, make off with my property, and damn everyone to purgatory.

Then I was asked for a story. I looked at their faces, shining in the gas light, and I must confess that the devil took a hold of me. I took a deep breath and caught the scent of roast pork from the kitchen in the basement. They want something from me, then I'll give to them but good, with vinegar and mustard on top!

This is what I told them:

"Once in Washington, during the winter, Riley a fellow-correspondent, who stayed in the same house with me, rushed into my room — it was past midnight — and said, 'Great God, what can the matter be! What makes that awful smell?'

"I said, 'Calm yourself, Mr. Riley. There is no occasion for alarm. You smell about as usual.'

"But he said there was no joke about this matter — the house was full of smoke — he had heard dreadful screams — he recognized the odor of burning human flesh. We soon found out that he was right. A poor old woman, a servant in the next house, had fallen on the stove and burned herself so badly that she soon died. It was a sad case, and at breakfast all spoke gloomily of the disaster, and felt low-spirited. The land-lady even cried, and that depressed us still more. She said:

"'Oh, to think of such a fate! She was so good, and so kind and so faithful. She had worked hard and honestly in that family for twenty-eight long years, and now she is roasted to death — yes, roasted to crisp, like so much beef. Poor faithful creature, how she was cooked! I am but a poor woman, but even if I have to scrimp to do it, I will put up a tombstone over that lone suf-ferer's grave! Mr. Riley, if you would have the goodness to think up a little epitaph to put on it which would sort of describe the awful way which she met her —'

"And Riley said, without a smile, 'Put it 'Well done, good and faithful servant!''

There were a few chuckles that were drowned by the ring-ing of a small gong in the hall.

"Is that the dinner bell?" I told the assembled. "Mighty fi-ne. I hope that's pork I smell! I would even eat a publisher!"

By the time the third course was being wheeled in, I was as jumpy as a cat on coals. There were footmen behind the chairs, servants bringing in wine and the platters, and still no sign of Holmes. The bruiser of a butler came in. He whispered into MacNaughton's ear. He dropped his napkin onto his plate and stood.

"I apologize, but I must leave ye for a moment."

I saw my opportunity. Holmes or no Holmes, I must see for myself to that blasted paper! I counted to a hundred, and then stood. The table fell silent. I excused myself and took care to look abashed, and they took my meaning. I must visit the water-closet immediately.

With the dining room door closed behind me, I rabbited across the hall to his office. The gas had been turned off, but I felt my way around by memory until I reached his desk. I struck a match and yanked opened the drawer. The key lay glittering in the feeble light. I pocketed it, tiptoed across the carpet, then peeped through the door. The staircase was free of servants. I vaulted the steps to the billiard room. With typical Scotch thriftiness, MacNaughton had the gas jets turned low to the point of gloominess in anticipation of our return. In a moment I was on my knees before the sideboard, my ears flapping for any noise. But all I could hear was the faint murmur of conversation from downstairs.

I opened the cabinet and pawed for the keyhole. The light did not penetrate, and I could not find it. Cursing, I struck a match. The brass keyhole gleamed in the flaring light. I jammed in the key, turned and the door popped, pushed by a hidden spring.

Then my blood froze. The hallway door opened. There was the sound of a woman's laughter, and MacNaughton shushing her.

I closed the secret door. The voices were growing nearer. I closed the outer door and sought a bolt-hole. Nothing suited. The room looked like a gentleman's club. Heavy couches against the wall; club chairs against the far wall. The voices were coming closer. I could hear her throaty chuckle.

I was in a desperate fix. I was a rabbit in the hunter's sights. The billiard table was nearest, so I spider-crawled across the carpet and dove underneath it, where I came face to face with Holmes.

"What—?"

He prevented further conversation with the palm of his hand, just in time for the hall door opened.

"We must hurry, my love," MacNaughton was purring. "I've left my guests at table and must return soon. Was it difficult getting the letters?"

"Naw," her Cockney voice cut through the gloom. "The old dear had 'em in plain sight, like he was waiting to hand them over. It was all I could do to not bust out laughing."

The crinkle of papers could be heard as MacNaughton shoved them in his jacket pocket.

"Aren't you going to keep them in the safe, love?"

"Not yet, not yet." MacNaughton sounded almost giddy over his newest acquisition. "The key's in my desk, and I don't have time."

"So when are we going to have time, dearie?" From under the gloom of the billiard table, I stifled a sneeze. The house servants did not do their master's duty by cleaning the cobwebs from here.

All we could see was the tail of her skirt as she was backed across the floor toward our hiding place. There were giggles. The silence was broken by moist smacks of the most disgusting kind. Surely they weren't going to . . . not above us!

"Oi!"

A pair of men's legs appeared at the door. The scene had spun on a point from lurid romance to a domestic drama. A man had entered the scene, stage center.

"Oi thought so!" he roared. "Ye said y'were going out for a drink, so I follows you and I find this!"

"No!" she screamed.

There was a bang. MacNaughton's legs jerked and he slid into view as he hit the floor with a moan, staring at the ceiling and clutching his chest.

"Clemens," Holmes hissed. "The gas! Turn up the gas!"

I crawled out from under the table, found a jet and turned the key, throwing light onto that scene of confusion. The man was gone, leaving behind a haze of gunpowder smoke. The woman was bent over and cradling MacNaughton's head. His shirtfront sprouted the red rose of blood in the center of his chest. Holmes bent over him and opened his jacket and shirt. MacNaughton was moaning, his face pale, his breathing rapid, but he was still moving, and even to an untutored eye that indicated that the fellow is still living.

"You better leave," Holmes said. Even then, I noticed he omitted my name.

"What about my paper?"

"There'll be a bigger scandal if you're seen at the home of a blackmailer who has been shot." He wiped his bloody fingers on MacNaughton's coat and stood. He led me out to the hall. I could hear the murmur of natives gathering at the foot of the stairs. They had heard gunfire, their host was absent, and soon someone would build up the nerve to climb up and see. The butler appeared at the top of the steps from the basement and was holding a confab with the other servants.

"You have seconds to avoid questions you can't answer," Holmes said, hustling me over to a baize door at the back of the landing. "That will take you down the servants' stairs to the back door."

I pressed the key into his hand and said, "You might find this useful. It opens the inner door of the sideboard."

I fled through the baize door and down the narrow back stairs. I shielded my face from the servants like a leper. Some were well-mannered enough to ask if I needed assistance; the rest observed my flight without comment. Perhaps it was a regular occurrence in this household. With memories of the bloody scene haunting me, I reached the door opening onto the back garden and fled into the night.

By the time the hansom reached my hotel, I fairly vibrated with anxiety and expected to pass a sleepless night. But the strain and nervous exhaustion had drained me. Fatigue was already pulling on my coattails as I unlocked the door to my hotel suite. The maid had left the gas jets on, turned low, and the dim golden light reminded me of that awful room. I turned off the jets and slipped into the bathroom where I made a hasty toilet. In the dark, I felt my way to my bed and slid under the cool covers next to my Livy. Before I could resume worrying about what tomorrow would bring, I dropped into a dreamless void.

By first light I was a subdued wraith. With her usual cheerfulness, Livy wanted to know what had happened last night. I tried to satisfy her curiosity about the guests, the food and the talk without mentioning the gunfire and the casualties. I also said that I would have breakfast out, as I had a morning appointment that I must keep.

The weather was as cool and still as the day before. The dampness was pervasive. But as I stepped out of the hansom onto Montague Street, the clouds broke and a weak sunlight chased the shadows into the alleys. It was the first change in the weather since we arrived, and I took it as a hopeful omen.

Holmes received me at the breakfast table. It appeared he hadn't started yet, as his place was surrounded by several covered plates.

"You missed much excitement last night," he said. "Have you seen the newspapers?"

I shook my head no and sat down. He nodded to the pile beside him on the table. "Then you will be pleased to know that, as of the late morning editions, there has been no mention of the affray. You seem surprised."

"Baffled. A shooting in Mayfair would have merited attention from any American reporter who wanted to keep his position."

"Your luck was in last night. The derringer was not charged enough for the bullet to penetrate deeply. The bullet stopped at the breastbone. MacNaughton damned Alf as a blackguard and ordered his guests not to breathe a word to anyone. Someone will talk eventually, but for now it will have the status of malicious gossip. If you keep your nerve and deny everything, it will be difficult for anyone other than your enemies to believe that you would be mixed up in it. Clemens, are you all right?"

I wasn't and I expressed myself in forceful words before admitting, "My hat and coat! I left them at the house."

"And I spirited them away before anyone noticed," Holmes said. "They are on the rack behind you. In the meantime, I believe this is yours."

He lifted one of the covers to reveal the dead man's hand. Cradled in his palm were several sheets of manuscript paper rolled up with a ribbon. I considered myself lucky to be sitting down, because the relief assumed a physical aspect, and I wouldn't have stood for long before such a scene.

I slid the roll of paper tenderly from its grasp, inspected it closely to ensure that no decayed flesh was attached, and tucked it in my side pocket. Holmes gently restored the dome to the plate.

"What perplexes me is who shot the blighter. And who was the woman?"

Holmes purred like a cat at the cream. "MacNaughton had many partners in his criminal enterprises. One of them was Mrs. Alf Randall. In addition to her other talents, he has been carrying on with her for some time. I suppose it was inevitable that Alf would find out, especially if someone met up with him in a pub and tipped him a wink. To be on the safe side, a discrete note was also sent to Mrs. MacNaughton. There was an excellent chance that one or the other, or perhaps both, would show up for dinner and nature take its course."

"But, but how did you cipher that Mrs. Randall was . . . involved."

"The cook mentioned that MacNaughton received several visitors. All of them were men except for Mrs. Randall. One could assume she was a member of the ring, but her status was confirmed in the snatch of song you quoted. In your country, a bobtail is a horse with a docked tail, but among certain classes it has quite a different meaning over here. It led me to suspect a different relationship between MacNaughton and Mrs. Randall."

For the first time in two days, my relaxation and satisfaction was complete. I struck a match on my shoe and lit my cigar. My stomach growled, and I looked forward to my breakfast.

Then I considered the covered dishes. If a hand was under one of them, what could be under the others was not worth considering.

"Speaking of cooks, I'd like to take you to the Langham Hotel for breakfast," I dropped my match and stood up. "But leave your friend."

Afterward

One advantage of doing a lot of historical reading is being able to take real-life incidents and tweak them into a story. The story almost writes itself.

Such was the case here. Twain really did give a speech titled "Some Thoughts on the Science of Onanism" to the Stomach Club in Paris. Unscrupulous foreign publishers did reprint unauthorized editions of his works. More insulting, they would add pieces by inferior authors and credit them to Twain. Unethical publishers were not above printing pornography for discriminating clients, the most notorious being John Camden Hotten, on whom I based Stuart MacNaughton.

While Twain never worried about his risqué pieces becoming widely known, he did withhold publication of some of his more volcanic opinions on lynching and religion until after his death. It didn't require a great stretch of imagination to shift the parameters to what you see in the story, or who he would call upon for help.

One more note: The cover illustration shows text from a small press edition of "1601," another irreverent risqué squib written by Twain and circulated in manuscript among a small group of friends.

The Adventure of the
Missing Mortician

The Adventure
of the Missing Mortician (1882)

This adventure takes place in the town Twain loved most — Hartford, Conn. — and in the house he designed and had built to reflect his unique personality and sense of style. It also gives us a chance to become better acquainted with two important members of his household: his butler, George Griffin, and his wife, the love of his life, Livy.

A LEOPARD CAN'T CHANGE ITS SPOTS. Neither can a man. I used to believe otherwise. I had seen this great nation grow into adulthood and stride onto the world's stage. I had said, "This will be wonderful. We have moved out of the nursery. Now we'll show those other nations something to be proud of."

I know better now. We change our surface topology. We dress our hair differently. We change the style of our fig leaves. We adopt the popular fancies as if we conceived of them. The heart still reveals itself.

Let me show you the difference between myself and my Livy. She's been gone these many years, and I hold on to these memories so that she'll never leave me. It was morning in Hartford. Livy was still asleep, an angel in gossamer. I was in the bathroom, dressing, when I became irate at the state of my shirts. It was apparent that they had been boiled in lye and dried in starch. The laundress had assumed I wanted my buttons loosened so they'd fall off when they had a mind to. As I found each shirt deficient, I ejected them out the bathroom window followed by a shower of boiling words. I added as celebratory confetti my ties, collars, and other objects at hand, so that I'd have the pleasure of watching them drift across the lawn like ghosts.

Then I froze. I heard a cough from our bedroom. Livy had awakened and no doubt heard my solo. There was no escape for me. The window was too high to leap from. I passed through the bedroom, and as I did, she called my name. I was mortified and unable to resist or object, as she repeated, word for word, everything she had heard. My shame at being caught turned to humor at her performance, and I told her:—

"You got the words right, Livy, but you don't know the tune."

That's what I mean about the inner person. Livy could no more convincingly portray my character than I could a sweet-tempered Lothario.

Which brings me to Sherlock Holmes, the man who plunged me into more chaos and misadventures than my San Francisco cronies. It was in May of 1882. We were staying at the Park Hotel in my hometown of Hannibal, where I had been gathering material for *Life on the Mississippi*. When we were finished there, it was clear that Holmes needed a rest. He had worked himself into a shadow of his former vitality resolving a mystery that, if I had put it on the stage, would be hooted off as mere melodrama, a romantic folly.[1] He had also put me in grave danger, which Watson enjoys and I find intolerable. I am not a hospitable man when it comes to lunatics, but he was alone in my country, without a safe bed to lay his head on. I invited Holmes to stay at Quarry Farm in upstate New York. It was owned by Livy's sister, and it was our custom then to spend our summers there.

When we went to bed that night, I was certain we had agreed on a plan, but when I woke the next morning, he had vanished. The room was completely devoid of Holmes. Laying there in my bed, drowsy and sore and brain-fagged, I heard the distant train whistle and the rumble of the engine. I wondered if any of it — the riverboat chase, the kidnapping, Hannibal, Holmes — had even happened. Or was it a fever dream?

It was the clerk downstairs who supplied an answer. When I returned the key, he handed me a message. It read:—

Clemens, Must leave. A wire I had been expecting from Chicago came in while you were

---

[1] The story behind this has not surfaced yet in the Twain Papers, if he ever committed it to paper.

asleep. I would ask you to come along, but you are not Watson. I hope to see you when this case is wrapped up. HOLMES.

Thank the heavens for that stroke of luck! There is no better feeling than to pretend to virtue only to see it was not needed. You get the credit without any of the labor. If Holmes wished to hare off on another case in the state he was in, then he bore the responsibility for whatever followed. He is correct: I am not that fool Watson, forever fawning over him and following him like a hound into too many kinds of danger. I took the measure of his character in San Francisco, and am glad to be well shot of him.

I returned to Hartford by way of Quincy, Keokuk, Muscatine, Davenport, Dubuque, Lake Pepin, and Saint Paul, and reveled being among my family. The summer passed slow and deliciously at Quarry Farm with my golden wife and my golden children. Susy was ten and serious and observant as a Puritan preacher. Clara, two years younger, was lively and curious, while Jean was just a toddler and developing. The days flew by. I was ensconced in my writing cabin overlooking the fields, wrestling with the book.[1] I read Dickens' account of his visit to America, and Francis Parkman's histories and copies of the *New Orleans Times-Democrat* to get the feel of how others saw the river. I heard the fate of poor Lem Gray, who let me pilot his steamboat at night on the safest part of the river.[2] While Lem slept, I smoked and gazed upon the moonlit

---

[1] Livy Clemens' sister had a special cabin built for Clemens' use at Quarry Farm. It was an eight-sided room with windows all around and heated by a chimney. During most of the summers from 1871 to 1899, Clemens wrote many of his major works there. It has since been moved to the campus of Elmira College.
[2] While aboard the *Gold Dust* from April 20-25, Clemens befriended its pilot, Lem Gray, and would be allowed to take the wheel during his watch: "He would lie down and sleep, and leave me there to dream that the years had not slipped away; that there had been no war, no mining days, no literary adventures; that I was still a pilot, happy and care-free as I had been

waters, feeling the weight of the craft responding to my hand, and wondering if I could wake up there, that I had never left the river and the job that gave me the most happiness.

❖   ❖   ❖   ❖

In late September, we returned to Hartford and reopened the home built on the backs of my books. I anticipated spending the rest of the year finishing the *Life* and indulging in my family.

Late one evening, Livy and I were in the main room. The children were asleep. The servants had been sent to bed. The end of the evening only needed me to turn off the gas.

There was a thump at the door, like a body had fallen against it. The noise startled Livy. Using her favored nickname for me, she said:—

"Who could that be, Youth?"

Before I could answer, there was a soft rapping on the glass, followed by a familiar voice that said:—

"Clemens? It's Holmes."

I swung back the door. He staggered past me into the foyer like a messenger from the battle. He cleared the archway into the main room, bowed to Livy and said:—

"I ... must apologize for visiting you in this fashion, Mrs. Clemens." He was dressed as a tramp. His coat was filthy, ill-fitting, and loose at the seams. His face was encrusted, his lips cracked and dry. He hadn't shaved, and unidentified matter was caught in his bristles. His shocking exhaustion under the thin light of the gas chandelier was matched only by his pungent scent. It was a combination of rotted polecat and a garbage scow in summertime, and so great that I recoiled.

While I gibbered at this apparition, Livy took charge. With the authority of a feminine General Grant, she ordered

---

twenty years before." Four months later, the boiler of the *Gold Dust* exploded at Hickman, Ky., killed 17 people, including its pilot. Clemens devoted a chapter of *Life* to the tragic fate of the steamboat and its pilot.

me to rouse the maids and prepare a bath. They bustled about, chattering "What is the matter?" and "Who could that man be?" Livy led Holmes into the Mahogany room off the foyer, and insisted that he undress and help himself to a dressing gown. His protests were few and feeble, and I must admit that I enjoyed seeing him meekly obey her. It made him seem nearly human. When he was ready, she led him to the bathroom and ordered him to scrape himself like a Christian.

An hour later, he was ready for bed. The application of cold water removed the first few layers of filth, and a cold supper took the edge off his hunger. His suitcase had been fetched from the porch and its contents, depending on its condition, sent to the laundry or burned. A cheerful fire was going in his room, and the security of the house, the darkened shades, and peace and quiet acted like a sleeping draught. Before we closed the bedroom door, he was asleep and breathing easy.

I figured we had an invalid for the next week, and I would be free to return to work on the book. You can imagine the shock when I walked into the dining room the next morning to find him dressed like a gentleman and finishing his coffee with Livy next to him. Only his freshly shaved cheeks and the wan complexion familiar to invalids and corpses betrayed his true condition. Livy stood to welcome me to the table, but without her usual peck on the cheek, then returned to her meal.

Holmes was leafing through the local newspapers. He had finished with the *Hartford Weekly Times* and started gorging on several months of the *Times Democrat* from the stack on the seat next to him. I couldn't believe he had walked through my door the night before looking like a shipwrecked mariner if I hadn't seen it myself. He looked fresh as a spring daisy, while I retained my usual appearance of a scalded cat. He even shaved without a single nick, something I rarely accomplish on my own. He said:—

"Ah, Clemens! Glad to see you're up."

"Thank you. Is there a great breakfast available or did you scarf it all?"

"There's rashers and eggs over on the sideboard. I'm sorry about your argument with your wife yesterday."

"My — what?" I glared at Livy over this breach of decorum. To my surprise, she did not show any sign that she had sinned by revealing our private business. This puzzled me. I sat at the table and covered my blushes by drinking my coffee. I had forgotten that it was freshly brewed, and it scalded my tongue.

"About the burglar alarm. I hope it was resolved to your satisfaction, even if your wife disagrees."

I tested my tongue and found it raw but functional. I said:—

"Did Livy tell you?" She said:—

"Of course I didn't, Sam! I didn't say one word about the alarm. You know—" Holmes cut in and said:—

"You didn't. Your mail did." He pointed the knife he was using to cut his ham at the stack of mail left next to my plate. "I can't help but notice the letter from the burglar alarm company. Your wife's behavior just now — her coolness toward your appearance — merely confirmed the matter. Besides, your butler mentioned the problems you've been having with the system."

My shock redoubled. George Griffin had been in our employ for nearly a decade, and he was the soul of discretion. I said:—

"Did he tell you? Why I'll have to speak to him—"

"Don't be hard on him. I saw the wiring over the window," Holmes pointed his knife at it. "I can see the wiring is deficient from here. He merely confirmed my observation."

Livy scolded me, saying it was sinful to jump to conclusions. She was correct, of course, and abashed and silent I resumed my breakfast. Over the course of the meal, Holmes kept up a steady flow of conversation. In between telling us about his adventures in Chicago — some botheration about an Italian marmot and an aluminum cow (pronounced in the English fashion with the stress on "min") — he commented on the maid's habit of sneaking out at night (confirmed by the scuff marks on her shoes and the presence of a key, the outline of which he spotted in her apron pocket), speculated that my friend, the Rev. Joe Twitchell, would call later today for a long walk (his card from yesterday left on the fireplace mantle, combined with my walking stick handy by the door), and deduced the solution to a murder that was extensively covered in the *Times Democrat*, that he proposed to wire the police later.

I then realized that the next few days would represent a desperate race to see what would happen first: Holmes recovering from his adventures or my braining him with a cannon ball.

After ferreting out all our secrets, Holmes settled into a new routine. I continued working on the book in my billiard room/office on the third floor. He went for long walks and read. With George's help, he rigged up a small lab in his bedroom and his mammoth brain was quickly engaged in an obscure and non-lethal point of chemistry. The staff and family were instructed to leave him be unless he desired otherwise. This meant that, when he emerged from his lair, everything he did was to a purpose. In the kitchen, he demonstrated to Susy, with a tomato and a mallet, how to judge the direction of blood spatters. That drove our cook to seek a new situation. He worked himself into Livy's good graces by performing her favorite airs on a borrowed violin. He also managed to make amends to myself by spending the afternoons shooting pool.

We were engaged in one such struggle when Livy entered to announce a caller. It was the middle of October, and the summer days were but a memory. The weather had turned chill. The wind was rattling the loose window sash and lashing the trees for having the temerity to hang onto their leaves. She came into the room and said:—

"Youth, Mr. Holmes has a visitor." He stroked a ball into the pocket, stood up, stretched, and accepted a card from her. She said to me:—

"It's Miss Newton. You remember the family. They're members of the church." She referred to Asylum Hill, where my long-time friend Joe Twitchell preaches. I nodded and said:—

"They're good people." Holmes said:—

"She wishes to see me?" Livy said to him:—

"She approached me yesterday at church, after you helped Rev. Twitchell find the Communion plate, and asked who you were. Don't look that way at me, Youth! She's worried sick about her uncle, so I told her about Mr. Holmes and his work in London." She turned back to him, massaging her hands with worry: "Perhaps you can help?"

"Maybe I can. I've enjoyed your hospitality and feel much fitter. It's time to leave my chemical studies and occupy my mind with more engaging work. Perhaps Miss Newton can provide it."

We received Miss Julia Newton downstairs in the library. She was a thin young woman who put one in mind of Emily Dickinson. Holmes placed her in an armchair next to the fire-place and sat opposite her. Just like in the drawings,[1] he observed her over his steepled fingertips as she worried a hand-kerchief in her lap. She said:—

"I appreciate your help, Mr. Holmes. Everyone tells me it's foolish to worry about Uncle Lysander. Even my Jerome says so. But I can't stop! I feel deep in my soul that something terrible has happened to him. You can help, won't you? Tell me you will." She dabbed at the tears that were coursing down.

Holmes said gently:—

"I would like to, but I must gather the facts before committing myself. What can you tell me about your uncle?"

"He is Lysander Mercer. He is a mortician over on Church Street. My mother is his sister, and he's been very good to us, on account of my father dying when I was but an infant. He's not married, but he's always said he considers me his daugh-

---

[1] Clemens refers to the drawings by Sidney Paget (1860-1908) that gave the deerstalker cap and Inverness cape to Holmes, despite them not appearing in the stories. He also drew the vivid illustration of Holmes and Moriarty at Reichenbach Falls.

ter. On Saturday, my mother received this note from him."

She pulled a sheet of paper from her small handbag and handed it to Holmes. In a wild, excitable hand, he wrote:—

> Must leave town for a few days. Will call upon return.
>
> L.M.

Holmes played with the paper, turning it this way and that, shooting a look down its edges, and sniffing the signature. He muttered a few words about the watermark and quality of the paper, then tucked it into his pocket notebook and said:—

"Does this look like his hand?" She said:—

"I'm not certain. He rarely has need to write to us. We see him so often."

"Has he left suddenly before?"

"Never. That is what has me concerned. The same day after we received this note, his assistant, Frederick Ord, knocked at our door, looking for Uncle Lysander. He had arrived at the business to find the door locked. He came to us for the spare." Holmes nodded and said:—

"When did you last see Uncle Lysander?"

"At Wednesday supper. Mrs. Clemens said that you helped ever so much to keep Mr. Clemens from getting himself murdered while in Hannibal and that you are a famous detectionist in London and — ."

I was prepared to leap to my defense but Holmes put up a hand and said:—

"How was your uncle's behavior at supper?"

"He was in very good spirits. We talked about my impending marriage to Jerome in the spring. They were even talking about combining their businesses as well."

"Jerome is a mortician as well?"

"He took the business last year upon the passing of his father."

"Have you consulted with the police? What do they say?"

Miss Newton's brow darkened at the memory. She said:—

"There was a horrid officer there who said Uncle Lysander was probably off on a 'spree' and would return when his money ran out. As if he would do such a thing! He is an upright citizen and a member of the Masons."

The interrogation ran its course. No, Uncle Lysander did not have any enemies. He had disputes with a few customers about payment on his bills, but that was the lot of every businessman. It appeared that the course of his life ran smooth and unbroken until Saturday. While she spoke, she absorbed with her handkerchief the silent tears that glistened her cheeks.

When Holmes finished his interrogation, he agreed to meet her at her home and accompany her to Lysander's business. Livy and I walked her to the door, cooing the usual bromides that everything will be all right. But I was troubled.

We returned to the room to see Holmes lost in thought, his pyramided hands supporting his chin. I pulled a cigar from the humidor from the mantle and lit it with a spill from the fireplace. Holmes said:—

"You know my methods, Clemens. What do you think of this?"

"I'm not your da—" I snapped, and then I caught Livy's eye and blushed. I amended my statement to: "I'm sure she's very much concerned for Lysander. Undertakers as a class are stable men. They must keep their heads clear and their manners calm in the face of distressed families. They're not known to perform impetuous acts, like leaving town suddenly, without good cause." He said:—

"You have nailed the issue. A traumatic disruption in his life is behind this. The lives of the poor and impoverished are nothing but change and struggle. The wealthy and aristocratic can afford to live their lives according to custom and the seasons. They visit London for the opening of Parliament and their shooting boxes for hunting season. Then there's the middle class, Clemens. The bourgeoisie the French call them. They have fewer disruptions than the lower classes and are not wealthy enough to move where they wish. They must work to earn their daily bread. When that is interrupted, there must be a reason."

His smug summation of humanity annoyed me. I burst out:—

"So you think people are herds, moving from field to field?"

Instead of being offended, Holmes considered my insult. He said:—

"We have few free choices in this world, Clemens. We have to eat, so we must find the means to do so. We live, so we must reproduce. We—" he waved a hand to express the thought that cannot be mentioned in polite company: "So we must raise children. We grow old, we perish. My position is unique. I stand outside humanity. The cycle of life is the same dance, performed over and over. We are not that far removed from the beasts in the fields, Clemens."

Livy said:—

"I hope there is room in your philosophy for the divine, Mr. Holmes." He bowed to her and said:—

"The divine rarely appears in my work, Mrs. Clemens. In fact, it is its absence that creates my profession. Clemens, can you lend me your assistance, today?"

I opened my mouth to suggest that my profession wasn't to ferret out lost morticians, but remembered Livy's presence, and said:—

"As much as I'm qualified to give."

"That is all I expect. We need to collect Miss Newton, visit Uncle Lysander's business, and speak to his assistant."

It was a balmy day, and I needed to walk. We ignored the horse-drawn trolley in favor of walking. Hartford was a bustling town in those days. It doesn't seem that way to anyone today who sees New York City where the tides of humanity wash up and down its streets. That's the way of the world. I rode a stagecoach over the West, piloted a steamboat up and down the crowded Mississippi, watched sailing ships disgorge miners who swarmed the California foothills, and sailed to Hawaii, the Holy Land, and around the world. Humanity is moving faster, but what did we leave behind? But these are an old man's thoughts, however, and have nothing to do with this story.

We found Julia Newton at her home with her mother. Mrs. Amoransa Newton was a woman whose surroundings bore the stamp of someone who was keeping up appearances and failing. We hadn't been introduced, but I had heard from Livy that she had aspirations to commit literature. This was reason enough to avoid her. She said:—

"Mr. Clemens, I'm sorry we had to meet under such circumstances. Despite my admiration for your works, I must confess that it was not my desire for Julia to consult with your friend, Mr. Holmes. Our family has been a part of Hartford for generations. Bad enough that she talked to a policeman. If word gets out that she hired a — a — I don't know what you characterize yourself as, but it cannot help but cause comment. But she is as stubborn as Mr. Mercer was." Her bare words made her sound mean, but she said this with such affection toward her daughter that it made you ashamed to intrude on her privacy. But to her plea Holmes said nothing. He had been walking around the room. He appeared distracted, so to keep the conversation going I said:—

"She cares very much about Lysander Mercer."

"As do I. But I can't see anything good coming from this." Holmes said:—

"Neither do I, Mrs. Newton. Do you believe that Mr. Mercer left on his own?"

"I can't imagine why he would. He is a most stable man. You could set your watch by his routine."

"Then it would follow that he is in some kind of trouble, perhaps even danger, wouldn't you agree?"

Her eyes grew wide and she said:—

"Is that a possibility?"

"It is a logical outcome. Either he decided to leave precip-itously and abandon his business, or he was compelled to un-willingly. If the police are convinced to investigate, then peo-ple will find out. Do you want that, Mrs. Newton?"

"Oh, heavens no! Then I suppose you must go ahead. You will be discreet?" I said:—

"As the grave, ma'am," and then instantly regretted it. Holmes said:—

"Then let us go to Mr. Mercer's business. We need to talk to his assistant and learn more. Good day to you, Mrs. Newton."

We walked with Miss Newton to the business. Holmes said:—

"We heard from your mother. We need to hear from you. Do you want me to proceed?" Julia said:—

"Mother was a bit hard, wasn't she? We had it out when I told her what I did. She's always concerned about what the neighbors think. But I must know what happened to Uncle Lysander."

"Then we shall proceed. I have heard that American girls tend to be more independent than their English cousins. Now I have seen it in action. And if I'm not mistaken, here we are."

Mercer's Mortuary was a prosperous shop on Church Street. A jingling bell on the door announced our presence to the young man sleeping in an office chair by the stove. He jerked awake and stood to receive us. Frederick Ord was a young man who tried to present himself as an older man. He wore his hair slicked down, and balanced a gold pince-nez on the bridge of his nose. He cultivated a sober mien befitting his profession, but still looked like a solemn baby owl. He adjust-ed his coat and smoothed his slicked-back hair and said:—

"Miss Julia, it is so good to see you. Has there been any word about Mr. Mercer?" She said:

"I'm afraid not. We're all so dreadfully worried for him. I'd like to introduce you to Mr. Holmes. He's agreed to help. He's ever so much a famous detective over in England." She made no mention of my appearance. I might as well have been one of the clients. Holmes said:—

"I hope you'll be able to shed light on this mysterious disappearance, Mr. Ord." He said:—

"Oh, how I wish I could! He's never done anything like this before. It's not like him to leave the shop unattended, especially since he's not trained me fully to take over." Holmes said:—

"How long have you been working for him?" Frederick said:—

"About six months. He's an excellent master. He taught me a lot about the trade, although I still have much to learn. I'm looking forward to opening a shop of my own someday, perhaps in Hartford, with a nice girl and settle down."

This last section he addressed to Miss Newton more than to Holmes. It's clear that he was a moonstruck calf around the girl, so clear that even she blushed at the compliment.

We were interrupted by the sound of a bell and a door opening behind us. A gentleman had walked in. He was well-fed and well-dressed, and judging by the strain placed on his waistcoat the effects of the former were clearly affecting the latter. He ignored us and walked over to Miss Newton and took her hand and said:—

"Any word from Lysander?" She repeated the news and introduced Holmes and I. Holmes said:—

"I'd like to talk to you about this case. Can we meet when we're through here?" He gripped Jerome Dawson's hand in a peculiar fashion. Dawson looked puzzled and said:—

"Of course, Lysander's disappearance concerns me greatly, seeing as I am to be a member of the family. My business is across the street. Drop in any time. Miss Julia, will you walk with me?" She took the hint, and made her farewells.

As soon as the door slammed shut behind them, Holmes said:—

"How long have you been in love with the girl, Frederick?"

The boy blushed down to his collar and beyond to his toes. He said:—

"From the first moment I saw her, Mr. Holmes. She's an angel, isn't she?" Holmes said:—

"Was she betrothed to Mr. Dawson then?"

"Oh, no, sir, that was only three months ago."

"Did you court her?" Frederick said:—

"I tried. I asked Mr. Mercer for permission, but he wouldn't give it to me. He said I was too inexperienced in the business to strike out on my own and support a family. Why, I don't even know how to embalm the body. But I've been working hard on learning everything I can about the profession." Holmes said:—

"What was Mr. Lysander like the last time you saw him?"

"He was feeling down. He went to Rafe McKee's funeral Wednesday evening. They've known each other for years, even before they were Masons. He'd been feeling poorly and Mr. Lysander knew he wasn't long for this world, but he was still right upset when he passed."

"Was it just about that? Or was there something else that was troubling him?" Frederick said:—

"Nothing that I could tell." He fixed Holmes with a quizzical look like a student who knew he wasn't answering the teacher's question.

When Holmes was finished, Frederick led us upstairs to Lysander's rooms. Lysander clearly cared that his clients were more comfortable than himself. The tables and chairs were worn and past their prime. His bulgy bed looked uncomfortable and was unmade. If he kept a servant, she came in rarely and was slatternly in her work when she appeared.

Holmes said nothing to me while we were there, a practice I found irritating. He walked through the rooms like a tax agent evaluating the value of the stock. At least he didn't perform his celebrated trick of crawling across the floor like a snake, or pulling a clue out from behind the sideboard.

When he had scoured Lysander's living quarters, we adjourned to the ground floor. Behind the front office was a large room, closed off to the public, where the mortician's real work was performed. Frederick unlocked the door. The air was faintly perfumed with the scent of formaldehyde. Between two gas chandeliers in the middle of the room stood a rectangular table that was slightly tilted. Its top was covered in sheets of zinc that curled up at the edge, and a notch at one narrow end had a bucket placed beneath it. With a wood block at the top end, it appeared to be a most uncomfortable bed, but I doubt any occupant ever complained. Against the far wall leaned a row of coffins, ranging from plain deal wood to the most elaborate hardwoods and gilded handles. We were about to go in when Holmes restrained us and said:—

"When was the last time anyone was in here?"

"On Friday. Mr. Mercer and I spent the day working on Mr. Toddhunter. He was to be interred in Waterbury. When we were finished, the teamster took him down to the station to catch the 5:05." Holmes said:—

"Excellent. Both of you will stay out of the room for a few minutes, while I work."

Holmes performed his impression of a bloodhound, but a slow-moving, ancient member of that breed. Borrowing a lantern from Frederick, he started by paying deep attention to the floor, which from my vantage point had appeared not to have been swept recently. He slowly walked along the walls like he was performing a cakewalk, pausing to bend over and sweeping the lantern back and forth repeatedly. At times, he took several steps back and performed this odd maneuver again before proceeding onward. Once he had circuited the room, he began a second round, but this time stepped toward the center where the table lay like an altar. This was accompanied by a melody of grunts, whistles, and other ejaculations in various moods. He ended his movements by standing still, casting his head about as if following a signal unheard by us. He said:—

"Clemens, come in and have a look around. Tell me what

you perceive."

While I wandered amongst the shelves, reading the labels and judging the quality of the silverware Mercer used on his customers, I said:—

"I wrote a sketch a few years back that might intrigue you, Holmes. I dreamed I was sitting on a porch. A procession of skeletons passed before me, bearing whatever they could carry, such as tombstones, shrouds, coffins, and the like. They were moving to a new burying ground because their ancestors — no, I mean descendants; I keep forgetting which way time goes — anyway, their great-granddescendents were not keeping up the cemetery. Nothing lasts forever, Holmes, not even the place where we were to stay planted forever. Someone must always keep up appearances.[1] Why—" Holmes interrupted and said:—

"Hello, what is over here in the corner?" Near the coffins was a large cabinet that contained supplies for the business. There was a shelf reserved for white linen sheets — carefully folded — a shelf for metal cans containing embalming powder, talc, putty, a shelf where rubber hoses were neatly coiled and tied, and a shelf large enough to hold a half-dozen large brown bottles. Holmes pointed to the cabinet and said:—

"Look between the cabinet and the corner. Let's shine the light there. Does that look like a stain on the wall?"

I looked where he pointed. About a foot from the floor were dark stains, small at first, that spread as they went down. Holmes said:—

"Look on that shelf, Clemens, the second from the bottom. Does it seem like there was room for one more bottle?"

"What do you mean?"

"Compare those two shelves that have jugs on them. The bottom one contains eight bottles, placed in an orderly fashion of two rows of four. The one above it contains seven, but

---

[1] Clemens refers to "A Curious Dream," which appeared in the *Buffalo Express* in 1870, when he was part-owner of the paper. Later, it was reprinted in *Sketches Old and New*.

in a way that's not as orderly as its brother. It looks like one went missing and someone tried to hide it." Holmes searched the room, then walked to another corner where a wooden barrel stood. He lifted the lid and looked inside. He reached in and something jingled. He said:—

"Broken glass, Clemens! The smell tells us it is embalming fluid. Someone was careless in their work, I suspect, and the bottle was dropped or knocked over. You realize its significance, of course."

"Of course." I didn't, of course, which was my typical response at this stage of any investigation Holmes undertakes.

We took our leave and walked across the street to Dawson's mortuary. Holmes said:—

"What do you know of Jerome Dawson?"

"He's been helping his fellow Hartfordians into the ground for more than a decade. He's a widower, ever since his wife had died delivering their child, who also did not survive. Ever since, he devoted himself to his business."

Mortician's businesses are all of a piece. They look more like offices where business was done. Dawson was reading a book at his roll-top desk when we came in. He slowly rose to welcome us. He said:—

"Has there been any news, Sam? Poor Julia's been out of her mind with worry."

"It's good of you to agree to help us in our time of need. We have been tracing Mr. Mercer's movements. Did you see him at Mr. McKee's funeral?"

"That I did, that I did. He was unhappy, of course. He knew the deceased for many years and was very attached to him. That made it difficult to make the arrangements, so I was solicited to perform that function."

"Did you see him after that?"

"No." A puzzled look crept over his face, and he said, "Maybe. I'm sorry. We've been working hard lately. I was in the business that Friday. As I closed up about 5 o'clock, I saw the lights were on in the office. 'Oh, ho!' I said to myself. 'Lysander's burning the midnight oil, he is. I wonder who he's working on.'" Holmes said:—

"Could it have been Frederick Ord working late?"

"Maybe, sir, maybe." He pressed his hand to his breast and was lost in thought for a moment. "But not alone. Lysander would have been standing by, making sure he doesn't commit a grievous error. The lad is still green."

There was more to report. Lysander had no major enemies beyond those a businessman collects through debts unpaid or unhappy customers. Dawson said that Frederick was angry about his impending marriage to Miss Newton. He had even raised the subject in a bar when the two men met. Dawson said:—

"The poor boy was deep in his cups when I saw him. He inquired earnestly if I was serious in my intentions toward her. He even threatened that he would do something if I ever mistreated her! I informed him that if he had paid more attention to his trade and to his master it was not my fault that her uncle preferred me to him. That put him in his place, let me tell you!"

Holmes nodded in agreement and said, "Then I think I've taken enough of your time." He extended his hand again and this time gripped Dawson's correctly. He turned Dawson's hand, revealing a pinky ring. He said:—

"An interesting design. A skull with a Latin phrase circling it. What does it say?" Dawson said:—

"Oh, something church-like, I've no doubt. I bought it more for the look of the thing." Holmes said:—

"It reminds me of a ring Mother Elspeth wears. Not the same, of course. Have you heard of her?"

"Of course. The noted Spiritualist."

"I met her in New York. We had a long correspondence and it was a great pleasure to meet her at last. She is particularly useful in criminal cases. She helped the victim of the Brighton Suitcase Murder identify her killer. In another case, she caused blood to appear on a dead man's body when his murderer passed by, astonishing the police and forcing a full confession from the terrified man. Are you interested in the afterlife and what we may learn from seers like her?"

"I have been for a long time. I've been a member of the Society for Psychical Research since its founding. I believe it's impossible not to practice our profession and not have some insights into the workings of the great beyond."

"Then you'll be interested in knowing that she will be coming to Hartford. I have engaged her to hold a séance at Clemens' home about Mr. Mercer's disappearance. Your presence, as a friend, would contribute to the psychic energies. Can you join us? It'll be tomorrow night."

The hour was set, they shook hands, and we left.

As soon as we were out of sight of the building, I pulled Holmes into an alley. I said:—

"Why didn't you ask me if my home was open for a séance?" He said:—

"I didn't know it would be until I suggested it to Mr. Dawson. But surely you could see that it would be necessary."

"What do you mean?"

"Did you not see the books on his shelves? *Where Are the Dead? or, Spiritualism Explained? Lights and Shadows of Spiritualism?* He even has *The Principles of Nature, Her Divine Revelations, and a Voice to Mankind,* the canonical work on the subject. This is a man who takes his ghosts seriously. If you let me go, we can catch the approaching trolley. We have more work ahead if we're to prepare for the séance." He trotted into the street and caught the car. I had to follow; he no doubt was expecting me to pay. When I sat down next to him, he said:—

"Did you catch him scratching?" I said:—

"Who? When?"

"Dawson. When we weren't looking."

"What do you mean? How can you see him if you didn't see him?"

"That, Clemens, is the best time to look at someone, when they think you're not looking at him. He was scratching him-

self but hiding it from us. You know what that means, of
course."

"No. Does that mean you have solved the case?" He said:—

"I have a glimmer of a solution. I must gather more data.
Here's my stop."

"But we're nowhere near home."

"Nevertheless. I have much work to do. In fact, I won't be
home tonight. I hope to see you tomorrow." He stepped off. For
the rest of the journey, I thought over everything I had seen today. Then I resolved to think no more of it and return to my
book.

Holmes was as good as his word. It wasn't until supper-time
was near the next day that Holmes knocked at our door. He was
in an excited state when he took me aside in the foyer and informed me that we were going cemetery-visiting that night.

Looking back over the many professions I labored in during my life, nothing was easier to master and provided me
with more terror than grave-robbing.

When Holmes informed me of his intentions, I acted
quickly. I hustled him up to my office, informing Livy of his
return as we passed through the library. Up two flights, I led
him into my office, closed the door, and turned up the gas.

Holmes paced around the billiard table, opening his
Chesterfield coat now that he was in the warmth. I could see
dirt and grass stains on his knees, and he looked like he had
been dragged through a hedge. I said:—

"What have you been up to out there, Holmes? And what
do you mean by visiting a graveyard?" He said:—

"I believe I know where Lysander is, but we need to make
sure." He continued to circle the table while I sunk into my
rocker by the stove and said:—

"Why not go to the police?"

"Because I have no proof, Clemens! None that would convince a policeman, anyway. Then we must consider the con-

sequences should my suspicions be confirmed. No, we must find out for ourselves, and I need your help."

I understood his meaning. Holmes had no reputation with the Hartford police, and neither did I, despite my numerous crimes against journalism, literature, and lecturing. Balanced against that was my reputation should we be caught in the act. Then I considered what I was being asked to do. I quailed at the thought. Graveyards can be comforting by day, even enjoyable. But a boneyard by night revived all my childhood terrors. Blast Holmes for putting me in this situation!

We conferred over what we needed for the task. As amateur gravediggers, we outfitted ourselves in a way that any professional corpse-taker could admire. I called up George and instructed him to set aside his butlering duties to attend to our tools. I said:—

"Bring out the shovels and file the blades sharp enough to cut West Texas hardpan. Polish the crowbars until they gleam like coal. Fill up the lantern and oil the handle so it moves quietly. Store them in an outbuilding. Do all this without your mistress knowing about it. Then, get the groom to hitch up the horses. We'll be leaving—" I turned to Holmes for advice, and he said:—

"Nine would do. If you'll excuse me, Clemens, I must prepare for dinner."

Holmes and I dined with the family. I was as nervous as a scalded cat. I jumped at the least provocation and walked around the table to tell a story or sing a snatch of a Negro spiritual to sooth my soul. It was my usual behavior, so it excited no more than the usual reaction from my family. Meanwhile, Holmes led the conversation into musical areas, especially his favorite artist, Sarasate.

We spent the rest of the evening with Livy in the library, reading to each other as the children played on the floor. It was as serene and comfortable a scene as would calm a minister. But underneath! Just the thought of walking into a graveyard, accompanied by memories of the clandestine visits I made as a child, as a way to test my courage, and I would falter in the conversation and feel my face heat up. I considered backing out, but I had promised Livy that I would help, and I knew that she must never know where my promise led to.

The children were put to bed, and soon it was dark enough for our work to commence. As we put our coats on, Livy was scribbling notes at her writing desk. I told her:—

"I must go out tonight, dearest. It's about finding Mercer, and Holmes has a theory he wants to test." She said:—

"Must it be so late? Do wear a warmer jacket than that, Youth. You'll catch your death. Where will you be going?" My mouth dropped, and strangled noises came out. Holmes jumped in:—

"To the Potter's Field. We must dig up a coffin."

"Holmes!" Thunder and lightning rang in my head. I wanted to grab the fireplace poker and brain him. Instead, I held my breath and waited for Livy's judgment. She stared at us over her glasses, then sighed deeply and looked at the clock. Clearly, she was ciphering. She said:—

"I suppose you have to do it. Take George with you. Lysander was a big man." Holmes said:—

"We have asked him." She nodded and said:—

"Then I shall pray to God for forgiveness. And, Youth, you must wear your greatcoat."

We walked by lantern light to the barn. The groom had the horses hitched to the wagon. We climbed in, and he led us into the yard. I shook the reins, and we rolled down the driveway and into the street.

The cemetery was on the southern edge of Hartford, at the end of a dirt road between the farmers' fields. Their houses were out of sight, so it was a long, lonely drive. The moon had sunk, so George walked ahead with the lantern to guide the way. When we reached the wrought-iron gate, he opened it. The metal hinges cried and groaned as if in pain.

Now it was Holmes' turn to lead us down the crushed-gravel path. George took his place on the wagon, and we moved on. The wheels sounded like they were crushing bones. The headstones gleamed like rows of teeth. I shivered. My skin was creeping and my ears were jumping at anything that sounded like chains rattling or footsteps sliding across the mould. All my childhood terrors about the land of the dead rose in me, so that I near jumped out my skin when Holmes said:—

"There! No. 132! We dig here!"

I yanked the reins and the horses whinnied and shuffled in fear. The wagon rocked, and George, who was sitting next to me, had to take the reins and croon soothing noises to calm the horses. We jumped down and gathered our tools. Holmes explained that the guests were stored close to the surface, stacked three-high, and that the box we wanted was in the second layer.

Oh, how I hope never again to hear the sound of a shovel rattling the earth ever after! The three of us worked steadily. George sang softly:—

I know moon-rise, I know star-rise,
Lay dis body down.
I walk in de moonlight, I walk in de starlight,
To lay dis body down.

I joined in, relying on my memory of when I first heard the song in Hannibal:

I'll walk in de graveyard, I'll walk through de graveyard,
To lay dis body down.
I'll lie in de grave and stretch out my arms;
Lay dis body down.

We fell silent when a blade struck wood. We turned the shovels over and scraped away the dirt. We finished the song with Holmes adding his baritone where he could.

I go to de judgment in de evenin' of de day,

When I lay dis body down;
And my soul and your soul will meet in de day
When I lay dis body down.

The lantern showed a long rectangle of fresh-cut wood. Holmes knelt, brushed a coat of dirt off, and searched the top for markings. He said:—

"Hutton! Just the man I was looking for. Lift him up. It's the one below him that's our prize."

I said:—

"I recognize that name. A mean, shiftless man. His family must not have wanted to pay for a decent burial." George said mournfully:—

"How we treat each other in life shall be repaid tenfold in death."

We set-to and dragged Hutton aside. The box below him had been protected from the soil and looked as fresh as when he was dropped a few days before. We pulled it out and Holmes knelt on top to read the name.

"Cruickshank. Not surprising he would be buried under an alias. He was meant to disappear. Hand me the crowbar."

The nails groaned like a dying man as we pulled each one out. The noise was so loud Livy could have heard it. Perhaps in her imagination she did. The long boards were pried off one by one, and when the majority had been cleared, George angled the light into the cavernous dark and revealed the pale face of Lysander Mercer. He looked troubled, as if wondering why his sleep was being disturbed, but he had the manners not to inquire about our business.

The trouble was scheduled to begin at half-eleven the next night. It was to be held in the drawing room off the entrance hall. The servants cleared the space before the three bay windows, placed the bier Frederick brought from the business, and encased the guest of honor in a newer model befitting his status. At Holmes' direction, the upper half of the coffin was opened to display Lysander. Frederick had worked on him all day to make him presentable. A round table was moved in along with the chairs. Holmes calculated the presence of seven guests from among the living. There would be the two of us, Jerome Dawson, Frederick Ord, Julia Newton, her mother Mrs. Newton, and Mother Elspeth.

Their invitations sparked a lively discussion that nearly caused me to cancel the festivities. While I have no qualms about contacting the dead, it seemed unseemly to have the relatives in the presence of the corporeal form of the host. To my concerns, Holmes was neither sympathetic nor comforting. He insisted that they should be present to lend tone to the proceedings. Otherwise, he argued, why would we be trying to contact Mercer from the Great Beyond? Besides, he had already discussed it with them, and he left to fetch them while I smoked and grumbled about not being told what was happening in my own home and oversaw the staging.

Much later, after the near-disaster, I realized where I erred. I had let Holmes out of my sight. You would think the man who knew the most about the devilment boys got up to when left to themselves would recognize that trait in others. Watson noticed it, and he didn't have enough sense not to stare at the rain with his mouth open. It never occurred to me that he'd — but let me start at the beginning.

The house was quiet. My girls were in their beds, long asleep. I walked about the house, turning the gas lamps low on the first floor, trailing cigar smoke and skittery as a cat. Mother Elspeth had arrived and was closeted in the drawing room with Holmes. She was a raggedy old stick swallowed in a profusion of lace capes and a mantilla. Her face seemed permanently shrouded in darkness. Yet she spoke in a soothing tone that could calm a fractious horse. She was the talk of New York spiritualist circles, so Holmes told me, able to summon passed-on relatives and even produce strands of heavenly ectoplasm.

Then I heard the clopping of horse's hooves, the rattle of metal-shod wheels on bricks, and the squeal as the carriage pulled to a halt. George was at the door, looking through the sidelights when I paused in the center of the foyer by the center table to await my cue.

The guests had arrived, as solemn as Puritan elders except for Dawson, who was excited about meeting Mother Elspeth. He made it a point to escort Mrs. Newton and Julia into the room. Frederick looked sick, and I took hold of his shoulder to ask after him.

"I've never attended one of these séance things," he said. "Do you think Mr. Mercer will really appear?"

"It is to be hoped, Frederick."

"And you think he'll tell us who did him?"

"That's the intention."

I nodded solemnly. He looked greenish, but that might have been the gaslight.

There were seven of us around the table. Mother Elspeth was backed against the wall. Across the table and beyond Dawson she faced Lysander before the bay windows. I was on her right and Holmes on her left. In between were the two Newtons and Frederick Ord.

The room was as dark as my conscience. A dim blue gas flare lit the coffin. All else was shrouded in gloom. Mother Elspeth was no treat to look upon during the day, but only her dim form could be perceived. She looked like one of Dickens's spirits threatening Ebenezer Scrooge.

The night was quiet. The house was slumbering, unaware of the unholy acts being committed within it. Livy and the children were safely stowed upstairs and beyond seeing or hearing anything in this room.

The disembodied voice of Mother Elspeth opened the proceedings by asking for the Lord's Prayer, followed by the 23rd Psalm. Then we launched into "Holy, Holy, Holy," a favorite from the Civil War. Unused to this spiritual practice, we sang softly and reluctantly until Holmes lent his voice to the proceeding, and we raised our ruckus in his wake. Midway through the song, Mother Elspeth sneezed. He pulled her hand from mine to maneuver a handkerchief, then firmly reestablished her claim on my palm after adjusting it to suit her comfort.

When we were finished, she said with a voice like gargled gravel:—

"There are spirits among us tonight! The gossamer veil separating our worlds have parted. Secrets will be revealed. Justice will be done. Anyone who fears either should flee! Mother Elspeth knows all and by her sacred bond with the spirit world must reveal all!"

The room quieted. Any attempt at a joke would be strangled for lack of oxygen. She said:—

"Amoransa Newton!" She cheeped at hearing her name called. "The one who was called Ammie by her husband. The woman who her family believed married beneath her, despite her love enriching them with a daughter! You hope Julia's marriage to a businessman would help the family reconcile, especially with your sister Rebekah. This is a false hope! Their affection is bound in a greater desire for status. To achieve this, you must be seen with the Clemens' family, the Stowes', the Gillettes, and others on Nook Farm. That is glory for you! Not in uniting with the dead."

"Now, hold on — " Dawson began. He was shushed by the table, especially Mrs. Newton, who was eager to hear more. Mother Elspeth continued:—

"Rebekah is a snob! Your brother Adam is as well. Claim the hand of friendship the Clemens' offer you and you will succeed!"

It was playing it high for my social card to be filled by the dead, but upon reflection the spirit was correct. Adam was proud of his ancestors. He claimed that several of them fought in the revolution. Just to goad him, I asked him on which side. His sister Rebekah, who ran the roost, had dropped hints that she was a poetess of great promise. Another Ina Coolbrith, in her estimation. I had known Ina in San

Francisco, and the notion that Rebekah could match her was pure moonshine.[1] I gently rebuffed reading any of her verse, but that must end if Mrs. Amoransa Newton would claim friendship and through her influence get to me. I ruefully reflected that if reconciling means being racked on the altar of literature like this, I must accept it.

A tambourine rattled through the air and at the end of its journey Mother Elspeth called my name:—

"The man with two names. The man with two faces. Smiling and angry. Comedy and sorrow! The drawling child in a man's suit. The childish father and the boyish lover."

"Now hold up!" I said. There was no call for the incorporeal to get personal like that.

"Clemens," grumbled Holmes. I bit back a retort in anger. Mother Elspeth growled on:—

"You are unhappy with your publisher. You suspect he is cheating you. You are unhappy with the sales of your latest novel. You believe the agents aren't pressing it hard enough. You fear your inspiration has fled and that you are grinding your talent down on a book no one will read."

A cold chill trickled down my back. Mother Elspeth was reading my soul to the assembled. These were fears I had expressed to no one. She continued:—

"Be of good cheer. Your publisher is cheating you. It is the way of their tribe. Yes, his agents are not working hard enough to suit you. The critics are asses and you are besieged by autograph seekers and investment offers of dubious merit. You see clearly. You are the one-eyed man in the kingdom of the blind. Is it any wonder that you are being driven insane?

---

[1] Ina Coolbrith (1841-1928) was a poet and former Mormon — being the niece of founder Joseph Smith — who was a longtime fixture on the San Francisco literary scene. She knew the major figures of the time, including Clemens, Ambrose Bierce, Bret Harte and Charles Warren Stoddard, and as city librarian of Oakland befriended Jack London and Isadora Duncan. She wrote poetry throughout her life and was honored by being named California's poet laureate in 1915.

Be of good cheer!"

I would've responded that for cheer it tasted awfully bitter, but I was interrupted by a blast from a horn. Mother Elspeth moved on to Julia. She said:—

"Julia! Your heart is open to me. You care for Dawson, but you are not sure you are in love with him." Julia was a dark shade, but her gasp confirmed the truth of this statement. "You admire Dawson. You revere him as one reveres a father. You agreed to give your heart to him. But it is an uncomfortable gift. You are young. You dream of more than a husband and family in Hartford. You dream of seeing the bright lights of New York City, or at least Schenectady. Marriage can make the heart grow in ways unseen even by the spirits. Look to the Clemens family as an example. Don't accept a coffin for a heart."

"That's quite enough—" Dawson began, but he was drowned out by both a tambourine and the horn. Somewhere, a bow scraped a single long and melancholy note on a violin. A shiver fled up my back. All the fears of the night, of threatening noise brewed the urge in me to flee the room and mother Elspeth croaked:—

"We have a spirit guide among us! Speak, spirit, and tell us who you are!"

"Hypatia," said the voice. "I was a resident of Alexandria, where I lived and was martyred in the year 415. I have been called here on behalf of one who was close to you all."

"Who sent you?"

"Rafe McKee."

This was puzzling. We had been expecting our guest. Mother Elspeth was of a similar mind. She said:—

"Not Lysander Mercer?"

"No." Mother Elspeth asked:—

"Do you know what you are here to tell us?"

"Yes. Who stole Brother Rafe's ring."

A silence settled on the table. Mother Elspeth said:—

"Not who killed Lysander Mercer?"

"No. Brother Rafe is burning with revenge on the man

who stole his ring."

I couldn't see Mother Elspeth from where I was sitting, but her voice made it clear she was thrown. "A ring?"

"Yes, Brother Rafe was fond of his ring. He wore it on his smallest finger. He earned it in ceremony with the Masons. It has a skull and inscription, and it was taken from him."

"Daw—" I began, then shut up. That's the ring he was wearing. But I couldn't finish the thought. He was out of his chair and roaring.

"Really, Mr. Holmes! I will not be bamboozled! I have been a Spiritualist for many years, so these shenanigans don't fool me for one minute. I know realistic phenomena when I see it."

"Be wary," Mother Elspeth said. "Dark forces are abroad tonight. It is the night when the dead walk again."

"So you say," Dawson spat on the carpet. He may have intended to keep the witch's evil eye at bay, but he earned from me a silent curse and the promise of a kick in the pants. "All this fuss about a ring. A ring! But the law walks at all hours, and I'll have it on you all." He paced to the door to turn on the jet, and I screamed:—

"Hell and damnation! He's out of his coffin!"

Somebody screamed. It might have been me. Mercer sat up and his head turned toward us. His mouth was opening and closing and from it a guttural voice declared, "Dawson. You killed me. In my basement."

"No!" Dawson had backed up against the door. He was breathing heavily as if outrunning the devil.

"Slammed me against the wall by the preservatives. Broke a jug of embalming fluid. Used one of my own coffins for the poor and hid me in Potter's Field. Now you take opium to drown your horror at what you've done. Confess!"

In the face of righteous anger, Dawson fled the room. No one stopped him.

Holmes had not said a word through all this. He had watched Dawson, his face as still and emotionless as a serpent awaiting to strike. I shivered as if someone crossed my grave.

His face was that of God, looking down at Sodom and pitilessly passing judgment. You say the benighted undertaker deserved it. Punishment should come to the unjust. But you weren't there. If you were, you can't help feel sorry for him, trapped under the gaze of implacable, inevitable justice.

I looked into the foyer. The front door stood open. I walked back into the drawing room, where Miss Julia was seated, being supported by her mother next to her. She was taking shallow breaths, and her face was so pale as to be bloodless. Holmes said:—

"George! You may lower Mr. Mercer. It's best we repair to the drawing room, and leave Frederick to his work." He escorted Julia and her mother from the room. Behind me, from under the coffin a voice said:—

"Right you are, Mr. Holmes." There was a sound of sliding wood, and the upper half of Lysander Mercer was lowered into his coffin. Frederick walked over to his former employer and gently adjusted his face so that he looked his old self again. He said in a tight voice:—

"George, would you get the men in the barn and we'll move Mr. Mercer home?"

"Right away, sir."

I joined the group in the dining room and helped revive them with tea. Holmes was kindness personified, but I could not forgive him. I boiled inside to tell him what I thought of his stunt. The tea tasted like boiled ditch water, but we drank it gratefully. Holmes said:—

"I most sincerely apologize for what we put you through."

"Even with your warning, it was a shock, I grant you," Mrs. Newton said. "I'm sure you have your reasons. But how did you know? How did you pull this off?"

"This is not an opportune moment with Miss Julia here." She was seated in a high-backed chair, and although she had mostly recovered from the initial shock, she had spirit and to spare. She waved a hand at Holmes as if banishing his objections and said:—

"I must know the truth, sir. In fact, I insist on it, no matter how coarse the details."

He nodded, and for a moment there seemed to be a hint of approval sneaking past his mask of cruel neutrality. "It was the ring that convinced me that he was responsible. He wore the ring of a 14th degree Mason, but didn't recognize the Masonic handshake. Where did he acquire the ring? I consulted that font of all local knowledge, the newspaper editor, and learned that a Rafe McKee, who recently passed, was a 14th degree Mason."

"He robbed a dead man," Miss Julia said.

"I'm sorry you should hear this," Holmes said. She refused the consolation and said:—

"You concluded that if he robbed one man, then he must have robbed others."

"Such behavior usually occurs in patterns," he said. "Mr. Mercer saw the ring and recognized it." Miss Julia said:—

"He was a member of the same lodge."

"That led to a confrontation, a fatal confrontation. Had the police questioned Mr. Dawson about it, he could have denied it all. Possession of McKee's ring would not have tied him to the murder. Another method needed to be found.

"His bookcases gave me an idea. To know a man's heart, look to the women who know him. To know the inner man, look to his books. He was a Spiritualist. I took advantage of that fact. He was also an egotist. He was well-satisfied with himself. He always had to show himself at his best. Sort of like Sam, here, who always has to be the ringleader of the circus when it comes to storytelling."

I felt abused. He had to lighten the mood, but at my expense, I ask you? "That may be true," I said, "and what's a circus without its star clown?" I meant it to sting.

"So you and Mr. Clemens," Miss Newton said. "You did that to Uncle — ?" Tears started to flow down her cheeks.

I couldn't speak around the lump in my throat. I had nothing to do with it, but this wasn't a time to explain. But I admit it: I feared the word spreading. Mark Twain, desecrating a corpse! No matter how justified the cause, it's still a terrible rock to hang around my neck. And the thought of it getting back to Livy!

Then fate came to my rescue. Frederick Ord entered the room and knelt beside her. Tenderly, cautiously, he took her hand and called her name. He told her:—

"Don't fault Mr. Clemens. He knew nothing of this. Mr. Holmes asked me to participate. He explained that if this worked, then no one outside the family will ever learn the truth. We can say he took ill suddenly and died out of town."

Holmes set his teacup in its saucer, rattling enough to catch our attention. He made a gentle motion toward the door, and we caught his signal flag. I went to warn Livy that she was needed, and asked George to help escort Lysander to the funeral home. The family would give him a private burial in the family plot.

Holmes and I met Mother Elspeth in the foyer and walked her to her boarding house. As we cleared the driveway and walked down the street, she straightened her back, dropped her shawl, and a dozen years. She turned to me with a delightful smile and Holmes said:—

"Let me introduce Mrs. Modjeska, star of the Polish stage. She has spent the last few years here and in London working on her English. Her performance in that Ibsen play promises to make that playwright as known here as Shakespeare, thanks to her."[1]

"Please, Mr. Holmes, you're making me blush!" But he fin-

---

[1] Helena Modjeska (1840-1909) was a star of the Polish national theater when she and her husband emigrated to the U.S. in 1876. They settled on a California ranch with other émigrés and tried to making a living there despite not knowing English, nor anything about ranching or farming. When the utopian experiment failed, she returned to the stage, performing in America and Great Britain. Some scholars have theorized that Irene Adler of "A Scandal in Bohemia" was modeled on her. With Clemens showing her on friendly terms with Holmes later in life, is it possible she could have been *the* woman after all?

ished:—

"But I think tonight was her greatest, most challenging performance. Its success certainly had the most riding upon it. She had attended several such séances, so she knew how to make tonight's performance convincing. I assisted where I could," I said:—

"It certainly convinced me, especially all those family details. Got 'em from Livy I suppose." He said:—

"Observation and deduction, my dear Clemens. Observation and deduction."

"Mrs. Newton's alienation from her family?"

"Family photos on the wall from when they were children. A wedding photo with her husband and his family only. No sister nor brother."

"Knowing her nickname?"

"Ammie is a common variant on Amoransa."

"Their desire for status? Of course, she mentioned it. Then what about your deductions about my publisher and his thieving agents?" Holmes nodded as if I had told a delicious joke and said:—

"I have been a guest in your home for several weeks. Do you never listen to your table talk?"

"I promise in the future to pay more attention. Julia's attitude to Dawson?"

"Her latest letter to him was open on his desk. Her posture as she received him. The body reflects the mind, Clemens. You can read a person as you would a book if only you pay attention to posture."

"Then what about Dawson taking opium? I don't recall seeing a syringe on his desk."

"The constricted pupils, the slow breathing, and his obvious fatigue. When he thought we weren't looking, he'd scratch himself. Taken as a whole, these are obvious signs of opium abuse."

By this time, we had reached Mrs. Modjeska's hotel. She again thanked Holmes for the opportunity and in return made arrangements for dinner later that month in New York. She ran up the steps to the porch as lightly as a young girl. She closed the door and silence returned to the street. I felt very tired, and longed for my bed. We turned away from the door and I said:—

"Thank heavens it's over. I'm for home, a cigar, and a glass in that order."

"Not quite, Clemens. The final act is yet to come. We need to pay a visit to Mr. Dawson."

As if in a dream, I followed him. We arrived there long after midnight. Holmes whistled. From the shadows of an alley across the street appeared a boy. He handled Holmes his pocket timepiece and said:—

"He's been in 'bout a half hour, Mr. Holmes. Running down the street like ghosts were after him. I could hear him wheezing."

"Good lad. Here's the rest as agreed. Cut along now, and stay out of trouble." The boy grinned, bit one of the coins, and ran off. Holmes said:—

"We need to check on Mr. Dawson, Clemens. I see his lights are on."

We crossed the street and Holmes knocked at the door. There was no answer. He tried the handle. It was unlocked. We entered into an unbroken silence that was oppressive. He led the way and I followed. The rooms on the first floor were empty, so we took the steps to the second, our shoes softly brushing the carpet in time to the ticking clock.

We reached the top step. The lights were lit up here as well. We looked into the bathroom. The tub had its fabric shower curtain drawn. Holmes drew it back. The tub was empty. Then he paused, cocked his head and said:—

"Where is that tapping coming from?"

I listened for it and heard the gentle rap-rap-rapping. We proceeded down the hall, dread rising in my gullet. The tapping was growing louder. I said:—

"Next the ghastly ticking of a deathwatch in the wall at

the bed's head made Tom shudder — it meant that some-body's days were numbered." Holmes stared at me. "Tom Sawyer," I said.

We found his bedroom. The tapping was coming from the closet. We were halfway across the room when it stopped.

Holmes yanked open the closet door. Hanging from the hook was Jerome Dawson, his suspenders wrapped around his neck. It was a spectacle too gruesome to describe, and even now, decades after the fact, I still shudder and feel my face flushing at the memory.

We took him down and laid him on the bed. I raced for a doctor, but by the time we returned it was clear that nothing on this side of the world was going to call him back.

We walked back to the house. The streets were quiet. Holmes seemed determined to say nothing, while I wanted to say everything. So I lit a cigar, blew smoke up to the gas lamps, and said:—

"You knew all along, didn't you?"

I don't know if he ever testified in court. I hope for his sake he doesn't, because he would have been jailed many times over for what he did to achieve what he saw as the right out-come. He needs a Watson to show off his genius. He said:—

"The data showed me. I recognized the Masonic ring and of-fered that organization's unique grip used to identify members. He didn't recognize it. That was not proof. It could be McKee had his ring on when he was buried and Dawson acquired his some other way. But Occam's Razor led me to suspect him."

"And the jar in Mercer's workshop. What of that?"

"Everoything we know about Lysander Mercer told us of a neat, meticulous man. His living quarters proclaim this. His personal relations are orderly and regular. But what of his workspace? The tracks on the floor, written in dust, and the blood on the wall told the story."

"Mercer recognized the ring on Dawson's hand and realized that it was Rafe McKee's. He confronted Dawson in his workshop. They circled the table, arguing. Dawson could see the end of his hopes. He would lose Julia, he would lose the merger of the two businesses. There was a struggle. It might have been an intentional attack, or perhaps Mercer tried to leave and Dawson restrained him. It ended with Mercer dead. Dawson decided to get rid of the body, and the best place to dispose of one is among other bodies. The chain of logic dictates the Potter's Field."

"So why not go to the police?"

He hunched his shoulders. A cold wind raced down the street, setting the flames in the glass lamps flickering. He said:—

"Proving murder is difficult in the absence of evidence. Dawson stole from one body. Chances are he was stealing from many more. To have that come out would bring anguish to a great many families. If necessary, it would have come to a trial. Let us be thankful that it won't."

"And for that you play judge, jury, and executioner?"

"I am a consulting detective, Clemens. I am not society's official representative. I act as I see best. I trust my judgment. It is what I have trained for. Let the curtain ring down on this tragedy, Clemens."

Afterward

The genesis of this story is peculiar. I wanted a story that reminded me of October, the crisp weather, the scuttling of leaves, and the hint of magic, like out of Ray Bradbury's "October Country" stories, or Neil Gaiman's "Graveyard Book." A story that described how Halloween was celebrated then, with less emphasis placed on children roaming the neighborhood in search of candy and more about how people celebrated at home playing spell-casting games to determine their future.

This story has nothing to do with that premise. Instead, it's about graveyards and morticians and the things they can get up to when nobody's looking.

That's the way my stories unfold. Over the years, I've gathered a mountain of information about Twain and Holmes: 4,000 computer files and eight feet of books. This inspired a number of story ideas, ranging from single-sentence concepts to complete scenes. After writing 15,000 words of notes and six stories, I realized that I wasn't writing stories so much as playing a card game. I fill my hand with cards, shuffle and sort through them, and figure out which combinations will work. I try to write the story, filling in some scenes and briefly mentioning others. Heavy thinking and long walks are involved, then I go over the pages again to firm up the story logic, then one more time to make sure it all makes sense.

That's how it worked in this story. It started with Holmes and Clemens on a walking tour of New England. Then they found themselves in an island village off the coast of Rhode Island (it's Block Island if you're curious). I had gotten as far as a full outline before realizing that the story didn't need Sherlock nor Twain. I moved them to a small town they encounter during a walking tour. When the mortician card appeared in my hand, I wondered: Why not set the story in Hartford? That would let me write about the most important people in Twain's life: his loving wife, Livy, his loyal butler, George, and his home. After that, it was a matter of writing and rewriting.

His house still stands in Hartford, Conn. It's worth making the trip to see it. Built at the height of his career, it was designed by Livy and him to reflect his passions — its exterior will remind you of the Mississippi steamships he piloted — and his status as a wealthy literary man. It was richly decorated and boasted technological marvels such as interior bathrooms, a telephone, and a burglar alarm. It is a character as much as its inhabitants.

The Adventure of the Fight Club

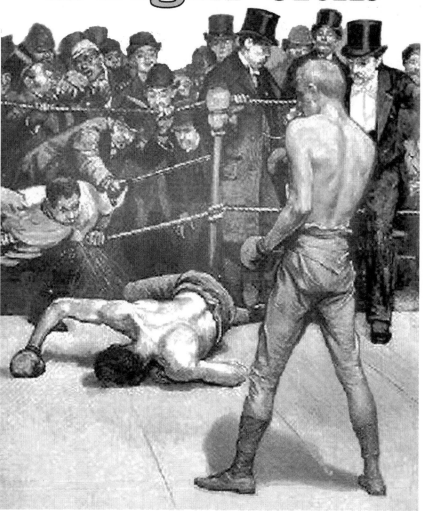

The Adventure of the Fight Club (1887)

———◆———

This story presents a mystery within the mystery. Previous stories in the series filled chronological gaps in Twain's life, such as when Twain met Mycroft Holmes in Tangier during a trip that inspired The Innocents Abroad, *or when he visited London as recounted in "The Adventure of the Stomach Club." There are few hints in this story as to when it took place. Holmes' references to Twain's Hartford home places this story after "The Adventure of the Missing Mortician" and before the events recounted in "The Adventure of the Whyos." For those reasons, a provisional date of May 1887 was chosen.*

This story is also unique in that it contains chronological errors, which the knowledgeable reader will recognize. It is also the only story in the papers that was narrated by Holmes' friend, Dr. Watson, who was known for fudging when some of Holmes' cases took place. But if Watson is the author, how did it get into the Twain papers? Handwriting analysis will not help, as the manuscript was typewritten. Could this be an account of a real story with the details disguised to protect the innocent, or a pastiche written as a joke? If it was the latter, was it Watson poking fun at Twain, or the other way around?

1. The Friend

DURING MY LONG ASSOCIATION with Sherlock Holmes, he never lost his capacity for surprises. I knew well his acting skill and ability with disguises. Yet he still confounded me with an unusual characterization. His deductive ability is unparalleled, yet he developed new ways of seeing deeper into the world what we skim over. His pronounced indifference to women was belied by his gentlemanly behavior towards them. His demeanour was as stern as a Glasgow preacher, yet ...

Imagine my surprise when I came downstairs in my dressing gown one unseasonably clement morning in early May and saw Holmes by the glowing coals of the fireplace. He was in his favorite attitude for listening, his head slightly forward, nodding as if asleep, his fingers steepled, but he was laughing! He emitted undignified snorts of merriment, like a train building a head of steam.

My surprise was redoubled when I saw in the chair opposite him a man I hadn't seen since we romped about San Francisco's Chinatown on the American Independence Day several decades before.

"Good morning, Watson," Holmes wiped a tear from his eye. "I assume you recognize our guest. Mr. Samuel Clemens was one of my clients early in my career when I was living in Montague Street."

"The honor of the introduction should be mine, Holmes, for I knew Sam out West before you did."

"Indeed? I wasn't aware of that." It was rare that I felt on the same level as Holmes and I resolved to enjoy it. "You must tell me about your adventure with him sometime."

It had been decades since I saw Clemens. Then, he was a young man whose spirits were as untamed as the West. He was older now, and his adventurous life and achievements had molded him. He was dressed in a proper suit, but it was rumpled. He slouched comfortably in the chair, smoking a cheroot that by the smell had been bought in a junk shop. He regarded me from underneath brows that could bristle with fire, then suddenly arch with good humor and warmth. Only a foot, bouncing on the floor like a piston, betrayed any anxiety.

"I'm pleased to shake the hand of friendship again after all these years, Watson," he drawled. "We've come up in the world since San Fran. How's your neck?" He went on to Holmes, "we've been swapping lies about our time on the stage, but your boy here has topped both of us. He played the most convincing imitation of a man being hanged it has ever been my pleasure to witness."

Holmes' surprise was startling. His confoundment by Irene Adler remained green in my memory, but that was minor compared to now.

"Your story intrigues me, Clemens. Watson will have to tell me about the measure he trod later. But we are awaiting a young lady, and it wouldn't do if two men were to receive her in dressing gowns."

"One is the room's limit," Clemens said grinning. "Or so I've read, John."

I took the hint, and rushed upstairs and changed. I returned to find my chair occupied by what I mistook for a girl in women's clothing. She barely occupied the seat, her feet barely touching the floor. She bore herself like a doll, but the tightness around her mouth and the twisting of her kerchief in her hands betrayed the state of her nerves.

Holmes said, "Dr. Watson, this is Lady Maud Tapp. Lady Maud, this is Dr. Watson, my companion on my cases. You may treat him as you would me. His discretion is on a par with my own."

She turned her attention to me, her gaze challenging. "And yet, you disclose your confidences to *The Strand*, do you not? And for money?"

"Only with the permission of the client," I said in my best bedside manner, as if I was talking to a fractious patient. I heard Clemens chuckling and felt my ears grow warm.

"She got you there, Johnny. Or do you go by Jack now?"

"Even so," Lady Maud said, "it would pain my father extremely if he knew that I told anyone about this. It would be terrible enough for him that I engaged your services, but if this appeared in The Strand, that would be–" she turned to Holmes as if he could divine her concerns.

Holmes's sympathy for her distress was palpable. "You need not fear. For every 'Speckled Band' or 'Hound' there are dozens that will never appear in the press."

"Simply to mention their existence would be indiscreet," I said.

She turned to me. "And yet, aren't your stories filled with mentions of other cases? We hear of the trained marmoset, the aluminum crutch, and Huret, the Boulevard assassin, do we not?"

"You're assuming, my dear, that those cases really exist," I said. "I mean, only a fool would believe in the existence of a giant rat in Sumatra, am I right, Holmes?"

Clemens choked on his cigar smoke. The mood was broken as he pounded his chest, and I leapt to his aid with a glass of water. Clearly, he had seen the look that had passed between Holmes and myself and found great merriment in it. Damn him!

When Clemens was settled, I moved to the breakfast table, pushed aside the remains of Mrs. Hudson's kippered herrings, unfolded my notebook, and with a warning glance at Clemens, set to work .

Maud Tapp was from the Tapp branch of the family that had resided in Liverpool since King James' reign. On the table next to me was one of Holmes' encyclopedic volumes, open to the T's, enabling me to learn that her father was Sir Henry Fawcett Tapp. It was a brief entry that made clear that this cadet branch played an insignificant role in the nation's affairs. I sighed and considered that it's the presence of these aristocratic families that make the achievements of our betters shine all the brighter.

"All his life," Lady Maud said, "Sir Henry preferred to spend his time tinkering in the basement of his castle near Rising Mildeau. We were a poor family for many generations, thanks to a duke with a taste for flashy women and paying blackmail, but we came into money recently."

"Married well?" Clemens said.

"Hardly," the lady spoke with a rasp. "My father had invented a new type of handle for the -- well, I can hardly say it out loud, it would not be proper -- but the porcelain throne that has lately come into fashion."

"The necessary box," Clemens said, the smoke from his

stogie wreathing his head like a Satanic undertaker.

Lady Maud nodded. "It was a small fortune, but most welcome. News of his success brought inquiries for my hand in marriage, to invest in company bonds, to finance inventions that only a simpleton would fall for: difference engines, perpetual-motion devices, typesetting machines."

Clemens' face grew as red as his hair. He had been a long-time investor in the Paige machine and no doubt had been filling Holmes' ear with his calculations for the fortune he would make. He considered raising an objection, but chose to clench his cheroot in his teeth and puff furiously.

"My father was subjected to all of these traps. I had been mostly successful in keeping him away from them."

"Until the moment when you weren't," Holmes said, catching the qualifying adjective.

"He invested thousands of pounds into a scheme to extract silver from the tailings of a Roman-era mine on the estate. He had been told that the process was nearly finished and needed only a few thousand pounds to finish it."

"How did they get to your father?" Holmes asked.

"They were very clever," she said, a faint blush mantling her cheeks. "I was being courted by Lord St. Simon."

Holmes and I shared a look. We had encountered his lordship in a previous case.

"He won an audience with my father under the pretense of discussing a settlement should we be married. Instead, he introduced to him the man behind the scheme, an odious man named Charles Stuart Everhardt."

Holmes was reaching for the "E" volume when an explosion of horrid language erupted from Clemens. He thrust himself from his chair and paced the sitting room, waving his arms in rage and scattering ashes on the furniture.

"Clemens, behave!" Holmes said.

"Fetch me a rope and I'll show you manners! Could it be the same jackass who infested the territories back in the 1870s?" He pointed his cigar at Lady Maud. "This man, you eyeballed him?" She nodded. "Was he a balding gent with scrub pads over his ears, a belly like jelly, who affected to talk like a pouncey Englishman?"

"I'm unfamiliar with 'pouncey,' but he matched your description, yes," she said.

"And he favors snuff over honest tobacco?"

"But not the proper use of the kerchief in containing it."

"And did he call this process of his 'The Secret of Erasmus'?"

This sent her rocketing from her chair. She gripped his arms and would have shaken him like a terrier with a rabbit in its teeth. "Yes! Yes! That's the man."

Clemens held her hands. "Then you have been fleeced by one of the greatest swindlers to hail from the Pacific Slope. By God, tell he where he is, and I'll horsewhip him, gratis!"

"He's staying at the Alexander."

"Then I'll corner him there. Why that —"

Propriety forbids me from transcribing any more of his monologue, which he conducted on his feet and between cigar puffs. It was plain that he knew Everhardt and did not approve of his company. Clemens in the grip of an emotion was unstoppable. I shot a look at Lady Maud when some of his more fruiter phrases hit the air, but she showed no signs of distress. In fact, it appeared from the glow of her cheeks and heightened breathing that she enjoyed it.

At the first sign of a pause, while Clemens was searching for an appropriate word to describe Everhardt's ancestors, Holmes interjected, "Clemens, are you willing to work with us on a plan to recover Lady Maud's fortune?"

"If it means seeing Everhardt dangle from the end of the rope, then I'm your man!"

"Lady Maud, is that your desire as well?"

She looked apologetically at Clemens. "I understand Mr. Clemens' feelings. I really do. But it is more important to me that it not be known that my father led himself to be embarrassed in this fashion. I prefer to recover the money Everhardt stole. So long as my heart's desire is fulfilled, I have no objection to a hanging."

Holmes clapped his hands in appreciation. "We'll need to discuss this matter in detail. First, I must reconnoiter." He got up and left the room. He returned wearing a rough coat, dusty pants, and a cloth cap. "I should return later tonight, but don't wait up, Watson. Clemens, let us meet here tomorrow and discuss the matter. Lady Maud, if you excuse me, I wish to begin work immediately."

2. The Plan

Holmes was as true as his word. He did not return that night. When I came down the next morning, he was taking his breakfast, looking trim and fresh as usual.

"I spent a most productive day yesterday with Mr. Everhardt, although he did not realize it," was all he said of the matter. He evaded my questions and said he preferred to wait until Clemens arrived. He spent the morning at the table digesting the pile of newspapers and clipping relevant stories for his scrapbooks. Sometimes, a piece of news would inspire commentary from him, and it was a delight to hear him outline how a scientific discovery in Germany could affect the future price of Newfoundland cod. Afterward, we went for a long walk, which allowed Holmes to gather fresh intelligence about the city, and we returned home well exercised.

When Clemens arrived that evening, Holmes suggested we dine out. "Simpson's serves an excellent roast, and with the help of a private table, we'll feed mind and body at the same time."

We engaged an upstairs room with a fireplace where we could talk in private. We laid our plans over platters of rare roast beef and Yorkshire pudding, that hearty English cooking that built and sustain our worldwide empire from John O'Groat, South Africa, India, Hong Kong, Vancouver, and Halifax. As the coal fire warmed us, Clemens described several schemes that he had encountered during his mining days out west.

"There were the stock schemes, where you form a company around a juicy land claim and sell shares in it. Reporters would be given shares in the mine, and in return pump up the noise about how much silver could be mined per foot. If need be, a visit to the test dig was arranged, and the mine 'salted' with silver so's the mark could discover the silver for himself. The stock would be bought and sold for ever-higher prices until the original investors had pulled out. Then it's revealed the claim contained dross and the company collapses."

"Would Everhardt know about that?" I asked.

"What he didn't know by experience he concocted himself. He's an old hand in that game. He took me for several hundred dollars, at a time when I didn't have them to spare."

"Does he know that?"

"Not as such. Shares get sold and resold. I was the one left holding the bag when the Conquistador mine folded. I've been itching for revenge ever since."

Holmes shook his head. "A stock scheme will take too long to get going."

Clemens suggested, "There's crooked games and bent sports like horse racing."

Holmes smiled, "England has a rich tradition of those kinds of fixes." He put his fingertips together and stared into the fire. "We need something big. There's the matter of several thousand pounds Lady Maud's father invested that needs to be recovered."

"A few fixed races won't cover that amount," Clemens agreed.

"Then you need a bigger scheme," I said.

"There is a possibility worth exploring. Last night, I shadowed Everhardt. In my guise as a common laborer, I waited outside the Alexander until he came out. He stopped at the Alhambra where Dan Leno has been such a success. He moved on to the Savage Club where he is a member. I was able to observe him from the window at the card table for awhile until the patrolman on his beat chased me off."

Clemens grumbled, "That's my club. Bad enough for their reputation that they let me in. Did you know he also loves boxing? He was a big one for staging bouts in the camps, just so's he could bet on them."

"Does he?" It appeared as if a light switched on inside Holmes. He gently tapped the arms of his chair. An idea was clearly forming. "There is a club in London called the Hellfire. Some of its members stage boxing matches with high-stakes wagers."

Clemens frowned, "Isn't that illegal here?"

"Yes. They organize their matches outside of the club, usually in isolated buildings south of the Thames. My observations revealed that Everhardt was a gambler who pushed a bet as far as it would go. We can take advantage of that." He outlined his plan, and the more Clemens heard, the more he was excited, to the point where he took to his feet and paced before the fire.

"That's a capital plan!" he said. "We'll need help to carry it off."

"I've already thought of someone who could help." Holmes suggested allies we could recruit from among the criminal class. Although we had roomed together for only a few years, we had experienced the events outlined in *A Study in Scarlet*, "The Speckled Band," and a few other stories. At that time, Holmes was a nonentity, known only by reputation to the Metropolitan Police and by word of mouth from grateful clients. It was at that moment that I understood how deep his knowledge of the criminal class ran. Had he chose to run an empire along the lines of Professor Moriarty, he would have at his fingertips a gang to run it.

Sated and feted, we were inclined to resume our labours to-morrow, but Holmes vetoed the motion. "You need to beard the lion in his den, or in this case, the Savage Club. Meet up with him, mention the fight club and the next match two days from now." He described further what he wanted Clemens to do, and suggested I go along with him.

"You'll play a member of the Hellfire Club, Watson, so you'll need a new name. Someone from the nobility. Americans do love a lordship. A minor noble, too obscure to be noticed by anyone and not easy to contradict." He searched his capacious memory. "I have it! You shall be Lord Dingwell. The title was recently revived in the Scottish highlands, so no one in London knows what he looks like."

Clemens objected. "If I'm to introduce him to that rapscallion as a friend, I won't be calling him Lord Dingwell. He'll need a plain name as well. Something easy to answer to. What's your middle name?"

"Hamish. After my grandfather."

"We'll call you Ham, how about that?"

I shuddered at the memory of the nicknames I was inflicted with at school. "How about Winston? It sounds similar to Watson. John Winston."

"Winston? For a last name?"

He was right. It is not a common name in Scotland. "How about Winston Moore?"

He puffed out the remains of his cheroot and tossed the stub into the fireplace. "It's your funeral. Anyway, once we're introduced, let me do the talking. Hang around if you must, but not with your ears flapping or your notebook open like you're a penny-a-word reporter." He pulled out another cheroot and sparked a wooden match alight with his thumbnail in the Western manner.

I should have taken umbrage at his insult, but I had grown accustomed to being treated this way by Holmes. "Tell me about it afterward," I said.

So instead of taking a hansom home, Clemens and I walked down The Strand and turned right on Savoy Street. The Savage Club was midway down the block, and beyond it the silent waters of the Thames shimmered in the moonlight. It was a cool night but our furious pace quickly warmed us. We rehearsed our scheme as Clemens' foul cigar scented the air.

The club's gaming room was jammed with bodies and the air damp with humidity. The uproar of shouted bets, cursing, and commentary on the table action was doubled and redoubled in the closed room. Coming in from the street, we welcomed the warmth at first, until we, too, were sweating and gasping for air like stranded trout like the rest of the members.

From underneath the thatch of his eyebrows, Clemens scanned the field like a native inhabitant of his country. Then he nudged me hard in the ribs and pointed.

"He's banking at the faro table with his back to the fireplace. Look for that ghastly olive-green checked coat."

Sitting stiffly in his chair, his arms spread and his palms caressing the green baize table, Charles Stuart Everhardt beamed at his fellow gamblers like a benevolent demon. His wool-pad sideburns were especially puffed, and most of his hair had fled to the nether regions of his scalp. He sat at the notch cut into the table, where the banker dealt the cards from a wooden box called the "shoe." The tabletop was marked with outlines of the 13 card suits where the bets were placed. Everhardt dealt the cards with one hand, while he rolled a thin flexible stick over the cloth with the other.

There was an outburst from the table. An elderly gentleman with a red beezer tossed his cards with a curse. He had been broken by Everhardt and was quitting the field. Clemens raced to snare the empty seat. He opened his folding leather case from his breast pocket and casually tossed a handful of bank notes on the table. He shouted:

"Pop in a fresh prayer book, banker, and prepare to be catawamptiously chawed up! Clemens is here from the Pacific rim, and I'm here to cavort until the cat wagon pulls up!"

Everhardt jerked like he had been electrified. His piggy eyes glittered in the candlelight, then he shouted, "Clemens! Cap the climax! I thought I recognized your clap-trap. When did you blow into England?"

"Long enough to hear you been raising hell like there's no

heaven." Clemens tapped the pile of bank notes and said, "Are you gonna fish or cut bait?"

"Fish!" Everhardt shouted. "We'll blather later."

Play resumed, and it wasn't long before Everhardt found an opportunity to employ his stick. While the bets were being settled and many hands were placing and removing their chips, one of the players risked sliding his marker from a losing suit to a nearby winner. Quick as a rattler, Everhardt slapped the young man's wrist with his stick. The youth yelped and gripped his injured wrist.

The sudden violence silenced the table. Everhardt smiled like a serpent: "Now, I know you weren't planning to honeyfuggle the house, but I wasn't sure if your hand knew it. We do it according to Hoyle, here, or we'll be on the proddy." He shook his stick at him for emphasis. "You twig?"

It was an incident that could have led to a tragic outcome. The young man was a member of an old, noble house, and while he commanded no authority, he was backed by powerful family members who could cause trouble on his behalf. Some of them were even in the room.

Clemens barked a laugh "We're burning daylight here. Let's play!" The young man was either intimidated or he couldn't understand a word he said. Either way, he nodded, still clutching his injured wrist.

The gentlemen resumed play, if only to catch up with Clemens' play. He had placed several bets and was calling for cards. I breathed a sigh of relief, grateful that I wouldn't have to explain to Holmes how we started a riot at the Savage Club.

The hours passed. I grew bored watching the play. I found an empty chair and kept an eye on the men and made use of the opportunity to discreetly scribble a few notes. I heard a name similar to mine being called. Then twice more and louder. Then I was grabbed by the arm and hauled to my feet.

"Winston, you blatherskite," Clemens pressed his face close to mine. I weathered a blast of stale tobacco and fresh whiskey. "Didn't you hear me yelling for you? Are you drunk already? Come on, we're going to eat!"

There was a cackle of laugher from the members at my discomfort. I glared at him resentfully, but mindful of Everhardt's presence, I stood on my dignity, removed his hand from my shirt and pulled it down. He turned on his heel, and walked away without a word, and we followed him.

We found ourselves at a table in the club's restaurant, and over toasted cheese on bread and more whiskey, Clemens and Everhardt reminisced about San Francisco and their days in the mining fields. If Everhardt knew of Clemens' stock misfortune, he didn't show it, and Clemens was good fellowship personified.

"One of my favorite games is Baccarat," Clemens said. "Have you seen it? The croupier uses this curved oar to gather in the money and chips."

"Are you good at it?" Everhardt said.

"Oh, I'd never play it," Clemens replied. "If I could have borrowed his oar I would have stayed. Otherwise, I didn't see the point."

As he told his stories, I watched the clock closely, and at the time we agreed, pulled my watch from my vest and opened it.

"It's getting on, Clemens," I said. I adopted a Scottish burr that I recalled a sergeant-major using from my soldiering days. "We need to get moving if want to get in a flutter before the first round."

"Is it? Ah, you are correct, Lord Dingwell."

"Round?" Everhardt said. "Where are you going?"

Clemens traced his lips with a finger. "I'm sorry, Everhardt. I can't let the cat out of the bag. His lordship invited me to a special event, but on the promise that I don't say a word about it."

"And yet you did, Clemens," Everhardt said maliciously. "You never could keep your yap shut. So you might as well spill to an old chum. Is it a sport? Ah ha! I see by your map that I twigged it. It's a boxing match, right? Why, I haven't seen a good mill since I left America. Where is it?"

Clemens shook his head, and I broke in to say, " 'Fraid we can't say. Strictly club business, you know. Enjoy your stay in London, Everhardt." I got up, and Clemens followed.

I walked out of the room without looking back, assuming the uncomfortable persona of a lordship. It was only when I reached the lobby that I realized Clemens had not followed me. I considered going back, then I remembered who I was, straightened my back, and stalked out.

I summoned a hansom and ordered the driver to wait. When Clemens appeared at the door, I waved to him, and he stepped up looking as pleased as the cat who lapped up the spilled cream.

"We hooked him, Johnny," he said as the carriage pulled away. "He stalled me to pinch out the location of the mill."

"What did you say?"

"Only that you knew and I didn't. But he's hungry for more. He wants to lunch with me tomorrow."

"Then we'll have to move quickly."

3. The Bait

The next day, while Clemens met Everhardt as arranged, Holmes and I traveled to St. Giles. The hansom slowly worked its way through the crowded streets until Holmes ordered the driver to pull up outside a large brick building. The building was shabby, but not quite as bad as those found several streets over. Several shops occupied the street level, while stairs led to the three floors of apartments above it.

Holmes opened the street door and led us upstairs to a landing with several doors. A knock on one was answered by a short man whose most prominent features were his jug ears and drooping moustache. Looking around his legs were two little girls. He caught sight of Holmes, paled, and attempted to close the door, but Holmes had already pushed his way in and grabbed his arm, the girls scattering in alarm. "Padraig Collins!" he said with good humor. "We come in peace this time."

Padraig eyed the taller man with suspicion. "So you say, Mr. Holmes? Then peace it shall be. Clara, Louisa, quit your grizzling! Mr. Holmes is a guest. But what would you be wanting with me otherwise?"

"We have need of your unique abilities. But, come, let's have a drink first, and then we'll talk."

Padraig brightened at the suggestion, but said there was none in the house. Holmes' offer to pay was accepted, and the girls were sent down to the pub for a bottle of gin.

At the table, his undrunk glass of gin in front of him, Holmes laid out the plan. Padraig drank his portion and set the glass carefully on the table, smacking his lips.

"This is a story for the ages, Mr. Holmes, I must say."

"Can you do it, Padraig? Can you help?"

"If I can't set this up then no one in the three kingdoms can. Let me see, you want to stage a fight, but in a place that'll attract the gents as well as people like us. I know of an abandoned warehouse across the river, Vauxhall way. We can do it up a treat, but cleaned up, like for the gentry on the slumnibuses. But you don't want the real moneyed gentlemen to be walking in, do you?"

"Correct. Only the men we hire will be in the room."

"So you'll need at least a hundred of them, some togged out as gentlemen and given roles to play. The rest will look like locals. They can outfit themselves. Then another dozen to run the fights, provide security. Some of them should be bruisers with fighting experience in case we need muscle." Padraig chuckled as he refilled his glass. "I've heard about plenty of cons, but don't this beat all! Setting up a scene to take in one gentleman. Will the payoff be worth it, you think?"

"If I know my man and his resources, enough to pay you all off and pay back the people he conned."

"You know," Padraig said thoughtfully. "If it works for one, it'll work for more. You could run several marks through the scene in a day. Spread the cost out with a chance for a greater return. Sure you won't consider — ? Ah, it's something to tuck in the back pocket for a rainy day. How soon do you need them?"

"To-morrow night."

"Ohhhh," Padraig frowned and rubbed his chin in contemplation. "That'll take some doing."

Holmes pulled from his pocket a heavy bag and dropped it on the table. "Will this provide enough incentive?"

Padraig's eyes widened as he lifted the bag of coins and weighed it in his palm. "This'll do nicely. In fact, I'm thinking of some shortcuts that will help."

"Send a message when you're ready."

On the way back to Baker Street in the hansom, Holmes was uncharacteristically jubilant. "Padraig was one of the best stage managers in the business. He was a field marshal when it came to organizing a cadre of actors and actresses, stagehands, and directors, and leading them into mounting the production. It was only his intense fondness for drink that rendered him unfit, even for the theater. Perhaps this exercise in stage managing will help him return to his true calling." Holmes stared at the passing scene, lost in thought. "I hope you are taking notes, Watson. There are elements to this case that have the potential to make it truly unique. I've never experienced planning a criminal act from the criminal's point of view. This will bring a unique perspective to bear on my future work. There may even be a monograph in it."

4. The Hook

Across the city of London, wheels were set in motion. Everhardt lobbied Clemens to intervene with Lord Dingwell on his behalf to admit him to the next round of fights. Padraig organized his work crews and seamstresses into setting the stage at the warehouse. Holmes sat and played his violin in a thoughtful manner, reviewing the details of his plan, while I organized my notes and set this account down to paper. That afternoon, Padraig sent one of his daughters with a message to Holmes stating that the warehouse was ready. Clemens and myself met Everhardt at the Savage Club that evening, and we took a hansom down the Embankment to Vauxhall Bridge.

We turned south of the notorious pleasure gardens and into the side streets where residences ran cheek by jowl with manufacturers. I filled Everhardt's ears with stories of our activities in the Hellfire Club, and how some of the members, bored with the round of sinister rituals and drunken revelries, had banded together to create what we called the Fight Club.

"We go about this business with the utmost discretion," I said. "Prize fighting is deeply frowned upon, and has been for many a year. So we formed this club and recruit bonny-looking pugilists to battle for prize money. We even have a club champion, 'Mad Mike' O'Connor from County Cork, fourteen stone of hard muscle with a right hand that strikes like lightning."

"Is this bare-knuckle or Queensbury rules?" Everhardt said, the gleam in his eye betraying his eagerness.

"Queensbury," I shook my head as if regretting the decline in standards since the days of bare-knuckle boxing. "Although the gloves they wear don't merit the name. And if during a match they fly off, well, the referee knows not to object."

"And betting. Is that allowed as well?"

"Of course! It wouldn't be sporting if we didn't."

At my order, we were dropped off on the South Lambeth Road. I led Clemens and Everhardt down several streets and into a darkened alley. A gas lamp at the street cast a reddish light that lightened the gloom and reflected off the damp cobblestones. At the far end, we stopped at a wooden door wide enough to admit a wagon. Behind it could be heard the muffled shouts and cheers of many men. I knocked up the door in a particular pattern. The sound of a bolt being drawn back could be heard, and a man's face glared at us from under his cloth cap. The effect was so startling that I stammered out the password.

His eyes shifted to my companions. "Who're they, then?"

"Friends of mine," I said in my most fruity and noble voice. "Stand aside and admit us."

He sneered and pulled back the door, and we walked into a cacophony of cheers, hoots, and shouts. The room had once been a staging area where wagons were loaded and unloaded. It was wide and high and lit by gas jets. The floor above was open in the center, offering a balcony-like view of the action below. The remains of ropes dangled from above like the remains of giant spiders.

At the center, a makeshift ring had been set up, and a crowd of gentlemen and locals were gathered about a fight already in progress. The boxers were shielded by the press of men, but we could see their heads bobbing above the spectators, and the sound of their punches punctuated the noise. The air was hot and fetid, dust motes drifted in the lamplight, and the violence stimulated the senses. My breathing grew heavy and deep, as it did in Afghanistan when battle was imminent.

Mindful of my role, I led us over to the far side of the room. On a platform of crates, Padraig had set up a table. A timekeeper was studying a watch. He rang a bell with a hammer and to the general cheering the fighters parted and returned to their seconds. As they swigged water and their friends staunched their wounds, men crowded around the table demanding to place bets. We could see more bookies walking through the crowd, calling the new odds and arranging bets.

The timekeeper rang the bell and the men returned to battle. One of them, a pale ginger-haired fellow, was clearly getting the worst of the fight. His swings were wild and unfocused, desperate measures to avoid the inevitable. Everhardt' face was flushed with excitement, and he took in the battle with evident pleasure. Clemens grabbed Everhardt' shoulder and leaned over to shout something in his ear.

I glanced over at Padraig and caught his eye. He nodded at my unspoken signal and waved his arms like a semaphore.

The ginger fighter seemed to take the message. He stepped in, swung and missed, took two punches to the head, and he collapsed to the floor. The fight was over. The referee raised the arm of the winner to a chorus of cheers, groans, and catcalls from the crowd. A few fistfights broke out, presumably by those who had bet on the loser. A couple of bruisers waded in with truncheons and quickly suppressed them.

Everhardt turned to us and said, "That was top-notch, Lord Dingwell."

"Wait for the next fight," I said. "He's a lad from Norfolk. Shows great promise. We've hopes of backing him against Mad Mike if he wins tonight."

"Are you?" he said. There was a thoughtful gleam in his eye. He pulled out a roll of bank notes and riffled through them. "Do you enjoy the sport, Clemens?"

"Oh, I enjoy making money off it more," he drawled. "Beats scribbling for thieving publishers for a living."

Two new men entered the ring. One was a fleshy older man, bull-faced, with a flattened Michelangelo nose. The other was younger, lighter, and considerably more energetic. He strutted around the ring, his arms up, as if he had already won, while his opponent contented himself with flexing and warming up.

"I recognize Warren the prizefighter," Everhardt said. "Who's the new buck?"

"Name's Ford. Sherrin Ford. The Norfolk man I was telling you about. He's the one I'm betting on."

"You're loony! Warren has got two stone on him. He nearly took down Nonpareil Dempsey in his prime."

"Stone and a half. If you're so sure, place a bet."

"That I will. Hi! You there!" Everhardt waved his bank notes at a nearby bookie. "What're the odds? All right. I'll lay ten pounds on Warren! No, twenty!"

"A hundred on the lad," Clemens said. Everhardt looked startled.

"You are flying high, Clemens." He shrugged at Everhardt's

comment as if risking a hundred pounds were nothing.

Nearly an hour later, the fight was over. Warren still had a powerful right, but Ford was quicker and evaded most of the blows. He wore down the boxer until two sharp rights and a powerful left laid the bigger man down.

The audience was thrilled, even the losers, by the display of fighting prowess. From behind the table, Padraig stood up and waved his arms to get the crowd's attention.

"Thank you all for coming to see our exhibition of pugilistic skill and tenacity." Cheers and laughter greeted him. "Come back again three nights from now, when we'll see Ford take on Mad Mike!" The audience dispersed, the winners to buy the drinks and the rest to hope to be the recipients of their largess.

"That's it?" Everhardt said.

"We have to be wary of the peelers," I said. "So we only run two fights, maybe three at a time. Wouldn't do to get run in, you know."

Clemens collected a wad of bills from the bookie. He commiserated with him and promised that he'd be back later and give him his chance at revenge.

We stepped out into the street. Clemens flagged a hansom and directed him to head back to the Ritz.

"I still can't suss it," Everhardt said. "Warren should have pounded him into the ground."

"Told you that you should have bet on him."

"That you did, that you did," he said slowly. He looked out the window at the people walking along the streets. "Is all this on the up and up?"

"To the ones in charge of the carnival, yes," Clemens said. "They set the odds so that the house don't lose at all. But there's a gang, see, who know how to get to the fighters. They sniff the wind, find a long shot, and figure out a way to make it pay off."

"And you know these people."

"We've done business," Clemens said simply. "They do me

a favor here, I do them a favor back home. Introduce them to people. Open doors."

"Yeah, I can see that," Everhardt said. "You're pretty tight with those Wall Street boys. Morgan. Diamond Jim. General Grant. Use your influence with 'em, eh?" He laughed with the knowledge he knew something dirty about his friend and pounded him on the back.

5. The Threat

"So, Holmes, what is next?" It was the next morning. A cheerful sun was shining through the bay windows, warming the brick fronts of Baker Street and polishing the streets of London to a golden glow. Holmes had taken a few bites of breakfast, pushed aside his plate, and lit a cigarette, watching the curlicues of smoke rise to the ceiling. He looked like he was calculating the atmospheric effects on smoke and its use in detection, possibly for another in his interminable series of monographs that he insist I read as if part of my obligation lodging with him was to act as his unpaid editor.

"Humph?" he blinked and focused his attention on me. "Pardon me, Watson, I was wool-gathering."

I swallowed my blood pudding and spoke. "We were successful last night in hooking Everhardt. He's looking forward to the match with Mad Mike. I assume that's when we'll fleece him, right?"

"Yes, yes, you're correct," he said. "However, not entirely. I have another wheel that I need to set in motion."

"Have you?" I resolved to update my notebook at the first opportunity.

"Yes, in fact —" There was a knock on the door. The voice of Mrs. Hudson could be heard asking the visitor his business. In his loud American voice, Everhardt asked if he could see Sherlock Holmes.

"Watson, into the alcove! Stand behind the curtain."

I fled to the bay window where a curtain had been installed to create a private reading nook. I pulled out my notebook and hurriedly scratched a few sentences until I froze, my breath caught in my throat, at the sound of the door opening.

"I got your note this morning demanding an interview," Everhardt gave the impression that he was in a terrible mood. Given the amount of brandy and whiskey we consumed last night after the fight, his head must have felt like he'd gone several rounds with Mad Mike. "What do you want?"

"Sit down, Mr. Everhardt, I prefer my conversations at eye level. Thank you. I asked you here for a favor."

"Oh? And who are you to ask a favor of me?"

"I am a consulting detective. No, sit down! We can have this conversation either here or at Scotland Yard. It is your choice. Good. Know this: I am not an official representative of the police. Sometimes, our goals and desires coincide, but sometimes not. This is not one of those times unless you insist. I asked you here to talk about Samuel Clemens."

"What do you want to know about him?"

"What he is doing in England."

"I assume doing whatever authors do in England. Beg publishers to accept their works. Pawn their watch to buy food for their families. Gossip about writers they hate and critics they despise."

"Your humor is typically American, but I am deadly serious. Clemens displays the appearance of a genial writer of humor, but behind the mask is a criminal mastermind of the first water."

The silence that followed was so long I thought Everhardt had left. Then he burst out laughing. He carried on for several minutes, and when it bubbled down, he caught another aspect of that remarkable statement and launched into another round of wheezes.

"Criminal ... mastermind. That is good turn of phrase. You should go on the stage. In moustache, tall hat, and cape. That is very good! Oh, let me wipe my eyes a moment. There. Sam and I have known of each other for too many years for that to pass muster. Why, I'd make a better criminal than he!"

"That, my dear Everhardt, is what makes him so effective. Have you seen his house in Connecticut? I have. It is a palace. He entertains on a lavish scale. He invests in numerous business enterprises. He counts President Grant and the wealthiest members of Wall Street his friends. When he published Grant's memoirs, he turned over the majority of the profits to the president's widow. Is that the action of a rational publisher? Of course not! He lives on a scale far beyond that of other best-selling writers. The inference is obvious: Clemens heads a criminal enterprise far beyond anything in history. He is here in England for a reason, and you're going to help me."

"You threaten me?"

"I make a promise, Everhardt." Even from behind the curtain, I could sense Holmes' power. When angry, he can present himself as a terrible, even avenging figure.

"You have nothing on me."

"Do I? See that scrapbook on the table? That is one of many I keep." There was a pause as Holmes walked to it and the sound of the cover opening could be heard. "Let us see, there's Eadweard, the nefarious terror of Eton. Dr. Evans, the notorious clairvoyant physician from Liverpool, who I helped hang. Here you are. Charles Stuart Everhardt, born Ryszard Scymanski in Piotrków. Why, here's an article in which one Harrison accuses the owners of the Stafford and Lone Star Silver Mines of swindling investors! I quote from the Marysville Daily Appeal: 'Harrison denounces by name Major J.D. Wooley, Cheyenne; Colonel W. J. Jones, of San Francisco; and Colonel C.S. Everhardt, of Salt Lake, as projectors of the swindle.'" Holmes punctuated his revelation by slamming the scrapbook shut. "Shall I go on?"

"All right, you got me," Everhardt lost much of his steam under the force of Holmes' personality. "What do you want?"

"What Clemens is planning."

"Then you'll have to wait. We went to a boxing match last night. Some setup involving the Hellfire Club. There's going to be another bout a few nights from now."

"Then I need for you to keep your eye on him. Accompany him everywhere. Tell me who he meets and what he says."

There was another pause, then Everhardt said, "I'll need money. He flies pretty high for a criminal mastermind."

"Here's twenty pounds. You shouldn't need more."

"Thankee."

"I expect daily reports. Telegram or messenger will do."

When I heard the door closing, I peeped through the curtains to see Holmes shaking in quiet laughter.

"There you are, Watson. Did you hear everything? Everhardt must think me a dangerous fool, conning me out of twenty of the best and lying about the fight as well."

"But why should he shadow Clemens? You don't really suspect him of criminal acts?"

"Only of letting improper manuscripts fall into the hands of unscrupulous publishers. No, my intentions are the opposite of my orders. I don't want Everhardt to watch Clemens, I want Clemens to watch Everhardt. Left to himself, he might see the flaws in our plan, or ask uncomfortable questions. He needs to be kept busy until we're ready to fleece him. In fact, that's where you come in. Clemens insists on spending his mornings and afternoons at his writing. That means you'll have to befriend Everhardt during those times."

"What will I do?"

"Play Lord Dingwell. Show him London. Lunch with him. Drink with him. Gamble with him. Whatever, but keep him occupied. You'll meet Clemens for dinner and pass him off then. Will you do that?"

"Of course. You can count on me. I confess I was also impressed by the quality of your intelligence. How did you get California newspapers here?"

"That was a mere subterfuge. I wired the San Francisco police after Lady Maud's visit and received the particulars. It looks more impressive if he thought I had my eye on him all along."

The next two days passed quickly in my memory, but

from the increasingly desperate tone in my notes that didn't appear to be the case at the time. In my guise as Lord Dingwell, I showed Everhardt cricket at Lord's, which bored him. We visited a Rugby League match between the Civil Service and Guy's, which he found more to his taste. We also visited the Savage Club and White's, where he left me to the reading room while he indulged his taste for cards. Every evening, we met Clemens at dinner where he read his day's writing to us before heading out for the evening.

This part of the plan was the hardest for Clemens to fulfill. Whatever injury Everhardt had done to him out West still hurt him deeply, for on the first evening, as we walked out of the restaurant, he grabbed my sleeve, leaned in, and hissed, "Even a damned soul as myself should be admitted to heaven for not stoving in his skull at the first opportunity."

Meanwhile, the clock continued its infinite turn, and day passed into night and back again. I saw little of Holmes, and when I did he refused to speak about the case, beyond rehearsing my part in what follows.

6. The Visitors

The day of the fight was more eventful than anyone expected. First, we received a visit from Padraig.

"I never expected to come here unless I was under arrest," he said. He settled into the basket chair by the fireplace and accepted a small glass of brandy. He downed the drink with evident enjoyment and set the empty glass on the small tray table.

"How go the preparations?"

"As you planned, Mr. Holmes. We installed a ring to give the proceedings some tone, and I've been recruiting a few more lads to fill the house. The seamstresses have been working late to finish dressing the toffs."

"And they understand the new script?"

"We rehearsed it until they could do it in their sleep. There is one question that I needed your advice on. I was approached by Lady Maud, see. She wanted to attend tonight's fight. In disguise, of course. But she wanted to see justice done, as she put it."

"Interesting. So long as she's well-costumed and unrecognizable."

Padraig nodded, "We'll have women in attendance, most of 'em serving drinks to the lads, like you'd see at any mill."

"We'll detail Watson to keep an eye on her. Anything else?" There wasn't, and he left to return to Vauxhall.

The next visitor was much more surprising.

Sherrin Ford was a tall, strapping lad whose wheat-colored hair poked from his bowler in unexpected places. For someone who faced violent men who outweighed him in the ring, his nervousness was unexpected and concerning.

"I appreciate this opportunity, Mr. Holmes, but something has come up that I think you should know about. Early this morning, I received a visitor at my home. I live with me mum in Spitalfields, you see, and this bald cove came with his bruiser to knock me up. He says he knew about the play and wanted in on it. I asked him what he was talking about, and he says, 'I know you're planning on throwing the fight. Don't worry, I want you to. I just want you to throw it when I say so.'"

Holmes said, "Everhardt."

"He didn't give me a name, sir. He says he'll make it worth my while, right now, and later. He wants me to come to America. Prizefighting's legal there, see, and he says he can manage me. If I do well enough, I could get a shot at a real championship." He looked down in shame.

"What did you say to that?"

"I didn't really know what to say. I know what you want me to do and why, so I said I'd have to think about it. That's when he said ... he said if I didn't do what he wanted, that I ..."

"That's all right, Sherrin. I think I know what he said."

"Mr. Holmes, what should I do?"

"I think you should agree. Did he say how he would tell

you?"

"He said he would signal my second during the fight. I'd have to stay up during the first dozen rounds, then he'd decide when I should take the fall. He'll tell the second, who will tell me. Are you sure you want me to do this?"

"Yes, I think you should. You didn't go into this to risk your life, or your mother's. I'm sorry it came to this, but we'll have to adjust the plan in light of this information."

"Will he come after me? If it don't go right for him?"

Holmes smiled and laid a reassuring hand on the lad's shoulder. "He'll be too busy trying to save his own skin to worry about you." Holmes continued to console the young man as he escorted him down the stairs to the street door.

"There's an example, should you need one, of the degradation to a society caused by gambling such as this," he said upon his return. He picked up his violin and began tuning the strings. "Take the clean competition and exercise that sport lets us indulge in, add a way to make money off it, and moral decay must follow sure as night follows day. Give me a moment, Watson. I must clear my head," and he launched into a long, plaintive movement that better expressed his feelings than mere words.

That afternoon saw our third visitor, this time from Everhardt himself. As before, I hastily retreated behind the curtain by the window, notebook in hand.

"Mr. Holmes, you asked me what I thought Clemens was doing," Everhardt said, "and at the time I would have called you insane at the suggestion of any criminal doings. But I admit you're right. Clemens has been fixing fights!"

"Indeed, tell me more," Holmes said, and together we heard about the fight he had witnessed a few nights ago, and Clemens' 'confession' to him.

"Thank you, Mr. Everhardt. That is most satisfactory."

"Now that you know this, Sherlock, what are you going to do about it?"

"Uphold the law. Apply to the police for a warrant for his

arrest. If we can catch him in the act, all the better."

"Excellent. You'll be able to catch him tomorrow."

"That's the next fight?"

"Yes, at the same place and time. And if he resists," he reached into his pocket to pull out a derringer, "we'll let Mr. Remington make the arrest."

"Impressive," Holmes said. "You don't see many of those these days." The men could be heard standing, and I received the impression Holmes was shaking his hand. "We'll see you to-morrow then."

"Holmes, I congratulate you," I said after Everhardt closed the street door behind him.

Holmes accepted my hand but more out of friendship than pride.

"Belief is a powerful human trait," he sat back in his chair and reached for his pipe. "The essence of a successful con is to convince the 'mark' of the veracity of the reality you construct. We created a nonexistent gentleman's club, faked a boxing match, and recruited a fake audience to watch and lay fake bets, all to fool one man that it was all real. On top of that, we had to ensure that Everhardt fooled me by lying about the date of the next fight. Running a criminal organization is much more work than I had anticipated. This has been a most educational exercise. I look forward to writing the monograph. But first, let's have dinner. Tonight's fight will tax our energies."

7. The Play

The fight had been going on for over two hours. True to his name, Mad Mike O'Connor came charging out of the corner early, forcing Sherrin Ford to backpedal repeatedly to avoid the Irishman's broad swings. This gave him the opportunity to step in and hammer the champion's midsection, then retreat to await the next onslaught.

I was seated on the large crate where Padraig Collins had set up his table. I had to play the cool, unflappable Lord

Dingwell, but my heart was hammering and restraining myself from showing anxiety was draining. Although I had been watching Everhardt palling about with Clemens, there was no sign that he had placed a bet. Clemens kept a rein on his true feelings as well, but several times during the match he looked my way and his bushy eyebrows signaled that he was just as perplexed.

Only Lady Maud felt free to express her concern. Dressed in filthy clothes common to the women of the neighborhood, a large hat shading her features, she looked nothing like the trim, self-possessed woman who had sat in our rooms a few days before.

"What's keeping him?" she hissed in my ear. "Why doesn't he bet?"

"I do not know," I answered, tilting my head in her direction so she could hear me better. Although Everhardt had not recognized her, it seemed prudent to not give him the idea we knew each other at all.

As for Holmes, I know he was around even though I could not see him.

The timekeeper next to Padraig ran the bell, and round 39 had finished.

The slam of a Gladstone bag on the table drew my attention. It was Everhardt. "Ten thousand pounds," he said in a clear, strong voice. "Ten thousand pounds that the champion puts away the lad in the next round. What odds?"

Padraig reached over and, his hands shaking, unclasped the lock and pulled the handles apart. The bag was crammed full of bank notes of various denominations. I know that I have never seen so much money in one place at one time.

Padraig gazed thoughtfully off in the distance and pursed his lips. "Three to one," he said. Everhardt nodded.

"Right," Padraig said and snapped the bag closed. "We'll mark this a provisional bet. We'll be wanting to count this first before we pay."

I looked over at Clemens, who was deep in conversation

with a laborer. They looked over briefly in my direction, and I thought I discerned the sharp features of Holmes under the cap! It took every particle of control not to wave back.

Then I heard my name. That is, I heard "Lord Dingwell! Your lordship!"

Padraig handed the case to me. "Mr. Everhardt does not feel comfortable with meself holding the stakes. Would you be so kind as to perform that function?"

I hadn't expected this. I knew most of what was to come, but I couldn't refuse. I clasped the bag and held it tight in my lap. The bell rang, and the fight was on. Everhardt leaped down and pushed his way to the ropes that formed the ring.

As before, Mad Mike stalked to the center. Two hours of hard fighting had taken its toll on him. His charges seemed to have no effect on the younger man, and he had taken enough blows to the head to make him cautious. A cut over one eye had opened, and a sheet of pale red painted his face. He had slowed down, jabbing to keep his opponent off-balance, and waiting for the right moment to unleash a still-powerful roundhouse.

There was a flurry of rapid blows between the two men. They parted, circled around each other energetically, then closed again. Then Sherrin went down on one knee! His gloves were down and he appeared to be clutching at his chest. The referee leaped in to protect him from Mad Mike, who backed away, a puzzled look spreading over his face.

Ford was breathing heavily, his face a mask of pain, and it was apparent to all he was suffering from a heart seizure. I leaped down. Padraig shouted "the bag," and I realized I was still holding the stake.

I thrust the bag into Maud Tapp's hands. "Keep an eye on her," I shouted to Padraig, and I pushed my way to the ring, and through the ropes.

Ford had fallen face-forward and was lying still. I kneeled beside him and rolled him over. He wasn't breathing. More men had entered the ring, and they were moving his limbs. Someone shouted, "Pick him up." I looked up and saw

Holmes, disguised as the laborer. Next to him was Everhardt. Together we lifted Ford's body.

His sudden collapse had thrown the crowd into a frenzy of cheers and boos. There were cries of "Murder!" and "Fake!" I heard the referee declare Mad Mike as the winner.

Then I heard screams and a chorus of police-whistles. Holmes looked over my shoulder. I turned my head, just enough to see Clemens. He looked furious, and he held a gun in his hand.

"Ford, you fraud!" he shouted over the noise. "I know you're shamming. Get up or I'll put you down for good!"

There were cries of "No!" and added to that were new cries of "Peelers!" "Crushers!" and "Coppers!" I could sense that men outside the ring trying to get out of the building at the same time more men were coming in, and Clemens continued to threaten to shoot Ford.

Then there was a shot. Everhardt looked stunned, his mouth falling open. Next to him, Holmes stood stock-still, frozen in amber, grimly aiming Everhardt's revolver at Clemens. Then he handed it back to Everhardt.

I looked around again, and Clemens was on the mat, blood trickling from his mouth. He still held the gun in his hand.

He was lost to sight as the policemen entered the ring, the ropes collapsing against their assault. They were led by Inspector Lestrade, who knelt briefly by Clemens, then stood and pointed out Everhardt and shouted "Arrest that man!" Some of them took Ford from us. I was pinioned in the arms of two policemen. The last I saw of Everhardt, he was being tugged away by Holmes, who was shouting something about not being caught up in a murder. Everhardt struggled and said something about his bag, but he realized the dangerous situation he was in and they fled toward the back of the building and out of sight.

The room slowly quieted down. I was still being held in place by the men, but they were no longer moving. They seemed frozen, looking around as if awaiting a signal.

Then we heard the cry, "They're gone!"

A general cheer went up. I was released. There were handshakes and jokes and even a few of the police officers clapping.

Clemens stood up and spat out the packet he had concealed in his mouth. "My that was filling," he pulled out a handkerchief, "but I wouldn't recommend it for the menu."

Padraig stood up from behind his table and said, "Thank you all. Police officers, please approach the table with your coats and helmets and give your name to the clerk. The gentlemen who are still around, please come to the address you were given tomorrow to return your clothes and pick up the rest of your pay. Teardown crew, please begin dismantling the ring. We want this place cleared in ten minutes!"

I was sore, sweat-drenched, and cheerful. It appears we had done it. We had cheated Everhardt of ten thousand pounds, and it looked like we got away with it.

Then I paused and looked around. Lady Maud was no longer in the room, and neither the money.

8. The Hangover

It was a glum gathering late that evening in Baker Street. I was laying on the couch, a damp rag cooling my forehead. Holmes was curled in his mouse-colored robe in his favorite chair. Clemens was furiously scowling and smoking by the fireplace. Only Padraig, seated at the table and dining on one of Mrs. Hudson's sandwiches, seemed unconcerned by the mood of the room.

Downstairs the door bell rang. I trudged downstairs and opened the door. Inspector Lestrade in his usual mode was sallow, sharp-featured and grumbling. He was in a much more cheerful mood tonight, going so far as to shake my hand and taking the steps two at a time. I caught up with him just as he was asking why it appeared like he was at a funeral rather than a celebration.

"It appears, Lestrade, that we were the biter bit," Holmes

said. "But let's not cause our mood to ruin our hospitality. The gasogene, tantalus and cigars are open for business."

"I'm not sad about this business at all," Lestrade poured himself a generous helping of whiskey. "Although I'll deny everything if this gets out. Where did you find those police officers for me to lead anyway?"

"The theater. They're from the production of *Penzance*. The costumes, too."

"Ah, I remember. They have a chorus of policemen singing that cheerful song. So what happened?"

"It turns out that we were played, Lestrade. On the way to Victoria Station, to put him on the train to Liverpool, a carriage passed us. A woman inside shouted, "Yoo hoo!" and waved a Gladstone bag at him. Everhardt was furious. He broke off from me and ran down the street after her and was lost from sight. It turns out that Lady Maud Tapp was not the daughter of his lordship, but Tilly Busby, an American actress with a talent for mimicking English ladies—"

"And the former partner of Charles Stuart Everhardt," Clemens said. "She was in on the scheme from the get-go. She let herself be courted by his lordship and introduced Everhardt to him. With her help, his lordship forked over thousands of pounds for his silver scam, then when they were back in London with the cash, Everhardt refused to pay her share."

Holmes took up the story, "She had heard about how Everhardt defrauded Clemens all those years ago and sought him out. When she discovered his connection to me, she decided to run a con of her own. Yes, laugh all you want Lestrade. I'm not ashamed to say I earned it. I assumed her story was correct. Why would she lie?"

"So all this was for nothing," Clemens said. "I don't even get a good story to tell out of it. That seems to happen every time I encounter you, Holmes, or one of your minions. No offense meant, Watson. And Holmes, my thanks to you for getting to his derringer and switching the bullets. It is an noble feeling to be shot at and missed, but I wouldn't want to make a habit of it. The odds are not worth the game."

Holmes nodded, then he chuckled thoughtfully. "The education of a consulting detective never ends. Fortunately, my earnings from my other cases have been generous, so Padraig and his band of merry schemers won't lose out by it. I will consider it tuition paid on a lesson well-learned: Crime does not pay."

"Well enough," Clemens said.

"Hand me my violin, Watson. I'm in the mood for a merry tune tonight!"

Afterward

I am an aficionado of true crime books, and one of my favorites is "The Big Con" by David W. Maurer. A linguistic professor researching criminal slang, he befriended several con men, and by gaining their trust gained entry into a subculture with its own rules and folkways. He discovered a community of nationwide con artists in which reputations matter, and where the tricks they played on marks would be refined, improved upon, and passed along.

I had read the book years ago, and loved "The Sting," the 1973 movie inspired by the book. When I picked it up again recently, I realized I wanted to use it in a story. The only question was how.

As I mentioned in the introduction, this story is unusual because it can't be fitted into the chronology of either Holmes or Twain. Those who count themselves as Sherlockians, who have not just the annotated editions but the 10-volume *Sherlock Holmes Reference Library*, will spot the obvious contradictions. Rather than decide, I chose to left it alone. There was a fun scene involving Lady Maud that would have to be cut. Rather than do that, I decided to leave it in.

The Adventure of the Whyos

The Adventure of the Whyos (1894)

I N THE LATE SPRING OF 1894, Mark Twain and I were getting along as well as two cats in a burlap bag. I was bankrupt. Henry Rogers, my good friend and the financial wizard behind Standard Oil, had convinced me to close my publishing concern, Webster & Co., and I was obliged to assume responsibility for its debts. I was a pauper, same as my father was fifty years before, and confirmed the old saw to those who knew the family back in Hannibal that "the apple doesn't fall far from the tree." People who knew me as Mark Twain expected tall tales and japes, and what they got instead was Sam Clemens, who held him responsible and was in no mood for jollity.

I had to close the house in Hartford that I had designed and lived in for nearly 20 years.[1] To live more cheaply, my family went to Paris. When I saw to the publishing house's corpse to the burial yard, I followed on the *SS City of New York*. The journey took a week, and I spent the whole of it in my stateroom, smoking cigars and immersed in my misery.

The ship docked in Southampton where Weatherwax shanghaied me. He was a florid bruiser-turned-business tycoon I was acquainted with in Hartford. He had read in the papers about my bankruptcy and my travel plans, and he wired me to expect him. He had a problem and needed my help.

Warned by Weatherwax's telegram, I laid low in my cabin and intended to plead ignorance of his cable as well as smallpox, but he bribed his way on board and barged in, acting like the wretched course of my life had been fated solely for the purpose of coming to his aid. I was overcome. The fight was

---

[1] Twain tended to conflate dates in his memoirs. Webster & Co. was closed in April of 1894, while Twain closed the Hartford house a year later after the failure of the Paige typesetting machine, at a loss of between $3 million and $5 million in today's currency.

not in me. My bags had been packed in anticipation of leaving at Le Havre six hours later, so he ordered them unloaded and bundled the whole of us into his growler.

Like me, Weatherwax had spent time in Nevada, but unlike me had struck it rich. A decade amid Eastern society had refined him; when he bit the end off his cigar, he opened the window before spitting out the stub. He set fire to the remainder and said, —

"Chloe's been in a bad way since you saw her last, Twain."

I winced at the mention of that cursed name. He said, —

"She's taken to her bed a week ago."

"My sympathies." I had known Chloe since she was a playmate to my daughters and thought she had the most sense in the family.

He explained that he was in England to get his only daughter knotted in matrimony to a fellow named Rannulph Winthrop, the son of a genuine copper-bottomed gold-plated English lord, only she wasn't having any of it. We were on our way to Chalkhills, his lordship's estate down the coast, where the lawyers were hammering out the contract, and he hoped that I could stop by and talk some sense into her.[1]

"I was afeared his lordship would call the match off, but he said he'd like nothing better but to carry on. Said it was obvious that the youngun's were meant for each other; Chloe just don't know it yet."

I eyed him critically. Was he a humbug or a hypocrite? I had met many aristocrats on my previous visits to the mother

---

[1] It was the fashion at that time for newly-rich Americans to marry their daughters into the aristocracy. The year before, Cornelia Martin wedded the 4th Earl of Craven in New York City. The Martins' bragging in the press about the wealth of the earl — whose demonstrated his interest in the ceremony by wearing boots with rolled-up pant legs — triggered a riot at the wedding. A side door into the church was found unlocked, and the public flooded in, disrupting the event and stealing anything that wasn't nailed down. The Martins fled to their home overseas, but the incident didn't deter them from seeking publicity. By their social-climbing standards, Paris Hilton and the Kardashians are pikers.

country, and if Rannulph's father was like them, Lord Winthrop had the morals of an imbecile and was chronically short of cash. Even if it meant his son marrying a near-corpse, Winthrop wasn't about to let pass this gold mine. Weatherwax poured smoke into the closed carriage like a steamship behind schedule and said, —

"Problem is, she's taken a dislike to Rannulph. You know what happens when a girl gets a notion into her head. Takes dynamite to blast it out."

He prattled on in this fashion, and I regretted my decision to join this fool's crusade. The carriage filled with smoke, and I had the notion of using it to screen my exit from the vehicle, but I decided against it. I wasn't as athletic as in my youth, and leaping from a speeding carriage no longer held any charm. Weatherwax let loose another chimney full of smoke and said, —

"I told my Chloe that it was her duty as a daughter to obey. Rannulph's as good as the next man, right Twain?"

"Assuming the next man was Jack the Ripper," I wanted to say, but the pressure in me was building like an overheated boiler. My concerns weighed heavily on my conscience, and it had been too long a voyage. Weatherwax fired another cannonade and said, —

"Don't know what to do. She's a girl, you know. We talk to her and talk to her. The lawyers are still tussling over the contract — and won't it make your eyes start to read the details in the Herald. Titled aristos are short on the market. Dukes and marquises have vanished, so viscounts are holding firm and asking for the moon — and getting it. You wouldn't believe what a mere baron without a castle would ask! Why —"

I fantasized shooting myself. Unfortunately, I missed, and instead, said, —

"Yes, yes, but what about Chloe? What's the matter with her?"

"Don't know. Doc won't say. Consumption, English cholera, the yim-yams. She's having trouble keeping her food down. I swear she's getting thinner by the day."

"So what do you want me to do?"

"Talk to her. Make her see reason. She loved playing with your Suzy and Clara. She looks to you as an uncle. She'll listen to you." He leaned closer. He had a glint in his eye that I used to see in the sharpest cards at the poker table. "I realize I'm keeping you away from your family when you're — I mean, I'll make it worth your while if you can swing this deal." And then he tapped the side of his nose and tipped me the wink.

Oh, how I wanted to tear him to pieces! In my palmier days, I would have raged at his effrontery. But I knew my financial situation, and while Livy has been the calm rock of reason, I still have to look to the family's future. So I denied my better nature and nodded as my conscience writhed.

Then he grew silent and worked his jaw some while the coastline rolled by. A notion arose that he was working up a head of steam to say something, and finally, he said, —

"This is strictly between us, Twain. We didn't meet out West, but I feel I can tell you things I can't tell a man like Beecher or Howell back in Hartford.[1] They're too refined for such sordid matters."

"And I'm a crude hayseed."

"Please! Please, Mark. I'm sorry. I didn't mean to insult you. But you know what I mean. I can tell you things."

He paused, then delivered his line like an actor on the Bowery stage, —

"Mark, I'm being blackmailed."

I gasped. I felt it was expected, but I sucked a large cloud of smoke that tickled my lungs, and I spoiled the effect by hacking into my handkerchief. Weatherwax pounded my back until the spasm passed and said, —

"A week back, Lord Winthrop's house was burgled. I

---

[1] Henry Ward Beecher (1813-1887) was a prominent clergyman and social reformer. He was the brother of Harriet Beecher Stowe, a neighbor of Twain in Hartford. William Dean Howell (1837-1920) was a literary critic and friend of Twain.

thought they hadn't touched us, but a few days later, I got this note." He pulled a crisp half-sheet out of his pocket.

It read, —

> "We found these prety notes. His lordship gits the rest of the stash unless you put £100 on the sundial at the Grecian folly at sundown. Tell no-one.
>
> "The Whyos"

"They had taken from Chloe's jewelry box letters she had written to some boy in Hartford."

"Who?" I couldn't help asking.

"I don't know! I never knew of this in the first place. She said it was a Lionel and that she had met him at church. She said the affair ended three years ago, and they returned each other's notes. But instead of burning the letters, she kept them! They sent a page from them with this demand."

As he blew on, I worked through the families we knew who might have a Lionel, but a candidate failed to appear. "It's no crime to fall in love," I said.

I swear Weatherwax blushed. It did not suit him. He said, —

"The . . . sentiments . . . were, well, I don't have to spell it out to you, do I, Twain? Even if his lordship didn't mind, if the New York papers got ahold of these, it would cause an uproar! You remember the Martin fiasco, don't you? They were forced to leave the country, with the papers hissing their spite at them."

"Did you pay?"

"Of course I paid! Cleaned me out of ready money. I had to send to Coutt's for more. I received the rest of the letter in next day's post."

"So your troubles are over."

Weatherwax's face grew red and he said, —

"But that's just one letter! They've got the rest. This gang will either bleed me dry or expose my daughter. I'm trapped, Twain, no two ways about it."

In the ordinary course of events, the prospect of extortion would have cheered me up considerable. I wasn't looking forward to playing Dutch uncle with the girl, but not even a broken-down pauper lecturer like Mark Twain was expected to play policeman. Help needed to be called in. But I knew only one man in England who would qualify, and after our last adventure, when I came within an inch of perdition, I swore that I'd rather let a tribe of Apaches skin me, or reread *The Deerslayer*,[1] before I darkened his threshold.

Then a vision of Chloe arose before me, and I knew I had no choice. I grumbled, —

"Weatherwax, I have this friend who might help . . . "

When Weatherwax heard of my proposal, he ordered the carriage to stop at the next station and shoved me onto an express to London. He would continue on to Chalkhills and talk his lordship into giving me room and board. I wired my family that I was delayed while he bought the ticket. It rankled me not to pay for it, but I swallowed the lie that he was obliged to do this because of the favor that I was doing him, not that I had no more on me than my name, a moth-destroyed purse and a stack of debts.

It was night by the time I reached that great metropolis, and the hansom cab bearing my remains to Baker Street rang on the cobblestones with that musical cadence familiar to all of London's visitors. The woman let me in at 221B and the moment I stood at the base of the staircase, I knew he was at home. The stench made my eyes water. My nose refused its

---

[1] From Twain's essay "Fentimore Cooper's Literary Offenses": "In one place in *Deerslayer*, and in the restricted space of two-thirds of a page, Cooper has scored 114 offences against literary art out of a possible 115. It breaks the record."

duty. I climbed into the sulfurous haze and, at my knock, was ordered to open the door.

Sherlock Holmes was deep into one of his chemical experiments. He brusquely begged me to park my corpse in the spare bed until he was finished. His rudeness when his mind was otherwise engaged was well-known to all, so I took no more offense than usual. I was exhausted from my long day's journey and quickly fell asleep amid the stink of bubbling gases and the clink of test-tubes.

I dreamed of Hell.

Holmes' mood improved dramatically with the coming day. He greeted me with the warmth born from our long association ¬reluctant on my part — and called downstairs for breakfast.

I like and admire the English, but my affection cannot extend to their cooking. It was designed by a remorseful Puritan hoping to achieve a state of grace by scouring the innards. And an English breakfast cooked by a Scot landlady must be intended as revenge for the occupation of her native heath.

We ate the kippered herrings and the grilled mess of tomatoes and bread and drank the strong coffee. I laid the case before Holmes and tried to make the mystery as enticing as my powers of speech could make it, but I needn't have worried. He said, —

"I have business that needs attending to in that part of the country. Are you familiar with the Whyos?"

His question startled me. Holmes has that nasty habit of asking questions to which only he knows the answer. But he couldn't dog me with this one.

"They're a gang of New York ruffians, found in the Five Points area."

Holmes nodded. He got up and searched among the line of scrapbooks on the wall until he pulled out one newspaper-sized volume. "One of the biggest," he said, opening the cover. I glanced over his shoulder and marveled at the stories culled from the city's newspapers. He said, —

"This concern has been in operation since your Civil War, and they have covered the range of criminal activities. At one time, they dominated Manhattan so thoroughly that other gangs needed to ask permission to operate there. Their crimes ranged from theft and extortion to murder. One of them even went so far as to carry a menu of their services."

He tapped his finger on a crudely-handwritten half-sheet that described such choice selections as "Punching $2," "Ear chawed off $15," "Shot in leg $25" and "Doing the big job $100 and up."

He closed the book and slid it back into its place on the shelf. "They're nearly finished as a major criminal force in New York, but it appears some of their number are attempting to rebuild their fortunes by exporting their expertise to our country. I suspect they may have a hand in the job I was hired for. We'll go down today. Are you willing to accompany me?"

"Of course. But where's Watson? Is he coming?"

He shook his head and the regret in his voice was apparent. "After my affair at Reichenbach, he returned to his practice and is there yet, dealing with consumption and dropsy and the membranous croup. Yet, if I know my man, he'll sell his practice soon and rejoin me at Baker Street."[1]

We left Baker Street and boarded the train at Waterloo accompanied by a stack of newspapers. I never saw a man who had such an appetite for news as Holmes. London was a great town for newspapers, too, with at least a dozen of them in all flavors. Our journey was quiet as we smoked and read, but presently he shoved the stack aside and we talked. He wanted to hear my views on the great financial panic of last year, when a number of railroads collapsed. Credit became as hard to find as a banker's smile, and no less than sixteen thousand businesses went under, one of them being mine.

---

[1] Which Watson would do three months later, unbeknownst to him at the time with Holmes' assistance, as recounted in "The Adventure of the Norwood Builder."

Holmes was a good listener, and when I had finished describing the panic on Wall Street, crowded with investors watching their fortunes disappear with each swipe of the chalkboard, he refilled his pipe and said, —

"A number of my countrymen had invested heavily in those railroads and suffered severe reverses as a result. Unfortunately, I expect we'll see more of these shocks. It was a shot across our bow when events in Argentina could cause a bank like Barings to fail.[1] But let us turn our minds to more profitable uses. Your news about events at Chalkhills was most welcome. Several country homes in that area have been robbed. The gang strikes when the home is empty or held by a few retainers. The valuables small and large are carried away, from the plate and paintings to furniture and statuary. This could be our best opportunity to get a line on this gang."

"How do the Whyos tie into this?"

"That remains to be seen. Even after Moriarty's fall, the Empire has more than enough experienced thieves for there to be no need to import more."

"And what about the extortion?"

Holmes smiled as toward a child asking where the sun goes at night. He said, —

"I won't fail you on that count. Surely a solution has already presented itself to you."

A caustic reply came to my mind about Holmes' indulgence in stagy jim-crack, but I bit it back. I can't stand this supercilious claptrap, but Holmes is a genius at what he does, and genius must be served. I'm sure people say the same about me.

A cart was waiting for us at the station. A young man in the rough clothes of the drover's trade transferred our bags

---

[1] Holmes was referring to the Panic of 1893, when overinvestment in railroads and stock manipulations had thrown the United States into a recession. The warning shot had been fired as far back as 1890, when Baring Brothers, England's largest banking house, collapsed due to overextended loans to Argentina.

and with a courtly "Arfter yew, gents," bade us to climb aboard. Holmes said, —

"You must be Rannulph, Lord Winthrop's son."

A grin split his face at being found out, and he offered his hand to shake. "Right as rain, sir. How d'yer guess?"

"The hands can tell much when one knows where to look. They are rough from use, but well-cared for. The nails are trimmed and squared, not thick and chipped. Your face is fair, telling me that either you are not out in the sun much, or you take care to wear that wide-brimmed hat when you are. This is confirmed by your tanned hands that end at the sleeve. Finally, you also bear a Roman nose, the hallmark of the Winthrop profile."

Rannulph chuckled as he parked himself on the bench in front of us and picked up the reins. He said, —

"That's as good a trick as any I seen on the stage. Helping out on the estate helps us keep an eye on the workers."

"What do you raise?" Holmes said.

"Mostly barley and potatoes. Quite a lot for this area. We set up a shipping concern to export the lot up the coast, even to France. I oversee that end."

I said, —

"The workers must appreciate the attention that you pay to their welfare."

"Oh, they hate it. They took great offense when I took to joining them in the fields. Complained to the governor, they did, when they caught him between routs, rides and revels. Now, I don't help 'em as much with the real work and they chalk the rest of it up as 'the young master's queer touches.'"

We drove on in silence as the town gave way to fields. Hoards of midges swarmed us. We swatted our hats at them for a time before giving up and letting them feast.

Holmes said, —

"I understand that you and Miss Weatherwax are engaged to be married. My congratulations to you both."

Watching his back gave me no clue to his mood, but the

quiet stretched far longer this time.

"Ah, weel, that has not happened, yet. Early days."

"Negotiations can drag on with so much at stake, but I'll wager they'll resolve themselves to everyone's satisfaction," Holmes said.

"Maybe," he said. "The governor wants the estate to stay on a sound financial footing. We just disagree on the means. Here's the turn into Chalkhills, gents. Mind your hats, the ride's going to be a little rough."

That's when the first ruts hit the axles amidships. We jostled about, our teeth banging and clashing, until a branch road turning toward some barn-like buildings took the ruts with them. Rannulph apologized; the combination of a rough winter and recent rains turned the road into muck and repairs had not commenced. Emulating the great detective methods, I concluded that whatever the source of his lordship's fortune, it did not lay with concrete or paving stones.

Weatherwax had been anxious for our arrival. He popped out of the mansion's front door at our approach, and arranged with a servant to move our luggage to our rooms. His lordship was out shooting, so Holmes asked Weatherwax to convey us to the invalid's room at once.

We followed Weatherwax through a maze of corridors and great halls until we reached the bedroom wing. Before the final door, he muttered, —

"I only hope that harridan isn't guarding the bedside."

What a pitiable sight! The shades were drawn and the gas lamp by the bed was the merest flicker. Chloe lay under the sheets, her eyes closed, her cheeks hollow and her eyes rimmed in red. Her hair spread like damp seaweed across her pillow, like Ophelia pulled from the brook. A small band of gold set with a single pearl on her left hand was the lone spot of cheerful color over the dismal scene.

Holmes crept to her bedside and gazed at her in that peculiar fashion that always gave me chills. A serpent eyeing his prey could not have been more still. He said, —

"Part the curtain, Clemens, if you would."

I did, but only for a moment. A sliver of light crossed Chloe's face and she flinched and cried, "No, no, leave the oysters be, for the love of God!"

Her outburst startled me so I slapped the heavy drapes closed. The door to a connecting room opened behind us and a young woman, slender as a reed and quick as a whippet, strode in and hissed, —

"What is all this? Who are you?"

Weatherwax spoke harshly and said, —

"This is Mr. Holmes and Mr. Twain. I asked them—"

"Oh, for shame, Mr. Weatherwax! Don't you recall the doctor's instructions?" She shooed us toward the door like she was herding a flock of geese. "No visitors and no disturbances. It could be fatal!" Chloe chimed in with a terrible moan and her babble pursued us as we fled. At the door, I looked back to see the woman dabbling at Chloe's forehead with a damp cloth and murmuring soothing words.

Weatherwax closed the door and Holmes gently led me away. I was horrified. Chloe looked far worse than I expected, and a dread rose in me that her time was near. It brought vividly to memory the suffering of my son, Langdon, dead these many years.

Weatherwax fumbled with his watch and turned to view its face by the light of the window. He stood there quietly for a moment with only the ticking of the hall clock for conversation, then he wiped his brow with a spotted red handkerchief and said, —

"Hotter than Hades in there. Come on, let's go see his lordship."

I linked his arm with mine and said, —

"She'll recover. She's young and vital."

Holmes — as unaffected with emotion as usual — asked, —

"Who was that young woman?"

"Her? That's Lord Winthrop's daughter, Judith. She's been looking after Chloe. That's her bedroom she came roaring out of."

"Is she solely responsible for Chloe's care?" Holmes said.

"She hovers over her like a mother hen when Dr. Conover's not here."

"Is he the local man, then?"

That roused Weatherwax. He said, —

"I should say not! He's one of the most eminent physicians in London, from Harley Street itself, with fees to match! Take a look at his latest bill."

Holmes glanced at the paper and I caught a glint of understanding in his eye. He handed it back and said, —

"Then she must be in very good hands. Now, I think it's time to beard the lion in his den."

His lordship was seated before the library fire, fresh from a morning spent massacring his kingdom's waterfowl. Since his wife died a few years back, he had been free to indulge his many hobbies involving the slaying of various beasts. He had been happy to leave Judith to run the household. It gave him the double the savings from treating a trusted family member as an employee while not having to dish out cash for a wedding dowry. All this galloped through my mind while watching his valet engaged in removing Winthrop's boot, which had not been scraped of bits of the countryside. His lordship assisted by pressing his still-shod counterpart against the man's backside.

Batting away the few midges that followed us inside, I mentioned my purpose in being there and introduced Holmes as a particular friend, here to advise me on the best way to solve the problem, keeping his true purpose under a bushel basket.

Winthrop repeated Weatherwax's arrangement to put us up for the night, and we accepted. He added, —

"I don't have to tell you gentlemen how anxious I am to have this wedding come off. I'm sure Mr. Weatherwax will richly reward you for your trouble."

Holmes said, —

"Your concern for your son's future wife is admirable, sir. Between the negotiations and the recent burglary, the strain must be burdensome. May I ask if any progress had been made in locating the gang?"

Lord Winthrop shook his head and said, —

"Constable Noakes is excellent only at chivvying the drunks and investigating the burning of hayricks."

We were interrupted by a servant bearing a coil of paper on a silver tray. Winthrop passed the strip through his fingers and I recognized it as a stock-ticker tape with the latest prices. He frowned, then he fixed me with his eye and said, —

"Mr. Clemens, you're from New York."

I admitted I was familiar with the metropolis.

"A fascinating city. I have not been there myself, but both Rannulph and Judith have visited friends there. You know Mr. Jay Gould. His railroad stock is profitable to buy, I believe."

I cannot fathom why a foreigner would assume that a resident — or in my case, a visitor only — to a city of over a million souls would be on good terms with them all. I said, —

"Men like Gould, Vanderbilt and Morgan don't enter business to lose money, but I can't say that's true for anyone who joins them."

He fumed at this, then rose and excused himself to get sluiced down before tea. Judith came in, and his lordship suggested that she show us about the place.

British mansions tend to be built on the notion that giants may someday decide to take up residence. We wandered amid soaring ceilings and oversized furniture. With Holmes' encouragement, Judith regaled us with the family history, mostly honest, and a complete description of the bric-a-brac. Her knowledge of furniture, its designers and provenance of the better pieces, was encyclopedic. We ended the tour in the billiard room, where she suggested we might relax before dinner.

This suited me something powerful. I had a table installed in my home in Hartford, and there is no better exercise to be found. I'm sure there are billiard parlors in heaven.

In England's better homes, a proper billiard room contains two tables, one for snooker and another with holes in it for the honest American game. While Holmes sat in a chair and smoked his pipe, I racked the balls and Weatherwax and I stroked for lead. But my heart wasn't in it. My concern for Chloe affected me, so much that my eye was off and Weatherwax was able to run the table and pocket a side bet I could ill-afford to lose. I was grateful when Holmes interrupted the transaction and asked Weatherwax for a list of Chloe's complaints. He said, —

"Fever, weakness in the limbs, sensitivity to light, headache, great fatigue, cramps, loss of appetite. She's been unable to keep down her food. You heard her babbling of oysters. She's like that when the fever's on her."

"What has Dr. Conover to say about this?"

"He prescribes what he calls blue pill and black draught and says that the disease will declare itself in a few days. Then he presents his bill."

He sat back in his chair and relit his pipe. "Let us turn to this threatening letter. How did you receive it?"

"By mail three days ago. A servant from the hall fetches the bag from the post office and Judith parcels it out at lunch."

"And it contained this note," he pulled the sheet Weatherwax had given me in the carriage, "and part of a letter?"

"That's right. It never occurred to me they were, well —"

"More than acquaintances. Yes, I understand. Have you talked to Chloe about it?"

"No, Judith forbade it. The doctor ordered complete rest."

"Do you still have the letter? I must see it."

The man shambled off, looking wretched. I shot a game in the ensuing silence while Holmes paced and smoked. He was cogitating hard, and I knew to let him be. He stopped and said, —

"A very pretty problem this is, Clemens."

"I'm glad you think so," I said with asperity. "A girl's dying and you're entertained. Her funeral will be the high point of your social calendar."

He idly rolled one of the balls on the table. "Oh, I don't think it'll go that far. I have a theory, but I need a day or so to pull it together, two at the outside."

I slammed the stick on the table.

"Confound you! Talk sense."

He put his hand on my shoulder like he was calming a skittish colt and said, —

"Miss Weatherwax is shamming, Clemens. Did you remark her face?"

"You saw her only for a moment."

"You see, but you do not think," he said in that superior way of his. "You shined a light on the truth, and a literal one at that. There was kohl under her eyes and a touch —the merest touch —of slap on her cheeks to emphasize the cadaverous effect. And one does not normally see smears of makeup on the pillows. You saw my Hamlet on the New York stage; I made the application of make-up a specialty of mine, and wrote a monograph on the subject. With the proper tools, Clemens, one can bring the dead to life and life to the dead."

I was so overjoyed at the news that I forgave Holmes his monstrous ego, and it was there that I blundered terribly. Weatherwax came in bearing the note for Holmes. He looked so miserable that it wrung my heart. As usual, Holmes ignored everything going on around him. He took the note to a French window and searched it intensely, so I laid a hand on Weatherwax's shoulder, and to comfort him, I said, —

"Put your mind at rest, Weatherwax. Holmes here has determined that Chloe's not sick at all. She's —"

"Twain!" Holmes said. But it was too late, as I realized what that meant.

Weatherwax pumped my hand and said, —

"So that's her game. Thank you, Twain. We'll see who's

shamming who—"

Judith encountered Weatherwax in the doorway, and he threw her the most terrible look. She was perplexed, but recovered and came to me and apologized most prettily for ordering us out of the sick-room. I assured her that I had been thrown out of worse places with less courtesy. I introduced her to Holmes, who was still studying Chloe's note by the light of a window.

Then Weatherwax returned, rubbing his hands with the air of a man who had performed a full day's work to his satisfaction and said, —

"That's that. I conceded the last few points. Chloe is now officially betrothed."

Judith turned pale and cried, —

"But her illness—"

"A sham, Twain assures me. Right, Mark?"

I babbled that I was guessing, but my stock sank rapidly under Judith's furious look. Holmes said, —

"I'm afraid that's true."

Judith said nothing but she played with a small pearl ring on her finger, and her look said it would please her if I had the courtesy to fall dead of apoplexy.

"I must inform Chloe," she said and left. Weatherwax said, —

"And I must tell my wife and see to the packing. Chloe's to be married in six weeks in New York and there's a mort of work to be done."

The door closed and it was left to Holmes to complete my humiliation:—

"There must be something in the American character that encourages babbling. Your lack of discretion makes me long for my Watson."

Holmes abandoned me in the billiard room, saying he had to move fast before we left the next morning. I spent the rest of the afternoon playing and smoking, but my heart wasn't into either pleasure. Afternoon tea held no charm for me, so I did not attend.

Then I heard a voice behind me. "May I join in?"

Chloe had walked into the room and picked up a cue stick. She looked frail as a reed, but she had scrubbed color back into her cheeks. But she still seemed weighed by her circumstances.

We did not play a game, but scattered the balls across the table and took shots as we saw them. We discussed Suzy and Clara and remembered happier times in Hartford, the tea parties and parlor concerts we held, and the hikes through the fields. I looked inside her for the bright flower of a girl that I knew, but she was gone.

Weatherwax's charge hung like a dark storm cloud over us. I had to, as the Bard said, screw my courage to the sticking point to bring up the subject and said, —

"Your father means the best for you, you know."

She knocked a ball across the table and into the corner pocket. I had long suspected that she and the girls had been practicing in my office while I was away, and her skill with the stick confirmed it. She said, —

"What do you think of Rannulph?"

"He seems like a fine lad," I said. "He has less of Lord Winthrop in him than you fear."

"Do you think I should marry him?" She turned to me for an answer. Her wide, brown eyes searched mine for any sign of humbug, as she did when she was a child, which meant, at the risk of repeating myself, that I had to lie like a congressman.

"Yes."

She held my gaze and then turned to study the table.

"Our minister in Hartford told us that families negotiated marriages in Jesus' time, like with Joseph and Mary."

"Yes, that is true."

"Do you think they were happy?"

"I do."

She shot again, a two-bank shot that failed to find the side pocket. As I bent over to return fire, she said, —

"Are you happy with Livy?"

I scratched, and she laughed with the cruelty native to girls.

"I'm sorry, Mr. Clemens. I didn't mean to corner you with such a personal question."

"Nonsense." I retreated to the table to pick up my cigar. "I can tell you that she is the light of my life. Without her, I would be a tramp miner. Or tramp writer."

"So she lifted you from the gutter and showed you the stars," she said. "But if Rannulph is as good as you say he is, I won't have as much work to do."

"Oh, I'm sure he has his faults. All men do."

She nodded as if I had confirmed her suspicions. The faint clamor of the dinner gong sounded. "I must leave you to your game and dress for dinner."

"Until then, Miss Weatherwax."

"Until then, Mr. Clemens."

Dinner that evening would have tried a saint's patience. Winthrop and Weatherwax kept up a fair rumble over the virtues of American versus English horses. Judith was glum and picked at her plate. Rannulph ignored me, since I was responsible for his future unhappiness. Chloe and her mother were civil to me but felt no obligation to sparkle. At one point, Weatherwax caught my eye. He nodded to Chloe and smiled at me. It had the feel of a pat on the head for being a good little boy.

To tell the truth, my feelings were in a tangle. Fulfilling my charge did not please me. The marriage would go forward, thanks to my —Holmes' —intervention, but I did not feel like celebrating. There was an ache in me without a clear source or cause.

Holmes walked in between removes and was in disgusting fine spirits. He joined in the men's talk about Shires and Morabs, Dale Ponies and Morgans like he had spent his life in the saddle.

The talk had turned from horses in general to Lord Winthrop's in particular. There was a particularly fine colt called Polestar he had his eye on for running at the Chester races.

Chloe said, —

"Lord Winthrop, I know so little about horses so I hope you can educate me. How can you be so sure this colt will run well?"

The old duffer preened at being able to act as an authority. "Because his bloodlines are sound, Miss Weatherwax. He was sired by Melbourne, out of Seaweed, both splendid runners."

"So you investigated the horse's parents?"

With a condescending chuckle he said "that's a pretty way of looking at it."

"Then may I ask after your bloodlines, sir?" A puzzled look crossed his face. "I ask on behalf of myself. If I am a filly charged with begetting an heir and a spare, I think I have a right to know. Is there insanity in your family? imbecility? Any whelps that needed putting down, lest they weaken the bloodline?"

The air around the table was charged. Mrs. Weatherwax, a female doppelganger of Mr. Weatherwax, cooed, "Oh, my," while his lordship's face turned beet red. Rannulph continued to dine as if he hadn't heard a word, while Judith cocked her head as if she were hearing an unusual birdcall.

"Pray, tell us, my lord," Chloe continued. "What are your qualities? I can see from your legs that you're not much of a runner, and your temper indicates you throw your riders too often. Were they bred out of your son?"

"Miss WEATHERWAX—" he said.

"Chloe, leave the table!" Mr. Weatherwax thundered. "Twain, what the hell are you braying at?"

I couldn't help it. I had been trying to suppress an outburst, but I had been flushed from the bushes, so I laughed my heart out. While Lord Winthrop sputtered his objections, tears sprang from my eyes and I slapped the table until the glasses chimed.

"Chloe's got you there, Lord Winthrop," I finally choked out. "And I think she has a point."

"Twain — " Weatherwax growled. "We agreed, — "

"Oh, stuff your agreement," I said. "Chloe," and I kept my face as straight as a card sharp. "You should marry who you want. Marry Polestar, if you like. I daresay he'd prove a fit husband."

"She'll marry Rannulph Winthrop," Weatherwax emphasized and raised his glass to him. "And no amount of rude behavior will change that."

"Hear, hear," Lord Winthrop said.

"And Twain," Weatherwax said. "Don't think you'll get one dime out of me."

"I wouldn't touch your tainted money," I said.

"That's right! Tain't yours at all!" He brightened at that. "Hey, I made a funny! Lord Winthrop, is it time for the port?"[1]

It was a relief when the cloth was drawn and the ladies excused themselves. In disgrace, I begged off an evening of claret and cigars and tottered to bed. Not that they were demanding that I stay. My propensity for speaking out of turn overwhelmed my reputation as a storyteller. Not that I minded, because speaking my piece greatly eased my tattered soul.

Still, it was an unhappy Sam Clemens who sat smoking in bed that night, writing a memoranda of the day's events. The ghost of my publishing house rose before me like the de-

---

[1] Years later, someone commented to Twain that his Standard Oil friend Henry Rogers "is a good fellow. It's a pity his money is tainted." Twain replied, "It's twice tainted. Tain't yours and tain't mine."

ceased Marley. I missed the comfort and counsel of my Livy, as well as my daughters. It seemed that everything I touched turned to ash, and I was not looking forward to resuming my journey tomorrow leaving Chloe stranded in a marriage unwanted by everyone except the fathers. I closed my notebook, extinguished my cigar, and lay back, but, as usual, sleep would not come to relieve my sorrows.

Blinking in the dark, my despair sunk as far as regretting disappointing Holmes, even if he does scrape my soul like a healthy conscience.

Then, a woman's shriek sent lightning down my spine. I leaped out of bed and was tucking my nightshirt into my pants when Holmes came to fetch me.

We tracked the hullabaloo to Chloe's sick-room. The place was a mess, with clothes thrown everywhere and the furniture tumbled about as evidence of a great struggle. Lord Winthrop was berating the maid with a letter in his hands and demanding answers, and she replied between sobs that she heard the sound of breaking glass and found the room empty and the French doors hanging shattered on their hinges.

He spotted us and charged, waving the letter in his hands and said, —

"These damned scoundrels kidnapped Miss Weatherwax!"
The note read, —

"We have the gurl. Will send word how much
to have her back in one peece.
                                   "The Whyos"

"What is this 'Whyos,' what? what?" his lordship demanded. I explained as best I could — leaving out the blackmail scheme — as he went on with the hellfire and damnation over the broken glass and the damage to the room, before returning the harass the maid some more.

I walked to the sideboard, where stood a decanter and

glass filled with a clear liquid. Next to it was a plate in which were floated several sheets of brown paper. The midges had found the open door, and I slapped at them, causing several to join their mates floating in the water. Holmes was on his hands and knees by the French doors, nosing over the glass shards with a magnifying glass. Behind him stood Weatherwax, white-faced and bearing a candelabra in a shaky hand that was dripping wax. He said, —

"We have to do something. We must call the police."

Winthrop ordered the maid to inform the head butler, then joined me at the sideboard. He picked up the glass and said, —

"It'll take an hour for Noakes to get here, but we have to act now." He was about to take a drink when, from the floor, Holmes spotted him out of the corner of his eye. He shouted "No!" and flipped his lens at Lord Winthrop. It caught the glass at the stem and dashed it from his hand. He whipped around in anger but Holmes spiked his guns.

"It would be worth your life to drink that," he said. "Come, Clemens. There's not a moment to lose."

We ran onto the terrace and raced for the stables where we secured two horses from the sleepy stable boy. I said, —

"Holmes, what happened?"

"You just witnessed the denouement of your revelation. More fool I was not to have anticipated this, but logic cannot always deduce the ways of the heart. Let's ride, Clemens. We have to get there before it's too late."

"Too late for what? Chloe's been kidnapped."

Holmes had mounted and was off as I shouted, "What are you on about?" after him. Cursing a streak that would have horrified Livy. I mounted my horse and followed.

We pounded down a road that moonlight had turned into a river of silver, past shrubbery turned into glowing fantastical shapes. I had not galloped like this for years, so the first mile racked my bones and panic tightened my grip on the reins. We reached the coast road and turned toward Southampton.

Our screws were thundering at a steady pace so I could lift myself in the saddle and looked about. Over the cliff to one side could be heard the rumble of the surf. On the other side, the rising moon illuminated the rolling fields of flax.

When we reached town, Holmes slowed his horse to a trot, giving me a chance to catch up. The chase had proved as beneficial as any tonic. Everything had been forgotten — my decrepitude, my financial worries, my failures. I was on an adventure, like Huck and Jim floating down my beloved Mississippi, and I must have sounded like a boy again when I said, —

"Where to, Holmes?"

"The wharf."

Even though it was late, there was still great activity as stevedores worked to load and unload their cargos. We rode past the slips and, at every boat, Holmes asked if any passengers had boarded within the last half-hour. All said no until we reached the steamer Lochinvar. Smoke poured from her stacks, and the mate of the watch said she was bound shortly for America. A half-crown bought us permission to come aboard and directions to their cabin.

At the door, Holmes said, —

"Do you have your gun?"

I told him it was at the wash.

"Then be on your guard for anything. They're desperate."

He knocked and sang out in a Boston accent that the captain would like to speak with them.

The door opened to reveal a tall, thin man in a moustache and bowler. He gasped and tried to close the door, but Holmes pushed in. The man raced for the table and pulled a pistol from a Gladstone bag, but Holmes twisted it from his hand. In two swipes, he pulled off the hat and moustache.

"Judith," I cried.

A connecting door opened and Chloe entered. It was an improved edition of the young woman I saw at dinner. The color was high in her cheeks, and her smile of welcome was charming. Kidnappings proved very agreeable to her. She said, —

"Hello, Mr. Clemens, Mr. Holmes. How lovely of you to see us off."

Holmes bowed and said, —

"Miss Weatherwax. You led us on a merry dance. I'm glad to see you've dropped the masquerade."

She laughed and said, —

"Oh yes! I was so looking forward to home again. How did you see through it?"

"Your extortion note spoke very clearly. Despite the misspelled words, the hand that wrote 'Grecian folly' could not be from a New York gang member. And I doubt that a Whyo would charge for blackmail five times the going rate for 'doing the big job.'"

Chloe said, —

"I apologize on their behalf, Mr. Holmes. I knew it was all the cash father had at hand."

I said, —

"What do you need the money for?"

"To pay Dr. Conover," Judith said. "He helped us so much with his lengthy treatment of Chloe's illness. It was only right to compensate him for his trouble. But now that we need the money for our passage, I'm afraid he'll never receive it."

Holmes said, —

"Don't worry about your friend. He's been billing your father at thrice the going rate for a Harley Street physician."

"How did you learn of our scheme?"

He pulled from his pocket Chloe's note to Lionel. "This love note. The ink is much too fresh for a three-year-old letter, and the paper bears the same watermark as the extortion and kidnapping notes."

Chloe laughed again, and, despite the trouble she had put us through, it did my heart good to hear her. Her mood turned serious, however, when a sailor knocked at the door and said it was time to cast off. She said, —

"Must we go with you?"

Holmes said, —

"I'm afraid so."

"But we meant no harm."

"This is about more than fleeing an unwanted attachment. My job was to unmask the Whyos and their connections on this side of the Atlantic, and I have done so."

He looked at Judith, but she stood firm and straight as a willow reed with a damn-your-eyes impudence.

He said, —

"There's no further need for dissimulation. The scheme was simple: the gang would steal from country homes, ship the swag to America in the guise of lawful goods and sell it there. But they needed someone with shipping connections, someone who knew where the treasures were located and who could be trusted not to preach on them. The coastal connection was vital to the solution, so I concentrated there, looking for large unexplained shipments of goods. I eliminated all of the ports but this one, and Clemens' call for help provided an ideal opportunity to visit this area.

"I must admit it was fortune that brought us to the right door. The only question was which family members were involved. You and your brother have been to America; your father had not. You're knowledgeable about the furnishings; your brother has the shipping connections. And, just to make sure, I visited your outbuildings down that rutted road before dinner and found the spoils of—."

Holmes' story was interrupted by another knock at the door. The sailor said, —

"Stay or leave, makes no matter to us. But if you stay, you gotta pay."

We took charge of the women and went off to roust the local constabulary. Holmes told Noakes that Inspector Lestrade was expected down from Scotland Yard by the first train to take control of the proceedings. Judith was arrested, and Chloe asked to stay behind to keep her company. As it was the shank of the night, we agreed, but not until I gave her a hug and informed her of where we were staying in Europe. There was more I wanted to say, but after the excitement of discovery had faded, it was clear she was worn to a nubbin.

We rode back slowly to the house on horseback, the moon lighting our way. The sea breeze picked up, keeping our cigars alight and whipping our smoke away.

I despise the moment in stories when the Great Detective is sitting high, wide and handsome, and prepared to reveal all to his adoring acolyte. After expending thousands of words in murder and mayhem, it seems obscene to take any pleasure in the wrecks of people's lives. That may suit a man of Watson's sheep-like demeanor, but we Westerners are made of sterner stuff. But as I mused over the events of the day, I came to an understanding. We were placed on this Earth to question, and the need for answers can become overpowering. I just didn't know how to ask.

But Holmes was an old hand at this game. He waded in and said, —

"It was a near-run thing in Chloe's bedroom, Clemens. You remark the paper in the basin? That was flypaper. Soaking it in water brings up the arsenic. His lordship would have been dissatisfied with his drink if I hadn't intervened."

I wished now I hadn't been told that. I said, —

"She meant to destroy herself."

"Until Judith interrupted with an alternative. She convinced Chloe to flee, packed what they could and tumbled the room to make it look like a kidnapping. Judith probably lashed out at the French doors for a touch of verisimilitude. But as the blackmail scheme was a fraud, I reasoned this probably was as well. Besides, the ladies took care not to crush the glass into the carpet, as it would have been if a gang of men had stomped into the room after kicking open the doors."

"And the boat to America, how did you figure that?"

"Logical inference from the available data."

"You mean you guessed."

Holmes ignored my jibe. He was in full lecture mode, which cannot be interrupted by any act short of dynamiting. "They had two choices: flee into England or away by boat. The authorities would be sure to watch the roads, the ports, and the railways, whereas no one would enquire after a couple seeking passage to the states."

"And the disguise?"

"Final proof of her criminality. She was prepared to flee before she entered Chloe's bedroom, probably as a result of my appearance. My name is not unknown in the criminal underworld, Clemens, and showing up on her doorstep made her suspicious. She used Chloe's affection for her, combined with your blowing up their scheme to derail the wedding plans, as a means of escape. Which was fortunate for Chloe's sake. Perhaps— ," he mused, "she used the disguise in her dealings with the gang. A minor point, but worth investigating."

We smoked quietly for awhile until I said, —

"Holmes, was it necessary to have Judith arrested?"

"Would you rather they sailed to America?"

"I'd rather Chloe was happy and away from her grasping, social-jumping scoundrel of a father."

"With only a few pounds between them?"

"I would have given her Rogers' address at Standard Oil. He would have seen after them on my word."

"And her brother? should he get away as well? Clemens, this gang robbed mansions of tens of thousands of pounds worth of goods."

"Oh, who cares a flip about the gee-gaws of the rich! You unmasked them. That should be plenty."

"I don't believe the owners or your public would agree."

I brooded about that. It seemed like Chloe was back where she started. Holmes — blast his genius for mind-reading — must have understood what I was getting at, for he clapped me on the shoulder and said, —

"Don't feel bad for Chloe. She won't be marrying after all, and I imagine that Mr. Weatherwax would be most grateful to us for being saved from the consequences of a scandalous match."

"Only to make another for her; perhaps with an even worse character."

"The answer to that is a closed book at present," he said solemnly, the ass. "We have a more pressing concern with the welcome we'll receive at Chalkhills. Will Lord Winthrop keep his promise to let us stay after unmasking his children as part of the Whyos gang, or must we doss somewhere else? It will be an interesting test of the English capacity for politeness."

Afterwards

This was the first story, published on the Amazon Kindle in 2014. What I had forgotten until I looked through my notes recently was that I had written it in 2001. So what follows is a recreation, based on the printed evidence, of how I came about to pair an American humorist with a fictional British consulting detective.

It all began in a sparsely decorated two-room basement apartment outside Harrisburg, Pa. I had moved there in 2001 from South Carolina to take up a copy editing job at a newspaper. While my wife stayed behind to take care of the kids, ages 11, 4, and 2, a dog and four cats, and sell the house, it was my job to go to work and hunt for a new place to live. That left me with a lot of time on my hands. I had no TV and dial-up Internet access, so I had plenty of time on my hands. Stimulus #1 for creativity: boredom.

The previous year, I had reviewed two collections of Sherlockian pastiches edited by Marvin Kaye. These books planted the seed for this series. The central conceit behind *Resurrected Holmes* was that a wealthy collector paid enormous sums to famous writers to concoct a pastiche story based on Watson's untold tales. So we got John Gregory

Betancourt writing "The Adventure of the Amateur Mendicant Society" in H.G. Wells' voice and Kaye inhabiting Rex Stout to pen "Too Many Stains (The Adventure of the Second Stain)." *The Confidential Casebook of Sherlock Holmes* imaginatively mingled the great detective with P.G. Wodehouse, Ida Tarbell, Consuelo Vanderbilt, and even Conan Doyle.

So with all these mash-ups in my head, eight years before Seth Grahame-Smith took it to the profitable extreme with *Pride and Prejudice and Zombies,* I decided to throw together Twain and Sherlock. Twain is one of my favorite writers, as my much-fondled copy of the two-volume *Unabridged Mark Twain* proves.

It wasn't the first time Twain had appeared in print as a detective. Peter J. Heck wrote six novels in the Mark Twain mysteries, two of which I have: *Death on the Mississippi* and *A Connecticut Yankee in Criminal Court.* In those stories, Twain took on the Sherlock role, with his fictional secretary, Wentworth Cabot, acting as his Watson. As I looked through them, I wondered: Could I do something like this as well? And what if I could tell it in an authorial voice, like the writers in *Resurrected Holmes*?

Only one way to find out.

To make it even more challenging, I decided to not just tell the story in Twain's distinctive voice, but I would set it against both men's chronology. I didn't want these stories to appear out of time, with a white-suited Twain — an affectation he adopted late in his life — dropping into Baker Street on a whim. In short, I decided to play the Game.

For those of you who aren't members of the Baker Street Irregulars, or who aren't Holmesians, let me explain. It consists of a group hallucination adopted by members of Sherlock Holmes fandom.

There are a few rules. First, Sherlock Holmes existed. Dr. Watson existed. The characters in the canonical stories existed. Conan Doyle existed, but merely as Watson's literary agent.

Second, all of these stories took place sometime in the

historical timeline of Britain. But when? That's the beginning of The Game.

Sometimes, Watson made it easy. In "A Scandal in Bohemia," he firmly states the story began "on the twentieth of March, 1888." Other stories are more vague, with perhaps the mention of the month, or a reference to the season, or to Watson's marriage. It's up to the Sherlockians to look at the evidence, pick a date, and make a case for it.

The chronology is not the only thing Sherlockians argue about. There's the question of Watson's wives. He mentions two, and the first one by name. Who was the second wife and when did they get married? Some speculated that he even married a third time. The questions can even go into some weird areas. Dorothy L. Sayers, a notable mystery writer herself, postulated that Watson wasn't a man, but a woman!

For my purposes, I decided not to play that part of the game. I had enough to do already! Sherlockian Les Klinger put together a fine chronology, so I adopted it. (If you want to see how deep the chronological rabbit hole goes, I heartily recommend Brad Keefauver's "A Basic Timeline of Terra 221b (https://basictimelineter-ra221b.blogspot.com/p/a-basic-timeline-of-terra-221b. html) I took R. Kent Rasmussen's *Mark Twain A-Z* with its detailed timeline and combined the two.

Writing the first story was easy. It was inspired by the forced marriage of Consuelo Vanderbilt to the Duke of Marlborough. I had written a mystery novel set at the Biltmore Estate in Asheville, N.C. It had been built by George Washington Vanderbilt, the grandson of Commodore Vanderbilt. This led to a lot of reading about the Vanderbilts, the Gilded Age, and the marriage market in which American robber barons acquired titles for their family by bartering their daughters to English aristocrats.

Once all that was settled, the writing came easy. It was the perfect combination of background knowledge and story telling. I sent it off to the major mystery magazines — *Ellery Queen* and *Alfred Hitchcock* — and it came rocketing back with printed rejection letters. So I put it in a drawer and forgot about it.

Flash forward a dozen years. I'm at the Pennwriters convention. My first book, "Writers Gone Wild," had come out, and I had given a talk on marketing. This earned me a seat at the book-signing table, and by chance I was seated next to Jonathan Maberry, the best-selling thriller novelist.

During a pause between signings (long for me, short for him), we talked about stories, and I mournfully mentioned the "Whyos," tucked away never to be seen by anyone.

Now, understand this: Jonathan is a pro. Writing is his business, and he attacks it like he does everything, with all his energy at his command. I had barely launched into my lamentation when he shot out the obvious question: "Why don't you publish it yourself?"

I suspect my brain short-circuited at the obvious logical answer. "I can do that?"

"Sure. Publish it for the Kindle." And then he turned to greet another wave of his fans, and I was left to think "well ... why not?"

Which seems, in retrospect, to be the motto for the entire series. Whenever I wondered if an observation was too audacious, if a plot twist too unbelievable, I ended up asking, "Why not?" and did it. I hope you enjoyed the stories.

Combined Bibliography

MARK TWAIN IN GENERAL

Fisher, Henry W. *Abroad with Mark Twain and Eugene Field.* New York: Nicholas L. Brown, 1922.

Griffin, Benjamin and Harriet Elinor Smith, eds. *Autobiography of Mark Twain, Vol. 3.* Oakland, Calif.: University of California Press, 2015.

Harriet Elinor Smith, ed. *Autobiography of Mark Twain, Vol. 1.* Oakland, Calif.: University of California Press, 2015.

Harriet Elinor Smith and Richard Bucci, eds. *Mark Twain's Letters, Vol. 2, 1867-1868.* Berkeley, Calif.: University of California Press, 1990.

Hoffman, Andrew. *Inventing Mark Twain: The Lives of Samuel Langhorne Clemens.* New York: Quill, 1977.

Howell, William Dean. *My Mark Twain.* New York: Harper and Brothers, 1910.

Neider, Charles. *The Complete Humorous Sketches and Tales of Mark Twain.* New York: Doubleday and Co., 1961.

Powers, Ron. *Mark Twain: A Life.* New York: Free Press, 2005.

Rasmussen, R. Kent. *Mark Twain A-Z.* New York: Oxford University Press, 1995.

Read, Opie. *Mark Twain and I.* Philadelphia: R. West, 1940

Sanborn, Margaret. *Mark Twain: The Bachelor Years.* New York: Doubleday, 1990.

Scharnhorst, Gary, ed., *Mark Twain: The Complete Interviews.* Tuscaloosa, Ala.: The University of Alabama Press, 2006.

Teacher, Lawrence. *The Unabridged Mark Twain.* Philadelphia: Running Press, 1976.

Teacher, Lawrence. *The Unabridged Mark Twain, Vol. 2.* Philadelphia: Running Press, 1979.

Twain, Mark. *A Tramp Abroad. Project Gutenberg,* http://www.gutenberg.org/ebooks/119.

Willis, Resa. *Mark and Livy: The Love Story of Mark Twain and the Woman Who Almost Tamed Him.* New York: Atheneum Publishers, 1992.

Zall, P.M. *Mark Twain Laughing.* Knoxville, Tenn.: The University of Tennessee Press, 1985.

OUR MAN IN TANGIER

Farr, Martin, and Xavier Guegan. *The British Abroad Since the Eight-*

eenth Century. New York: Palgrave Macmillan, 2013.

Macnab, Frances. *A Ride in Morocco Among Believers and Traders.*

Mayo, William Starbuck. *The Berber; or the Mountaineer of the Atlas.* New York, G.P. Putnam, 1850.

Meakin, Budgett. *Life in Morocco and Glimpses Beyond.* New York: E.P. Dutton, Co., 1903.

Rohlfs, Gerhard. *Adventures in Morocco.* London: Sampson Low, Marston, Low & Searle, 1874.

Strang, Herbert. *King of the Air: Or, To Morocco on an Aeroplane.* New York: Bobbs-Merrill Co., 1907.

Wharton, Edith. *In Morocco.* Hopewell, N.J. : Ecco Press, 1996.

THE ADVENTURE OF THE DANCING MAN

----------------------, "Done Gone Up to De Angels," *The Herald,* July 2, 1896.

Heintze, James R., "Chronology of Fourth of July Celebrations during the 18th-20th Centuries along the Frontier and in the West," *Fourth of July Celebrations Database,* http://gurukul.american.edu/heintze/fourth.htm.

Langley, Henry G. *The San Francisco Directory; Chronological History of Principal Events.* 1871.

Leslie, Mrs. Frank. *California: A Pleasure Trip from Gotham to the Golden Gate.* New York: G.W. Carleton & Co., 1877.

Lloyd, Benjamin Estelle. *Lights and Shades of San Francisco.* San Francisco, 1876.

Radford, John, "Dr. Watson to 1878," *The Baker Street Journal,* www.bakerstreetjournal.com/images/Radford_Watson_to_1878_JF.pdf

THE ADVENTURE OF THE JERSEY GIRL

Howitt, William. *Life in Germany: Or, Scenes, Impressions, and Everyday Life of the Germans.* London: George Routledge, 1849.

Körner, Gustav Philipp. *Memoirs of Gustave Koerner, 1809-1896.* Cedar Rapids, Iowa: The Torch Press, 1909.

THE ADVENTURE OF THE MISSING MORTICIAN

--------------------, *Hartford and Its Points of Interest; Illustrated from Original Photographs.* New York: Mercantile Illustrating Co., 1895.

--------------------, "Interior and Grounds," *The Mark Twain House and Museum,* https://marktwainhouse.org/about/the-house/interior-grounds/.

The Adventure of the Whyos

MacColl, Gail, and Carol McD. Wallace. *To Marry an English Lord*. New York: Workman Publishing, 2012.

Patterson, Jerry E. *The Vanderbilts*. New York: Abrams, 1989.

The Adventure of the Fight Club

Byrnes, Inspector Thomas. *1886 Professional Criminals of America*. New York: The Lyons Press, 2000.

Gorn, Elliott J. *The Manly Art: Bare-Knuckle Prize Fighting in America*. Ithaca, N.Y.: Cornell University Press, 1986.

Watson, Aaron. *The Savage Club: A Medley of History, Anecdote and Reminiscence*. London: T. Fisher Unwin, 1907.

Weiser, Kathy, "Western Slang, Lingo, and Phrases – A Writer's Guide to the Old West," *Legends of America,* https://www.legendsof america.com/we-slang/15/.

Copyright Acknowledgments

"Our Man in Tangier," copyright © 2017 by Bill Peschel, first appeared in *Sherlock Holmes Great War Parodies and Pastiches I: 1910-1914,* reprinted by permission of the publisher.

"The Adventure of the Dancing Man," copyright © 2014 by Bill Peschel, first published as "The Humorist's Curse" in *The Early Punch Parodies of Sherlock Holmes*, reprinted by permission of the publisher.

"The Adventure of the Jersey Girl," copyright © 2015 by Bill Peschel, first appeared in *Sherlock Holmes Edwardian Parodies and Pastiches I: 1900-1904*, reprinted by permission of the publisher.

"The Adventure of the Stomach Club," copyright © 2015 by Bill Peschel, first published as "The Adventure of the Stomach Club Papers," appeared in *Sherlock Holmes Victorian Parodies and Pastiches: 1888-1899*, reprinted by permission of the publisher.

"The Adventure of the Missing Mortician," copyright © 2018 by Bill Peschel, first appeared in *Sherlock Holmes Jazz Age Parodies and Pastiches I: 1920-1924*, reprinted by permission of the publisher.

"The Adventure of the Fight Club," copyright © 2018 by Bill Peschel, appears here for the first time.

"The Adventure of the Whyos," copyright © 2011 by Bill Peschel, reprinted by permission of the publisher.

Bill Peschel
AUTHOR
travel ⟩

About the Author

Bill Peschel is a former journalist who shares a Pulitzer Prize with the staff of *The Patriot-News* in Harrisburg, Pa. He is also a mystery fan who runs the Wimsey Annotations at Planetpeschel.com.

The author of *Writers Gone Wild* (Penguin), he publishes through Peschel Press the 223B Casebook Series of Sherlockian parodies and pastiches and annotated editions of Dorothy L. Sayers' *Whose Body?* and Agatha Christie's *The Mysterious Affair at Styles* and *The Secret Adversary*. An interest in Victorian crime led to the republication of three books on the William Palmer poisoning case.

Peschel was born in Warren, Ohio, grew up in Charlotte, N.C., and graduated from the University of North Carolina in Chapel Hill. He lives with his family and animal menagerie in Hershey, where the air really does smell like chocolate.

Visit Bill at Peschel Press (www.peschelpress.com) or his personal website at Planet Peschel (planetpeschel. com). He can be reached at peschel@Peschel press.com or at Peschel Press, P.O. Box 132, Hershey, PA 17033.

PESCHEL PRESS

Suburban Stockade
Strengthening Your Life
Against an Uncertain Future

Build A Resilient Future

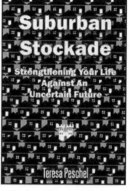

It's our paradox for the 21st century. The richer we've grown in material goods, the less we seem able to cope. We have access to borrowed money, but we can't save $500 for an emergency. Many families are one paycheck from financial disaster, yet the culture discourages us from saving money. We're told to spend more, even to go into debt for a new car, an oversized home, or a college education. We're bankrupting our future to pay interest on our past spending. We've become slaves to debt.

"Suburban Stockade" is Teresa Peschel's manifesto memoir about her quest to drop out of the rat race, embrace her peasant ancestry, and prepare her family for an uncertain future. She describes how our emphasis on a consumer economy and cheap goods blinded us to the personal and moral costs of economic growth. To pursue material wealth, we're taught to ignore the value of family, friends, and community, and the pleasures of a comfortable home and good food.

Peschel describes how to win by paying down debts, saving money, buying a home we can age in, and keeping ourselves secure. Although not a how-to book, Peschel describes how she cut expenses through simple tasks such as insulating her home, hanging laundry, searching for mongo and obtainium, and effective grocery shopping.

Peschel dares you to build your suburban stockade by not playing the game where the rules are set by corporations and economists and rigged by politicians and the media.

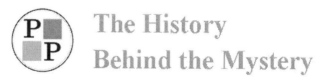

The History
Behind the Mystery

PESCHEL PRESS; P.O. BOX 132, HERSHEY, PA 17033

TRADE PAPERBACKS AND EBOOKS • WWW.PESCHELPRESS.COM

The Complete, Annotated Series

Available in Trade Paperback and Ebook editions

Return to your favorite novels by Agatha Christie & Dorothy L. Sayers with added material exclusive to these editions!

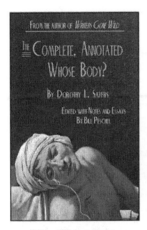
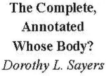

The Complete, Annotated Whose Body?
Dorothy L. Sayers

Sayers' first novel introduces the witty Lord Peter Wimsey investigating the mystery of the body in the bath. Three maps and essays on notorious crimes, anti-Semitism, Sayers and Wimsey, plus two timelines. *282 pages.*

The Complete, Annotated Mysterious Affair at Styles
Agatha Christie

Mystery's most auspicious debut, Christie was only 25 when she introduced Hercule Poirot! With essays on Poirot, Christie, strychnine, women during the war, plus chronology and book lists. *352 pages.*

The Complete, Annotated Deluxe Secret Adversary
Agatha Christie

Christie's conspiracy thriller in which Tommy and Tuppence —based on herself and her husband?—fight socialists plotting to ruin England! With art from the newspaper edition and essays on thrillers and her 11-day disappearance and more! *478 pages.*

Don't miss future Peschel Press books: Visit Peschelpress.com or PlanetPeschel.com and sign up for our newsletter.

The 223B Casebook Series

Available in Trade Paperback and Ebook editions

Reprints of classic and newly discovered fanfiction written during Arthur Conan Doyle's lifetime, with original art plus extensive historical notes.

The Early Punch Parodies of Sherlock Holmes

- Parodies, pastiches, book reviews, cartoons, and jokes from 1890 to 1928.
- Includes 17-story cycle by R.C. Lehmann.
- Two parodies by P.G. Wodehouse, and a story by Arthur Conan Doyle.
- Essays on Punch, Lehmann, Wodehouse, and an interview with Conan Doyle. *281 pages.*

Victorian Parodies & Pastiches: 1888-1899
With stories by Conan Doyle, Robert Barr, Jack Butler Yeats, and J.M. Barrie. *279 pages.*

Great War Parodies and Pastiches I: 1910-1914
With stories by O. Henry, Maurice Baring, and Stephen Leacock. *362 pages.*

Edwardian Parodies & Pastiches I: 1900-1904
With stories by Mark Twain, Finley Peter Dunn, John Kendrick Bangs, and P.G. Wodehouse. *390 pages.*

Great War Parodies and Pastiches II: 1915-1919
With stories by Ring Lardner, Carolyn Wells, and a young George Orwell. *390 pages.*

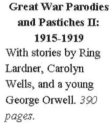

Edwardian Parodies & Pastiches II: 1905-1909
With stories by 'Banjo' Paterson, Max Beerbohm, Carolyn Wells, and Lincoln Steffens. *401 pages.*

Jazz Age Parodies and Pastiches I: 1920-1924
With stories by Dashiell Hammett, James Thurber, and Arthur Conan Doyle. *353 pages.*

The Rugeley Poisoner Series

A 3-book series from Peschel Press reprinting seminal works
about Victorian poisoner Dr. William Palmer

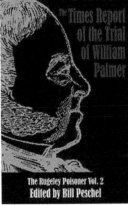

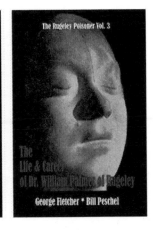

The Illustrated Life and Career of William Palmer 1856	The Times Report of the Trial of William Palmer 1856	The Life and Career of William Palmer of Rugeley 1925
• A "quickie biography" written to cash in on the trial. • Gossip about Palmer's family, betting scams, and the stews of London. • More than 50 restored woodcuts. • Essays on medical training and racing. • Excerpts from Palmer's love letters. *225 pages*	• A trial transcript created by the Times newspaper, edited, corrected, and annotated. • More than 50 original woodcuts restored to better-than-new condition. • Essays on the trial judges and barristers, glossary of medical terms, and index to witnesses. *426 pages*	• Written by a doctor who interviewed witnesses and jurors. • Rare photos and art not seen since 1925. • Annotations define medical and legal terms and clarify obscure points. • Essays on Palmer's impact on modern culture, strychnine, and Rugeley today. *227 pages*

45801573R00148

Made in the USA
Columbia, SC
23 December 2018